I0576540

Henry C. Pearson

His Opportunity

Henry C. Pearson

His Opportunity

ISBN/EAN: 9783337288914

Printed in Europe, USA, Canada, Australia, Japan

Cover: Foto ©Andreas Hilbeck / pixelio.de

More available books at **www.hansebooks.com**

HIS

OPPORTUNITY.

BY

HENRY CLEMENS PEARSON.

BOSTON:
JAMES H. EARLE, PUBLISHER,
178 WASHINGTON STREET.
1888.

Copyright, 1886.

BY JAMES H. EARLE.

All rights reserved.

TO MY WIFE.

CONTENTS.

HIS OPPORTUNITY.

I.

A . Lazy . Resolve.

A YOUNG man, in tight-fitting bicycle-suit, was walking leisurely down one of the broad, gravelled walks of a city park. A little in his rear followed a half-dozen street-boys. Huddled together, earnestly agitating something, they appeared like an animated bale of woolen rags, studded with blacking boxes and shocks of towy hair. That they were discussing the young man could not be doubted. Yet the usual street-methods of emphasizing a debate, — with apple-cores, lumps of mud, and gutter slang, — were entirely absent. There was a subdued air about them that argued respect.

"Starting an orphan asylum, Chamberlain?" said a pleasant voice.

The saunterer turned half round, and a look of genuine pleasure lighted his face.

"Hello, Will," he said; "glad to see you."

"Are you so distinguished that even the bootblacks tender you an ovation, and follow at your heels in admiring reverence?" continued the other.

"I guess so. They seem to think I am worth following."

Then halting, he said, "Well, boys, what is it?"

"We seen you pull Bob out from under the horse-car," said one awkwardly.

"Yes."

"An' us fellers thought we'd like ter know where a feller like you lived. Your sort is awful scarce 'round here."

The young man laughed.

"Here is my address," said he, handing a card to the speaker. "Any time you or any of your friends wish to see me, come to my home. Now don't follow us any further, please; it will draw a crowd."

The boys slowly dispersed, and the young man and his friend passed on.

"I want you to come up to my room and explain this little episode. It promises to be interesting," said the new comer.

A short walk brought them to a building crowded with lawyers' offices. On one of the doors was the name William Marshall; this they entered.

"Now, fire away," said Will.

"There is hardly any thing to tell," replied his friend, with a litttle reluctance. "I was coming up the street just before you met me, and started to cross when a horse-car came booming along. I hate to hurry when I have plenty of time, so I waited to let it pass. Meanwhile, one of these street-rats, a boot-black, —a mite of a fellow,—who was running in the middle of the street, dodged a 'bus, and slipping, fell right in front of the horses of the car. It was down-grade, and I saw that the youngster would be run over, so I pulled him away."

"How did you get the tear in your jacket? What means all that mud on your limbs, and why do you hold your right hand so queerly?" asked his friend.

Chamberlain blushed.

"You do beat the Dutch, Will, for using your eyes. I did not imagine I was so conspicuously ragged, muddy, and sprained, as you represent The fact is, when I had the little fellow well under my arm, the pole between the horses knocked me down; and if I hadn't managed to grasp it with my right hand, and allow myself to be dragged a short distance, I'm afraid we should have been hurt."

"It was a splendid thing to do, and I'm proud of you, old boy," exclaimed Will, heartily. "I don't wonder the boot-blacks followed you. They recognized the real grit in the action. Is your hand badly hurt?"

"Only sprained a little. I was on my way here to tell you that I am going to leave the city," said Chamberlain, adroitly turning the conversation, which was becoming uncomfortably full of praise.

"For the summer?"

"For two years."

"Two years! Where?" exclaimed the other.

"That I cannot tell. If it were possible for me to make known to any one my destination and my plans, it should be to you, old fellow; but it cannot be done," was the sober reply.

Will Marshall was silent for some moments. He loved his friend with his whole heart, and knew that he was in the main a manly, generous, good-hearted fellow, but without any particular aim in life. Was he going abroad in fast company, to spend his fortune in riotous living? Was he——

"I am not going on any sort of pleasure-trip; I am going where I shall have to buckle right down to hard work," said the other, as if he divined his friend's thoughts.

"I am glad to hear you say that; but you are not ashamed of it?" was the hearty comment.

"Am I apt to be ashamed of what I do? Was I ever ashamed of being lazy?"

His friend smiled.

"Two years," said Chamberlain, as if to himself; "by that time all my friends will have forgotten me. I wish I could tell you all about the matter, Will; it is for all the world like a fairy-tale, — but I can't."

"But you will write?"

"You will receive an occasional letter from me through Doctor Ponsonby, and any letters left with him will be forwarded to me."

"One thing," said his friend, "would make me feel that this mysterious expedition was all right: If I knew that you had chosen the one Friend to go with you."

Chamberlain was silent. He looked at the floor and then out of the window, but said nothing.

"Is it not the common-sense way, to drop a foolish pride and do right?"

"Perhaps so; but you know you said that I must give up my wine," was the light reply.

"I simply told you what I had done," replied Will, earnestly. "If I thought that by foregoing any sort of pleasure I could save one soul, I would do it."

"I verily believe you would, for you are generous and self-sacrificing; as for me, I'm a crooked stick, and always shall be. It runs in the blood. There's a car. Good-bye, old boy; see you again Saturday."

Closing the interview summarily, the young man ran down the stairs, boarded the car, and in the course of half an hour was at home.

Left an orphan in the care of a busy guardian when but a child, Tom Chamberlain had not been brought up,—he had grown up as he could. He had been sent to the best schools, had enjoyed excellent instruction in all knowledge except that which is the beginning of wisdom. His chum, Will, was an earnest Christian, and he viewed his religion with profound respect, but when it was offered him, shook his head. It had no charm for him. He wished to be lazy; and that sort of life, to his mind, meant work.

As he sat in his handsomely-furnished room, smoking a choice cigar, he drew from his pocket a letter, and opening it, began to read. It was written in a fine, careful hand, with old-fashioned curves and flourishes, and quaint crosses instead of periods at the end of sentences. It read:—

"STEELVILLE, May 1, 18—.

"*Nephew Thomas,*— Being about to end a long and useless life, I venture to address you. Undoubtedly you are aware of the enmity that formerly existed between your father and myself. If you are, I beg that you will not let it influence you in the least in deciding what I am about to request. I can live but a few hours. My physician forbids me to write even this.

"I have made a great deal of money in my life-time. If you visit my factory you will see more than a thousand operatives that I have gathered. They are my slaves. I have bound them and ground them under my heel for years. Their wretched tenement-houses were of my building. The dram-shops were allowed by me, and I alone am responsible for their existence. Wretched Steep Street, where live my slaves, is weighing me down to perdition! It is too late for me to do anything; my race is run. You are the last of the family,—my dead sister's son. Will you then take my property, take the mill, take Steep Street, and do with it as I ought to have done? My lawyer will call upon you soon, and acquaint you with the contents of my will.

"And now, my nephew, I charge you that you be

stow upon Steep Street what I have denied it. Visit it and see for yourself its many needs.

"Farewell,

"ROBERT FLINT."

The young man read and re-read this letter. It was, in his life, a strange occurrence. Heretofore he had taken almost everything without surprise, until he was thought to be one of the young Americans whom nothing astonishes. He wondered if his uncle knew of his laziness; of his distaste for labor of any kind; of his belief that, however good religion might be for others, it could be of little advantage to him?

What sort of an evangelist would he make? The more he pondered the deeper he sank into profound astonishment. Had it been his chum who had been chosen he would have thought it the right thing exactly; but the idea of making Tom Chamberlain a missionary was too absurd! Of course he could refuse to have anything to do with it, for he had property enough to live comfortably; but when he reached this point he always read the letter again, and once or twice finished with very moist eyes.

About this time the lawyer spoken of called. He was a short, florid man of forty-five, with reddish hair and whiskers, and keen blue eyes that had a look of steel in their depths.

For some years, he informed Chamberlain, he had been the confidential clerk of Robert Flint, and agent of the file-works. He spoke of Mr. Flint as a hard worker, an eccentric and benevolent gentleman, but rather unpractical.

Surprised at this latter statement the listener said, —

"My letter spoke of some conditions in the matter."

"What letter?" inquired the lawyer.

"My last letter from my uncle."

"Ah, yes," was the somewhat astonished reply, "the conditions were that you should become a common laborer in the factory for a term of two years, in order that you might learn the business, and at the end of that time you should have full control of the property, otherwise it goes to some benevolent institutions; but," added the lawyer, hastily, "you are the only lawful heir, and in case you refuse to do as the will demands, as you justly can, you may release yourself; I have abundant proof that the lamented Mr. Flint was not in full possession of his reason at the time he framed the document. It can, therefore, very easily be broken."

Mr. Lamson, after these long and telling sentences, wiped his moist brow with a fine handkerchief and looked slyly at his auditor.

"What is the condition of the factory people?"

"O, about the same as in other places like Steelville. They are a happy, thoughtless, hand-to-mouth people, with a fervent wish to be let alone," was the careless reply.

"My uncle wished me to get an insight into the whole business, did he?" was the next question.

"That is what he put in the will. The conditions were that you should come to Steelville, where of course no one would know you, and that you should begin in the 'grinding room,' learn what there was to be done there, then go to another room, and so on. At the end of the two years, if you have followed out his instructions, you will be declared his nephew and receive the property. Until then you are to remain *incognito.*"

"Not much pleasure in such an outlook?" said Chamberlain, interrogatively.

"I should say not, sir. It would be a dog's life. Only the strongest constitutions can stand it. If I were you I should think twice before I decided to do it," was the quick reply.

"You are right," said the other, with a lazy look that delighted the lawyer. "I have thought twice; once when I received my uncle's letter, and once when you explained the conditions.

You may expect me at the factory, as a workman, in one week."

With a promptness that one would hardly have expected, Chamberlain at once began preparations for the new life. There was a chance for adventure in this affair that lent it a tinge of romance, yet there are few of the young aristocrats of the world that are willing to step down, — to lower their caste, even for the novelty of it, and he had many doubts. A return to the letter dispelled them when they became too thick, and the getting ready went steadily on.

At length the time for departure came, — the good-byes to Doctor Ponsonby and Marshall were said, and with only a valise for baggage he started for the station. The reasons for taking no trunk were two, — he had no clothing suitable for work, and wished to purchase such as would be fitting when on the ground, and, second, the old doctor earnestly advised it. Had the young man known that his guardian's purpose in so doing was to make it all the easier for his ward to return, it is possible that he would not have been so complaisant.

When once aboard the cars and speeding on his journey, Chamberlain had time to meditate. His imagination, fired by the possibilities of the whole affair, painted the strongest pictures of drunken operatives, brutal task-masters, and close, filthy work-rooms. Part of this the letter was responsible for, and part, as he assured himself, reining in his runaway fancy, was something that he knew nothing about. Whatever train of thought he attempted to follow, ran into a file-factory, and he found himself, much to his vexation, planning all kinds of ways out of various hard places, which his common sense warned him would probably never occur.

After a long ride, as he approached the village where the steel-works were situated, he became interested in the conversation of two gentlemen who occupied the seat directly in front of him. They appeared to be small politicians, and were unconscious that anything that they said might be heard by fellow-passengers, or else were so calloused that they did not care.

"The vote of Steep Street is yours at the price named," said the first speaker.

Chamberlain pricked up his ears. Steep Street was the factory settlement of his uncle.

"But you were to be fair with me. If I run it must be because there is money in it. Now I am willing to put out one dollar any time if it will bring in two. But that I must be tolerably sure of. Let's see your figures."

Two heads bent over a paper and went through

with a calculation that covered apparently thousands of dollars, or of votes, Chamberlain could
not decide which, and then the document was
folded up, put away, and the negotiations continued.

"If I pleased I could go in and, by the proper
use of two-thirds of the money you ask, buy the
important votes of the village," said the buyer.

"You could n't do it. You can't get the inside track of the man who holds these people.
He has them right where he wants them. There
is n't a move in that village but he knows all
about it. To outsiders it appears like a slipshod,
reckless, unthinking mass of humanity. That 's
what it is, but a master hand is on it. Lamson has his thumb on every soul in the place.
He knows that as long as they are down he can
put his heel on them, and that 's why they are
kept down."

"I rather doubt that. He is too pious a man
to deliberately destroy people that way. If I
am not mistaken I have heard him bitterly deplore the wretchedness in the place. He is tied
up in some way and cannot do any thing. You
are wrong in your conclusions, I am sure, and
I think, as you are so willing to draw the long
bow on things I know about, that it will be
well for me to go slowly on this bargain. Lam-

son is no friend of mine, but I'm not quite blind, and I say that he is just the reverse of what you have pictured."

"Steelville! Steelville!" called the brakeman, and the gentlemen, followed by Chamberlain, got out. The latter was in a ferment. Which of the two was right? One of them must be very much mistaken in his estimate of the bland lawyer.

"Carriage, sir?" said a voice, which woke Chamberlain from his reveries, and set him wondering what had possessed a "cabby" to ask him, a plainly-dressed workman, if he wished a carriage. Something was wrong. What could it be? His hat was not fashionable: he had seen to that. His suit was ready-made; his cane, — here he stopped, flushed, and laughed. According to the custom he unconsciously carried a cane. It almost upset his dignity, so amused and provoked was he, and the first hedge he came to he broke the article in two and threw it away, hoping that none of his future acquaintances had noticed the folly.

As was natural he promptly made his way toward the seat of interest, the mill village, instead of following the stream of passengers up the hill to the town proper. Erelong he came in sight of the mill turrets, and then passing

around a curve, suddenly stood at the foot of a
hill that was lined with houses of the tenement
stamp. The dilapidated street-sign, defaced by
tobacco quids, covered with scrawling names,
hacked, and whittled, was not needed to inform
him that this was Steep Street.

II.

A · Stranger · in · Town.

STEEP Street was a condensation of wretch·edness in every form. From the rotten, river-swept sills of the houses at the foot of the street, to the ragged chimneys at the upper end, there reigned an air of reckless want. The buildings were huddled together at all angles, in inextricable confusion; the fences that separated them having vanished up the wide-throated chimneys years before. Window-panes long since demolished, were replaced by boards, hats, or coarse sacking; door-latches were wanting, hinges were broken, door-steps sunken and displaced. The yards about the houses were trodden hard and smooth as concrete walks, by scores of bare feet. The only signs of thrift in the settlement were the pig-pens that, like unwholesome fungi, clung to the sides of the houses, and mingled their stench with the uncovered sink-drains that slid sluggishly toward the river.

Throughout the yards, on the steps, on the low roofs of the swine-pens, quarreling in the street, were swarms of ragged, unwashed children of all ages, in every variety of filthy dress and undress.

Across the river rose the buildings of the file-works. Even from a distance one could not fail to notice the good repair in which that part of the manufacturing settlement was kept. Evidently the owner of the village saw that it was for his advantage to do his business in an orderly, cleanly manner, however he managed the tenements.

It was after a close scrutiny of the squaliu dwellings that a young man stopped in front of the house at the head of the street, and asked for a drink of water. This house had one advantage over the rest: it was on higher ground and had no sink drain running through its front yard. There was good reason for this singularity, — no drain being available for the purpose. A tall, muscular woman, with sad yet good-humored face, answered his knock.

"May I trouble you for a glass of water?" said the caller.

"If you'll step inside I'll see if we've got any that's fit ter drink," she replied, with an attempt at politeness.

Chamberlain, for it was he, followed her in, and taking a seat in a chair which had no back and

decidedly rickety legs, waited for the liquid re-
freshment.

"Stranger here?" asked the woman.

"Yes; I'm going to work in the file-factory,"
was the reply.

"O, in the office, I s'pose; clerk it?"

"No, ma'am; in the grinding-room."

His questioner looked at him doubtfully.

"My name is Bowman," she remarked, as if
his might mitigate her wonder.

"Mine is Chamberlain."

"The boys will be down on such a swell as
you," she said, after a pause. "Have you quit
a good job?"

"Pretty good."

"Well, take my advice and go back to it.
Them slim fingers of yours war n't never made
to handle pig iron. You aint got the strength."

"What I'm thinking about especially is a boarding place. I wish to be somewhere near the
works."

"Yes," said the woman, taking a ragged-edged
tumbler that had once been filled with five-cent's
worth of sham currant jelly. "Yes, you'd want
a boardin' place, sure. You look kinder stuck
up, sort of as if you belonged to the big bugs
in the town above; but if you intend to have
any peace among the grindin'-room hands, you'd

best board somewhere on Steep Street. If you should try to live up among the swells, all the boys would be down on you."

This speech was quite a damper to the listener's hopes. He had dressed plainly and flattered himself that he looked quite like a laborer, but this sad-appearing woman had known at once that he was not used to hard labor. To be sure she made a mistake in taking it for granted that he was weak because his fingers were not thick and brown. He doubted if many of the mill-hands could compete with him on the horizontal bar, or in leaping, running, or boxing, but, of course, he would have to prove this to them by deeds rather than words, if they attempted to crowd him because of his gentlemanly appearance.

The thought that he must live on the factory street was repulsive to him. In the week that had elapsed since his decision he had revolved the matter very carefully, and had determined to fulfill the trust imposed upon him the best he could. The last words of his lonely, miserly, repentent uncle had sunk deep into his heart, and now as he beheld the abject misery of the operatives, he felt a new and strange sense of pity and responsibility. A desire to do this people good was growing in his heart. He realized his own unfitness for the work, but he also saw that is things were, he alone could not raise this mass of diseased humanity up to health.

From the outset he was almost morbidly anxious to get the sympathy of the operatives. When the woman therefore spoke of the feelings that would be engendered if he chose himself a boarding place among the pleasant families in the upper town, where there were no mill operatives, he at once gave up the idea, and turned his attention to the accommodations of Steep Street. As yet he had not seen Mr. Lamson, for he had a feeling that it would be better for him to make all outside arrangements without asking advice. For this feeling the astute lawyer himself was to blame, — his manner on the occasion of his first visit having prejudiced the young man against him to a certain degree.

"Do you know any boarding place about here?" he inquired.

"There are two reg'lar boardin' houses down yonder," answered the woman, pointing in the direction in which the drains ran, "but they are awful rough places; you wouldn't git much sleep nights. They drink and carouse almost all night long. I was goin' to say that I didn't know but we might be able to put ye up. What would you be willin' to pay?"

Chamberlain had a vague thought of twelve
dollars a week, but deciding not to state the
price, said, cautiously, —

"What should you charge?"

"We should have to put it pretty high," said
the other.

The young man mentally raised it to fifteen,
but ventured nothing.

"Would four dollars and a half be more than
you could pay?" she asked finally.

"O, no; I will pay that. Can I come to-night?"
was the ready response.

"Yes, I guess so, if you pay a week in advance," she replied, a sudden suspicion being
developed by the extreme willingness of the lat
ter to pay the price named.

The money was promptly paid, and the bargain completed. This done, it occurred to the
young man that he would like to see his room.
He learned, to his dismay, that he was expected
to share his cot with the landlady's son, a youth
of eighteen. An extra half dollar per week, however, secured the tiny bed-room for himself
alone, and he left to seek Mr. Lamson and
make known his arrival in Steelville, and his
plans for carrying out his uncle's wishes.

It was with a curious feeling that he stood
in the handsomely-furnished outer office, waiting

for the agent. From the mighty engines, hammers, and rollers within the stone buildings, came a steady roar that jarred even the floor on which he stood. The strong men in blue shirts, who occasionally passed him on their way in and out of the busy rooms, the clatter of the trucks in the packing-room, the piles of files in neat packages, gave him a glimpse of a new world. He felt like a Columbus setting foot upon strange shores, where he might find almost any kind of queer and terrible beasts, and experience dangers of which heretofore he had no idea. Not that he in the least regretted his decision; on the contrary, the further he went, the more he felt that he was doing right, and that he might yet give his uncle's slaves their freedom.

"Ah, Mr. Chamberlain, you are here I see," said a bland voice; and waking from his reverie, he saw the agent.

"Well," said he, when they were seated, "you are still determined to carry out your uncle's ideas?"

"Certainly."

"Had you not better let me show you over the place before you decide? The work is of the heaviest kind, and intensely disagreeable."

Mr. Lamson, please understand me once for

all: I intend to carry out my uncle's wishes. I see many young men here in the factory who are physically weaker than I am; I know what I can stand. I wish my *incognito* kept a secret. If you showed me about the place, would it look as if I were a common laborer? My boarding place is decided upon, and all I need is to have my work assigned me for to-morrow."

"You will at least spend this first night at my house?"

"Have you ever had any of the grinding room help at your house over-night?"

"I can't say that I have," was the reply.

"Then I must refuse, with thanks. I am very much in earnest in this, Mr. Lamson; and while I appreciate your courtesy, I must beg that from this moment I may be to you simply, Tom Chamberlain, workman."

"Your wish shall be respected," said the lawyer; but it was with a look of disappoinment that he made the promise.

Chamberlain had said that he was very much in earnest, and he spoke truly. At last he was fairly roused. The covert opposition that his uncle's confidential manager manifested toward his becoming acquainted with the details of the business, from whatever cause it might spring, only served to increase his desire to carry it through. Beyond this, however, was the honest wish to help the operatives. He easily saw that Lamson had no pity for, and no thought of alleviating, their glaring misery. Indeed, he suspected that he should find in him an enemy to all enterprises for their welfare. With new resolution at the thought of this possible opposition, he determined to work alone if need be, and effectually destroy this monument of his uncle's sin, and build in its stead a beautiful little township of tenements that should be filled with sober, industrious, God-fearing people.

But why God-fearing? questioned his heart. Because, he answered himself, they would n't be sober, and industrious, and respectable, unless they were God-fearing. This thought came into his mind and took up its abode there, and was a most powerful every-day sermon to the young man.

Meanwhile, Lamson stood looking at him, as if to fathom the thoughts that were passing in his mind. With returning suavity, he said, —

"As you suggest, it will be better for you to enter the mill as all the beginners do, being registered and assigned a place, and a stated amount of pay. I see you are thoroughly in earnest, and you may count on me for help in the furtherance of your plans. Just step this way, if you please, and give your name to the clerk."

After going through the usual formula, Chamberláin was given a "pay-roll number," and felt that he actually was a part of the throbbing life of the factory.

A touch of a bell, and a few words through a speaking-tube, summoned a foreman, and placing him in his care, with an every-day air that delighted the novice, Lamson went back to his office.

"Don't stand staring 'round all day," said the new boss. "Come along and I'll set you at work. We don't need you. There are plenty in my room; but I s'pose we shall have to find something for you to do. What's your name?"

"Chamberlain."

"Got any chewin'-tobacco with you?"

"No."

"Well, next time I ask you, see that you have some. I most generally forget mine during work hours, and have to borrow."

As a green hand, he was set at work upon the least important jobs in the room; and he began with the task of polishing the brass couplings of a long row of steam-pipes. Around the valve-stems was an encrustation of dirt that nothing but muscle would remove, and ere long his arms were aching and his back had a "crick" in it. There was, however, no give up in Chamberlain's nature, so he toiled and sweat till the brass looked like molten gold, and even the crusty foreman admired. He had a suspicion,— which, by the way, hit the nail on the head,— that this job was a "tester," and that there was little time spent, as a usual thing, in the polishing of couplings in that room. He therefore resolved to give his boss an elevated idea of his capabilities, and did his very best. The noon whistle was a welcome release, and he went to his dinner with an appetite as good as any laborer in the place. On his return, he found the men grouped in different parts of the room, lounging away the remnant of their nooning. His advent did not appear to be noticed till one of them came toward him with an aggressive swagger and said, roughly,—

"You're a green hand at this business, aint you?"

"Yes."

"Well, I s'pose you know the custom of the place?"

"With regard to what?"

"With regard to what? Don't try your kid-glove language with me. Why don't you say, ''bout what?'"

"'Bout what?" said he, imperturbly; so per-

fectly copying the other's accents that the listeners smiled, while the questioner scowled.

"Every green hand is expected to 'wet down,'
—to treat,—and it's your turn; so pony up!
My name is Gaffney — Thirsty Gaffney, some call
me. I was born thirsty, and I've been growing
dryer every year. Now I intend you shall wet
me down."

When first the insulting swagger had been
indulged in, Chamberlain had flushed angrily,
and been ready to resent the bully's demand;
but a new thought overcame his irritation, an
amused light came into his eyes, and he stood
facing the man with almost a smile on his face.
The reason was this: Gaffney stood almost
under a broad shelf that was used for the "fire
buckets," which were pails, ten in number, filled
with water, ready for instant use in case of fire.
The insurance companies were very strict in that
section, and the pails were examined and re-
filled whenever the water got low in them. One
of Chamberlain's minor chores that morning had
been to climb up and look them over. Directly
under the first of the line stood the aggressive
file-grinder. From where the young man stood,
an inch steam-pipe ran up from the floor nearly
to the ceiling, then took a half turn and followed the wall close behind the line of water-

pails. The pipe was cold, and the young man held to it with one hand in a natural lounging attitude.

"I'm perfectly willing to wet you down if you really wish it," he said.

"Cert'nly I wish it; and the sooner you do it, the better it will be fer you," was the savage reply, for the man was sure that the youth was quaking with fear.

In obedience to this threatening request, Chamberlain gave the pipe a sudden vigorous pull. As he hoped, it caught pail number one an inch below the top and tumbled it down, drenching Gaffney to the skin, and frightening him almost out of his wits. A howl of laughter burst from the men; and as the wrathful grinder caught up an iron rod and started for the "green hand," he suddenly found himself confronted by a half dozen burly, laughing workmen.

"Ye brought it on yourself! Ye asked fer it' Let the lad alone!" they shouted, and the bully slunk away, for once unable to say he was "dry."

"That's the best 'wettin' down' that ever any green hand gave. You'll do, me boy! We are proud to have you in our room," said a man who had been particularly surly that morning.

"I'm mighty glad I hired you. This will learn them file-grinding hands not to try to pick on us sorters," said the foreman.

III.

"Sam."

IN the office of the file-works sat Mr. Lamson. On all sides beautiful finishings, the oaken paneling, the handsome desk, and the stained-glass door, bespoke the thriving business. The gentleman, although at the head of the firm, and lord of the gem of an office, did not seem content. A restless, dissatisfied look that partook also of perplexity, expressed itself in his features; something was wrong. One so schooled in complacency as the crafty lawyer, would not worry over nothing. Touching a bell he summoned a boy.

"Call Sam," he said.

In a few moments a tall, broad-shouldered man stood blocking the doorway. Six feet three in his stockings was Sam Putnam. Among all the strong men who worked in "the iron," he was the most muscular and the best proportioned. In his scant working clothes, which consisted of a short-sleeved undershirt, dark blue pants, and slippers, the bulging muscles swelling on arm and chest, he looked the personification of strength.

"Come in and close the door," said the agent.

"There is no one near. I dont want to be cooped up in that little pen," returned Sam, carelessly.

The gentleman flushed and frowned, looking as if he were about to give some sharp command, but instead said, —

"How does young Chamberlain come on?"

"All right," was the short answer.

"Does he really learn all he is set at, or is he shamming?"

"O, he learns thoroughly enough. Works as if his life depended upon it."

"Do the men like him?"

"They always like any one that minds his own business."

"How do you take to him, Sam?" was the next question, accompanied by a searching glance.

The giant returned the look with a half contemptuous smile, saying, —

"I think he is a likely chap, Deacon; a trifle too pious, perhaps."

"Pious! You don't know him," exclaimed the other.

"Hump! Perhaps you do," was the reply.

"Sam," said the agent, impressively, "if this

young Chamberlain learns the whole business, it will be the worst thing that ever happened to you and me."

"What do you mean?"

"I can't explain, but remember this, he is here for a purpose, and if he accomplishes it, you and I and some of the rest are going to be much the worse for it."

"I suppose you would like to make a second Tam of him?" remarked Sam, with a return of the old ironical smile.

A look of hate sprang to Lamson's face.

"How many times have I told you never to mention Tam to me?" he said, angrily.

"A good many times," replied the other, with a laugh.

Lamson grew white with rage, but the looks that he turned upon the imperturbable figure in the door were entirely without effect.

"Speaking of Tam, is he still about the mill?" said the agent at last.

"Of course."

"Well, I won't have it," exclaimed Lamson, breaking out afresh. "He is no use here. He is a positive damage. I won't have him around here any longer."

"When he goes, I go," remarked Sam, with a gleam in his deep-set eyes.

"Sam," said Lamson, suddenly regaining his self-poise, "we cannot afford to quarrel. We are necessary to each other. Now it would please me exceedingly if you would accede to my request in this matter, and allow me to remove Tam to a place where he could be cared for, and where he would be much happier than he is here. Perhaps, too, he might be cured."

The giant always felt ill at ease when his employer addressed him in court phrases. He therefore remained silent.

"You surely won't object?" said Lamson.

"But I will. You hate the sight of him, and no wonder; but you had better not lay a finger on him. Tam is going to stay," said Sam, with sudden emphasis.

Turning on his heel the man strode away, muttering angrily to himself.

The agent closed the door with a slam, and began pacing the office floor with a most disagreeable frown on his brow. He was accustomed to success when he attempted to manage men. He understood Sam perfectly, yet he could not twist him as he did many others. The thought made him exceedingly wrathful, so much so that few of the acquaintances of "cool Lamson" would have recognized his changed face, had they happened in upon him just then.

Sam had called him "Deacon" with a scorn-
ful emphasis that brought the blood to his cheek
and the fire to his eye.

So the help know it, do they, he thought.
"Deacon Lamson!" That sounds well, does it
not? Yet his cheeks burned at the thought of
the comments of the men. In the town above,
where were churches, schools, and wealthy families, it had caused no surprise when he had been
elected deacon of the largest church. He even
had felt a deal of self-gratulation, and possibly
the shadow of the shadow of a thrill of piety
and resolve for future usefulness. Down in the
mill village, however, it was entirely different.
There he was known. To be sure the deceased
owner of the works was still blamed for the
misery in the desolate tenements, and for the
grinding of the operatives. "Old Skinflint," as
Robert Flint was generally called, was still hated,
and his memory often cursed, but little by little
the keen-eyed sufferers were discerning the fact
that smooth-spoken Lamson was perhaps a little
harder, and more merciless, than the owner had
been. When it was known that he had become
deacon there was a breeze of comment throughout the mill village.

"I tell yer, my fren's," said Gaffney, from
the steps of "Hole in the Wall," the popular

saloon, "he deserves to be a deakin. Ain't he got caperbillities in the way of bein' a cheatin', lyin', slippery deakin? Course he has. He's bound for the Kingdom, he is, 'cause he owns a pew, an' a hymn-book. A pew is a reserve seat for Heaven; a hymn-book is the check for it. I don't blame him. I'd be a deakin myself, if I had money enough. Here comes Sam Putnam, my fren's, an' I invite you all to take a drink at his expense, with this sentiment: 'Health to the Deakin!'"

Most of the dwellers on Steep Street agreed with Gaffney that Lamson was fitted to be a deacon, which to their minds meant a hypocrite. They felt that it was a move either to pull wool over the eyes of his fellow-men or the Powers above; either of which, to their misty minds, was deemed equally possible.

There were to be sure a few faithful hearts, cowed by a fruitless struggling against the prevalent unbelief, who secretly cherished the hope that the new dignity might be a forerunner of a reign of justice, but they were soon disappointed Their longings were never expressed in words, and no one but the great and pitiful Searcher of hearts knew of the faith-germ that ever and anon quickened with vague hope.

One result of the honor which had been be-

stowed upon Lamson had been that he was thereafter called "the deacon" from one end of the
village to the other, and with the same contemptuous intonation that Sam had used when
summoned to the office. Another result was the
aversion that the majority of the people held
toward the church was intensified. It was perhaps a quiet hatred that they bore toward the
congregation who had honored their oppressor,
but it was none the less real.

As for the people in the town above, they
were entirely unconscious of the feeling that existed among the factory folk. When any kind
of mission work was undertaken by them, it
failed, unless bolstered up by picnics, festivals,
and entertainments; and when these were removed, there was found to be not an atom of
religious interest. There were those in the upper
town who honestly grieved and prayed over this
state of things, and who used all their wisdom
to overcome the apathy into which the people
were plunged, but their efforts were singularly
unsuccessful. Nor was the reason ever suspected.
It is but simple justice to say, that if Mr. Lamson's true character had been known, he would
never have been received into the church. In
the upper world he was kind, charitable; to all
appearance, "full of good works." Many times

he was heard to deplore the state of things on Steep Street; and it was generally understood that through some clause in the will of Robert Flint, who had been an outspoken church-hater, there could be nothing done, at least for a term of years.

The mill people, believing all others knew Lamson as well as they did, but shut their eyes to his true character, because of his wealth, despised and hated the church, as they did the agent, and joined hands in vowing enmity to both.

Among those who learned that the lawyer was a deacon, was Chamberlain. He also was fully enlightened as to what the people thought of his fitness for the position.

About this time he was absorbed in serious thinking. Although not a professing Christian himself, he had a high respect for such men as his friend Marshall. He knew that there were disciples of Christ whose very presence in that village would be a protest against the prevalent sin, — an overwhelming rebuke to such professing Christians as the grasping agent. The thought that the whole settlement was so given over to the service of Satan, that all actually believed that there was no goodness, no real piety, nothing but hypocrisy among the well-to-do dwellers

of the upper town,—was a great burden to the
young man. It seemed as if every knee had
bowed to Baal, and he stood alone in his respect
for the religion of Christ. Of course he was
wrong in this, for there were a few who, crushed
under the prevailing wickedness, forced to spend
all their energies in a bitter struggle with poverty, yet called upon the name of the Lord.
Of their existence he knew nothing, and he
really believed that from one limit of the settlement to the other, all ages and sexes were in-
dulging in a frantic rush to destruction. Among
other plans for the mitigation of this state of
affairs, he seriously meditated sending to a missionary society for a laborer to come among
these people. A talk with one of the more intelligent of the "puddlers" dispelled the idea.

"A missionary!" the man said in amazement.
"What for? There is n't a soul here will take
any stock in one. Folks know too well the hum-
bug of the whole thing. If any one wants to
convince me that they believe in the Bible, and
all that, let them do as it says,—let them live
it."

"Would not a missionary do that?"

"Yes, if he was hired to. A man will do
'most anything for a salary. Now let me tell
you, young feller, if you have been gulled into

thinking there is a shadow of truth in what these
folks try to force on us, you are deceived.   I
have made this a sort of study, and as far as
I can see, the ministers are a pretty good set
of men; they are paid to be.   A low-down,
sloven, drinking parson would n't stand any show
at all, and they know it.   So you don't want
to look there for your examples; but you want
to look at the people that profess to believe as
the ministers do, and yet don't get no pay for
it.   Look at them, and what do you see?"

"Some hypocrites, and some good, earnest
men who would lay down their lives before
doing a mean or a wicked thing," replied Chamberlain, warmly.

"Not much," was the bitter reply.   "You find
a set of grasping, hard-fisted, stuck-up fellers,
who grind the life out of such of us as are
under them; who cheat and lie about bargains,
and who pretend to be one thing and are something else.   I am only telling what I see every
day.   If you can bring a Christian who can run
a mill like that down yonder, and deal justly
with his help; who will live himself as his Bible
teaches; who is charitable and generous, and who
values human beings a bit above the profit they
pay him in their daily work, — I 'll believe, and
not till then."

.Chamberlain groaned inwardly. The great want
was apparent: There was need of an earnest
follower of the Master, who should *live* a se
mon, not preach one. There must be such in
Steelville; yet they were as far removed from
this people as though an ocean flowed between.
The man's argument caused the missionary idea
to drop out of sight.

Would it be possible to get Marshall to come
and live in this community? He hurried to his
boarding-place and wrote a long letter to his
friend, sealed and directed it, and then after a
long struggle with his own thoughts, destroyed
it. All of the long Saturday afternoon he
thought and planned. There must be some way
out of this. On him rested a heavy responsibility — a legacy left by his repentant uncle.
More and more the burden weighed. All day
long Sunday he wrestled with the problem, and
could see no way out. When the spirit of the
Lord is striving with man, no compromise will
answer; and Chamberlain, although he taxed his
ingenuity to the utmost, found no solution except
one, to which he would not for an instant
listen. Yet this suggestion, no matter how often
hurried out of his mind, came back and whispered its tender invitation over and over again.

At the time that he was so sorely tempted to

put all responsibility upon the shoulders of others, a fellow-workman, — a file-grinder, — also tempted, was, by the guiding of God's Spirit, being led toward the light.

Twenty miles from Steelville was a city of some size, where those of the file-workers who could afford it, went on occasional sprees. Once or twice a year select parties took the Saturday night train and spent a riotous Sabbath in the slums of the city, returning on the "Sunday night freight." From one of those parties that had already wasted one-half of the beautiful summer's day in carousing, two men detached themselves, and straying into the city park, sat down to talk. The younger of the twain was a man of forty odd years; healthy, vigorous, yet bearing the marks of dissipation. A costly meerschaum between his teeth, he sat and smoked, waiting for the other to speak. Ever and anon he took the pipe from his lips and looked at it with that admiration that inveterate smokers are wont to bestow upon their idols. To him this pipe, a present from his companion, meant comfort and ease. It was the only valuable he owned. With a longing for the good things of life, which his friend possessed, he looked at the pipe and rubbed it as if it were an Aladdin's lamp, and would fulfil his wish.

The man by his side was in every way more diminutive and much older — if the bleached appearance which pervaded his whole person could be truly taken as an index of increasing years. The two began to speak on indifferent topics, in which neither appeared deeply interested, yet to which both clung, as if feeling that the power of conversation would forever leave them if not encouraged by some sort of votive offering. From factory topics they drifted to horse-racing; from that to the latest variety at the lowest theatres; from that to the Sabbath excursions, and from this topic, which approached the nearest to the religious of anything, they swung around upon one which seemed at once to awaken their interest.

"I tell yer," said the lesser man, with an attempt at energy in his attenuated voice, "there is lots of money in it. No other business makes such profits. Why, there's Mulhern, that's in the city council here, and was once a sweeper for Lamson! I remember when he bought his first barrel of beer and started selling, and now look at him: He's just rolling in money, and has got the finest saloon in the city! Then there's Bill Guesclin; look at the position he occupies! He stands a fair chance for being mayor one of these days, and ten years ago he kept the meanest little rum-hole in the village, next to yours. I tell yer, Temple, if only a man drink light, and sell fair, he's sure of fortune. I've got the cash and the experience, and you understand the grocery-business; there is your hold. You can run Pfaff under ground in a month. I'll back you in good shape, and no one will know it either."

"The fact is, I don't want to sell rum," said the man, a flush rising to his face.

"O, pshaw!" replied the other; "you make me tired. A feller that'll drink rum the way you have, and that'll go the rounds and be into everything from a gin-mill to a prize-fight, and that's slept under the bar many a night when he was too drunk to get home,—to be afraid to sell rum, is more than I can understand."

His companion winced perceptibly, but made no reply.

"Now, look here," continued the smaller man; "I've got the papers right here in my pocket, and if you want to know it, they're all signed, too, so sure was I of getting your consent. All that is needed is to settle on the profits, and we will set you up in less than a week. No more file-grinding for you. I will guarantee two years from to-day you'll have as much money as any of them, and be able to own just as fine horses, and have things as good, as Lamson has. Why should n't you have a profit out of this as well as he?"

"I tell you, I don't want to sell rum," said the man, but less positively than before.

"Well, what are you going to do? Grind files till you get so bad a drunkard that they'll fire you out, and then go to cleaning out spittoons, and washing bar-room floors, and hanging 'round for the slops that are left in the bottoms of the beer-glasses? You're proud, I know, but you ain't no prouder than lots of fellers that have come to just that same thing."

"Where are the papers?" said Temple, brokenly.

With a thin, white smile, the man drew them from his pocket and handed them over. His fingers trembling, and his eyes blurred by sudden moisture, the other took the documents, and slowly opening them began to read, his companion watching his every move with a keenness that none would ever have guessed him to be able to command.

During the conversation, two men, in citizens' dress, and of quiet appearance, had come down one of the broad paths of the park and now stood quite near. One of them mounted a mound of earth, opened a hymn-book, and began in a clear, pleasant voice to sing.

At first, when the words of the song rang out on the still air, Temple moved his head impatiently, and crumpled the paper with a nervous grasp, as if protesting against this interruption to his thoughts; but as the song proceeded, the frown gradually faded from his heavy brow, and the document appeared forgotten, as he listened with increasing pleasure. Not to his ears alone had the song come, for from all parts of the pleasure-ground, rising from recumbent positions in the shade, leaving the rustic seats, breaking from gossiping knots of smokers, young men and boys, and some whose heads were gray, were converging toward the spot.

"Why don't you read?"

There was no answer.

"Say, is it a bargain?" continued the other, after a lengthy pause, and holding out a shrunken hand.

But Temple rose suddenly, brushed him aside, and lounged up to a better position for hearing. His companion followed, and ere long they were wedged into a dense crowd that had collected in front of the turfy rostrum. The reading of the Scriptures followed the singing, and then came brief remarks; and by the time the service was a half-hour old, there had gathered two thousand people. As Temple glanced around over the faces, — many of them seared and scarred with sin; many old and wrinkled; a few fresh and young,—thoughts came to him to which he had long been a stranger, and of which his companion never dreamed. Seeing the gravity that had settled over his chum's face, his friend thought to relieve it by chaffing the preacher, so in his husky voice he called out,—

"Oh, give us a rest!" looking about for approval, and was much surprised to see on Temple's face a look of contempt, such as he had never before encountered. A few loafers who laughed weakly at his outburst, and who gathered closer to enjoy whatever fun he might be able to produce, afforded him little consolation. The experiment was not repeated, and the services went on.

Nearly an hour had passed when the little man, who was thoroughly weary of the whole proceeding, suddenly made a momentous and alarming discovery. Looking down upon the ground he saw protruding from beneath Temple's substantial boot-heel, the stem of his costly meerschaum.

"Jack," he said, in a horrified tone, "you are smashing your pipe."

There was no reply.

"Say, Jack," tugging at his sleeve, "you 've got your foot on your pipe, man, and you 'll smash it all to flinders!"

With a sudden, strange glance, Temple turned and looked into the face of the man whom for two riotous years he had called "friend." Then grinding the pipe more deeply into the gravelly earth, and setting his lips firmly together, he bestowed his whole attention upon the chapter then being read from the Bible.

Aghast, subdued, utterly overcome, by this most eccentric behavior, the other stood, not knowing what to do, and wishing most heartily that some policeman would make away with the disturbers of his peace. But none did so, and the agony went on. Finally, the last song was sung, the last word spoken, and the two preachers, descending from their improvised pulpit, departed as quietly as they had come, and the congregation as quietly resumed their favorite and usual lounging-places.

"Pretty long-winded fellers, are n't they?" suggested the liquor-dealer, as they walked away toward the depot.

This remark received neither rebuke nor approbation, and another was ventured upon.

"Say, Jack, I s'pose you 've 'bout made up your mind to come into that, have n't you? Of course it ought to be settled this afternoon."

Temple turned and again looked at his companion with the same gaze he had bestowed upon him during the service, and then he said, slowly,—

"Ed. Crabtree, you've known me for two years, — known me pretty well, — can you tell any good of me?"

"Why, yes," was the startled reply.

"Well, don't you do it, because lying is some-thing I everlastingly abominate," said Temple, with decision. "But, look here, that proposition is for me to join you in setting up that bar-room?"

"Yes."

"And I was going to do it?"

"Yes," with an eager intonation.

"I had almost shaken hands on it, when that fellow began to sing?"

"Yes; it was about the same as settled," said the other, with a satisfied accent.

"Well, now let me tell you, since I've heard that reading, and that speaking, and that sing-ing, I've changed my mind. Sooner than be a Steep-street rumseller, I'd live as the rats do, on the best picking in the garbage-barrels. Sooner than make other men what I have been and you are, I'd travel the streets from morning till night as a broom-pedler."

"Why, them fellers did n't talk temperance."

"I know that," was the energetic reply, "but what they did talk made me remember who I was, and what my father was. Those songs they sung brought back the old Connecticut homestead that I, since father's death, have poured down my throat and the throats of other fools. The chapters that were read, brought back to me my godly father, the deacon, whom everybody loved and respected, and who would no more do a wrong thing than he would lose his own right arm. And, I tell you, when I remembered all those things, I made up my mind that if it was selling rum or starvation, I'd starve; so that's your answer, and here's your papers, and now get; I don't want to see you again to-day!"

There was a ring in the voice that admitted of no argument, and the liquor-dealer, accepting the fact, left, while Temple, his face flushed with excitement, waited impatiently for the night freight.

IV.

In·the·Saddle.

CHAMBERLAIN had been a workman for several weeks. He now felt assured that he could, without injury to his health, stand almost any work in the place. Mr. Lamson and Doctor Ponsonby had predicted that he could not endure the hardships to which he would unavoidably be subjected, — that he would find the workmen coarse, illiterate, and quarrelsome, accustomed to severe labor, jealously demanding that all in their company share alike; that he would be obliged to work, fight, swear, and drink with the worst, to make himself even tolerable to them. These statements he found to be greatly overdrawn. The men were profane, were hard drinkers, and settled many differences with their fists; but, as a rule, they allowed a noisy man to be noisy, a quiet man to be quiet. Strangers of a peaceable turn of mind were not molested.

Chamberlain had adopted the regulation sleeveless flannel shirt, and dark pantaloons belted about the waist. His lithe figure looked well in this costume, and his white arms, symmetrically developed by gymnasium practice, brought many rough compliments from the workmen. Unaccustomed though he was to labor and self-denial, he did not find it especially hard to spend ten hours a day in the factory. He went into the work with a vim that was altogether unusual, and provoked amusement among the men.

In taking his place he had been obliged to answer questions as to his past life, but although his replies were wordy and amply satisfied the questioner, the actual information obtained was meagre. They learned that he had been at school up to his entry into the file-works, and that information, while it accounted for some of his peculiarities, made him of importance in settling minor disputes. On the whole, therefore, the young man had been well received, and was pleased with the prospect of the two years' adventure to which he had now fully determined to treat himself. In addition to this was also the often-present thought of wretched Steep Street. It was his to renovate, and he vowed, if it were within the bounds of possibility, to make it one of the best-ordered streets in the town. In this he was honest, but as yet, little knew the task that lay before him.

His work at the end of the third week was "grinding files." In the great "grinding-room" were, in a long row, ten grind-stones ; not the diminutive stone that one sees in the farm-yard or carpenter's shop, but monsters weighing tons. Above each was built a wooden-saddle, on which the grinder sat, as the stone whirled swiftly between his knees, smoothing the rough file-stock into proper shape for "cutting." The work of grinding required considerable skill, and, as a rule, only the older hands were allowed to do it ; but he had shown such aptitude, that as a special favor he was assigned a place and allowed to grind with the rest.

As he bent over his work one afternoon, the perspiration standing in beads on his brow, and mingling with the splashes of slate-colored mud that flew in all directions, he heard near him a clear, feminine voice. Glancing down he saw Mr. Lamson and a young lady standing close by. The agent, with marked politeness, was explaining the machines and processes to his companion. With some curiosity Chamberlain looked at the latter. She was strikingly beautiful. That she was the daughter of wealth and culture, her dress and manner at once proclaimed ; and that she regarded the men about her as of different clay from those whom she knew as friends and associates seemed probable. Apparently she thought the young aristocrat to have been born to the work, for he received the same well-bred look of carelessness that the rest did.

He was a trifle chagrined that his patrician bearing even in the wooden-saddle should not be recognized; yet, beneath his disappointment, he laughed at his own absurd pride. He was not wont to worry about the good or ill opinion of young ladies; but for some reason that he did not seek to explain, it would have greatly flattered him to receive notice from this lovely visitor. Her lack of discrimination wounded his self-pride, even while he recognized his own foolishness.

From Lamson's attentions, it was plain that the lawyer was very eager for her good opinion; but whether or not she was pleased with him was not apparent.

The men in all parts of the room looked at the visitor admiringly. She seemed insensible to the compliment which their eyes were paying, and observed them with the same quiet air that she bestowed upon the queer saddle-covered stones. Hitherto, Chamberlain had believed that he should never feel ashamed of any honest calling, but now for the moment he felt awk

ward and out of place. With strong mental
protest at his own foolishness, he bent to his
work, grasping the file with so much force that
when it came in contact with the whirling
stone, a large spatter of mud flew from it,
striking the young lady full in the face. Chamberlain was aghast.

In response to her startled exclamation, the
agent turned wrathfully toward the stone, but
seeing who was the aggressor said nothing. Instead he proffered his handkerchief, and the stain
was quickly wiped away. From the wave of
crimson that flooded the young lady's cheeks, it
was evident that she was vexed. Mr. Lamson
apologized as well as he could for his awkward
workman, saying that he was a new hand and
careless, and that he should be reprimanded.

Had Chamberlain been himself and in his
own clothes, he would at once have apologized
gracefully; but in a workman's garb, his face
smeared with mud, his hands covered with huge
leather-mittens, he felt like a boor, and could
no more frame a fitting excuse than could any
of the callow apprentices of the place. He
therefore sat and blushed, smarting under the
indignant glance that he had received when
Lamson had said that it was " sheer careless
ness."

A little later the visitor passed from the room, all chance for apology was gone, and he felt as if he should never have the courage to go into society again. The courtesy which he had formerly known so well how to bestow, seemed to belong to the good clothes he had discarded.

"Say, Chamberlain," said one of the men, halting before his stone, "did you douse that Whitney gal a puppus?"

"Who?"

"Why, Miriam Whitney, the agent's gal. You spattered her, didn't you?"

"Yes; but it was an accident; I ought to have apologized."

"Humph, I'm glad you didn't. She's too stuck-up to live. She looked as if she would like to have seen you hangin' fur it. Shouldn't wonder if she made the boss fire you," returned the other.

"Oh, I guess not," was the reply, and the other moved off.

"Miriam Whitney," thought he; "a pretty name. So she is the agent's 'gal,' is she?"

"Say, the boss wants you in the office at wunst," said the sweeper, appearing at that moment.

"I told you so. The deakin never gives a man his black look twice."

With much wonderment, Chamberlain walked directly to the office, and stood before the glass-paneled door of Lamson's sanctum. Within were two ladies; one the fair girl whom he had spattered, and an older lady. The agent's face darkened when he saw him.

"What do you wish?" he said harshly, opening the door.

"You sent for me," replied Chamberlain, a trifle disconcerted.

"You are mistaken; I did nothing of the kind. If I had, there is no excuse for your appearing here covered with mud and filth."

"The message said 'at once.'"

"That will do. You were not sent for. Return to your work," was the stern reply.

Chamberlain realized that the little sweeper had played a joke on him, and he replied, —

"The next time your special messenger comes for me, I suppose I need n't notice it?"

"Chamberlain," replied the agent, "remember you are only a common laborer here. Go back to your work, or I shall summon the day watch man to remove you."

This was said in a low, intense tone; and the other, realizing at once the power that this man had, and the consequences that would surely follow open rebellion, swallowed his wrath and

walked back to his work. Poor fellow, he was
more excited than he knew, for when he mounted
his stone again, his hand trembled so that he
could with difficulty work. What could be Lamson's thought in so insulting him? Up to this time
there had been only kindness and sympathy.
Was it anger on account of the awkwardness
that caused that trifling accident? or did the
shrewd lawyer intend to humiliate him till he
rebelled and left? The ferment in his mind was
not in the least allayed when the foreman of
the room came along and shouted savagely, with
a string of oaths that made him shudder:—

"What kind of work are you doing up there,
you college idiot? Look at the face of this file!
Don't let me see any more of that, or you'll
get down and go to sweeping again. Now
mind!"

Chamberlain made no reply. He recognized the
work as some of his, done since the accident,
and saw that it was faulty. There came to him
the thought, that the foreman spoke to few of
the others as roughly; and certainly, if he were
a judge, their work was fully as often badly finished. Was not this part of a train of humilia-
tions purposely laid to explode the magazine of
his temper? With a firmer purpose and a cooler
head, the young man set himself harder than

ever at work to turn out the best file-stock in
the room. There never had been any complaint
as to the quantity accomplished,—now for the
quality. One thing rejoiced him so much that
it took away nearly all of the sting of the rebuke, and that was, that under this sort of training he could not help but be the best workman
in the room. When they had been easy with
him, and smoothed his path, and granted him
half-holidays unasked, it was much harder to be
faithful and conscientious in his labor; but now
with every faculty on the alert, with jealous eyes
on him, eager for opportunities to reprimand, he
progressed finely, and above all, with grim determination, kept his temper.

"You had better leave," suggested one of the
more friendly of the men. "Swinert will never
give you any peace. He hates you for some
reason or other, and when he gets down on a
man, it's all day with him. Give in your notice;
you can get a job somewhere else."

"I guess I'll stay a while longer."

"Well, you are a fool if you do. No other
man but Gaffney would stand what you have.
Next thing the boss will do will be to strike
you."

"Swinert strike me? Oh, no! I guess not,"
was the confident reply.

"Why would n't I strike you," said a new voice, and the foreman stood in front of him.

"If you will listen, I will tell you," said Chamberlain, assuming a confidential air. "In the first place, you are too noisy a man to be dangerous. A man who exercises the muscles of his jaws so constantly as you, never does much telling work with his hands."

"Look here, you——"

"L'ave the lad explain; you invited it," said one of the men.

"Yes, let him go on, it 's the noon hour; you ain't boss now," said others, and Chamberlain continued.

"In the second place, you are all broken up through rum and tobacco. Physically, you are a wreck. No doubt you were once a strong man, but you are now a very weak one."

The man made a movement forward as if to carry out his threat, but the bystanders restrained him, and the lecture went on.

"In the third place, you lack one essential, which I doubt if you ever possessed, and that is, real grit. No plucky man will hit a boy as you struck the sweeper yesterday. No brave man will curse a woman as you cursed your own sister at the mill door last week; and lastly, no one but a ruffianly coward will *be bought* to drive another man out of the mill."

At the last shot, the man turned white, and as the whistle blew, hurried into the factory. The men dispersed, discussing the matter and casting ugly looks at the door through which he had disappeared.

In the middle of the afternoon, ostensibly to examine his work, Swinert drew near and said, anxiously, —

"For Heaven's sake, Chamberlain, don't spread that report; the men will mob me! I have a wife and five children to support. Don't ruin me."

"It depends on yourself. Do what is right, and I will see to the men; and remember—I am here to stay."

V.

"One·of·Us."

"HOLE in the Wall," the popular groggery of Steep Street, was the evening resort of most of the able-bodied men of the settlement. The proprietor, a short, stout man of German-Irish parentage, named Pfaff, was said to be wealthy. In addition to his stock of liquors he kept a small grocery, which, occupying the room directly in front of the groggery, gave ample opportunity for sly drinks. His customers embraced most of the adults of the village, and indeed some of the children might be so called, as they invariably tasted the beer which they carried home by the pitcherful. Pfaff was thought a very jolly fellow, — a trifle obstinate in his opinions, but generally as fond of friendly converse as he was of American dimes. He was ever ready to drink with his guests, at their expense, and on rare occasions "stood treat" himself

Not only in the mill village, but in the town above, Pfaff was noted for the excellence of his drinks. For this reason numbers of the liquor-loving from the upper settlement frequently dropped in to taste " Jacob's Best," and the fact was enlarged upon by the liquor-dealer with loud-voiced pride to the evening loungers.

The laborer, in a factory where the water is poor, is like the desert traveler, often morbidly thirsty. The wells in the file-works furnished water that was brackish and hardly fit to drink. The homes on Steep Street were not better off. The people used the water for washing, but no more than was absolutely necessary. In drinking it was frequently neutralized by a portion from the family bottle, in the proportion of one part of water to three parts of liquor, and sometimes the hurtful water was entirely left out. It had naturally come to pass that a special prejudice existed against it in the minds of the villagers. If any one was sick, it was laid to the water. Every ill seemed to have its origin in the unwholesome furnishings of the wells. Had it been within the bounds of reason, there is cause to believe that most cases of delirium tremens would have been traced directly to "bad water." This being the case, it was not strange that Jacob Pfaff grew rich and bloated; that men,

women, and children drank his beer and other
liquors; that the traces of excessive drinking
were on masculine countenances, otherwise intelligent and manly; on feminine faces, that, free
from it, would have been womanly and attractive.

Pfaff had no sign over his door, but he had
many a sign through the hamlet. What were
the old hats stuffed in broken windows, the filthy
door-yards, the noisome fumes, the bloated fathers
and mothers, the rickety children, the rags, vice,
and squalor, but Jacob Pfaff's signs? The people
did not read them thus, however. Their thought
was "the water is bad; we must drink something."

It happened one evening, as Chamberlain was
returning from work, he was overtaken by one
of the grinding-room hands with whom he had
often spoken. Pleasanter and better informed
than most of the men, he had taken pains to
give timely and valuable hints about the work.
These he appreciated and remembered, as John
Temple joined him, and the thought gave an
unusual cordiality to his greeting. As they came
in sight of "Hole in the Wall" the new-comer
began to speak of the excellent beverages sold
there. Perhaps the German name had something
to do with it; but the speaker asserted that

no saloon he had ever patronized furnished such thirst-quenching liquor. Jacob, he said, had just renovated his bar, and now the place was clean and wholesome, would n't Mr. Chamberlain come in and try a glass?

Our friend, as we know, was not a teetotaller; he believed that it was right for any one to take wines or beer when they wished, provided they did not overdo the matter. Indeed this had been impressed upon him by his guardian when he was quite young. Only a few times in his life had he tasted liquor over a bar, and then in the company of those who were considered high-toned gentlemen. The invitation that he now received was, for the moment, a puzzle to him. He had no sympathy with those who guzzled liquor as did the people who patronized Pfaff; yet, here was a file-grinder, a gentleman in his way, asking him to drink with him. With no religious scruples to bring for ward, no excuse to offer, for he instinctively ac knowledged that were it in a first-class hotel, and his companion a society man, he should say yes, he consented, and for the first time, and with a feeling of shame-facedness that was entirely new to him, entered the saloon and went up to the bar.

The proprietor saw the new face and bestirred himself. A fresh customer always roused him to an awkward politeness,—a courtesy flavored with cupidity.

While Chamberlain waited for his glass, a hand was laid on his shoulder, and a rough voice said,—

"Well, if here ain't Chamberlain, our youngest; the chap that the boys said was pious! They did n't know ye, did they, lad?"

It was Gaffney, who apparently had forgotten the "wetting-down," and was now as dry as ever.

"I told 'em," continued the man, keeping his hand on the young man's shoulder, to steady himself, "I told 'em to hold on and wait till ye showed yer hand; I felt from the first that you was one of us."

Chamberlain set down his glass untasted.

"Drink your beer, don't mind Gaffney," said his friend.

"Yes, drink it, it is good; never mind Gaffney," echoed the dealer.

"Thank you, I don't think I **wish** for any now," was the reply; a strange gravity settling over the young face.

"Perhaps there is something wrong with it; shall I draw another?" asked the proprietor a trifle anxiously.

"No, I thank you," was the positive reply, and Chamberlain moved toward the door.

"Fernald," close the door for a minute," said Pfaff.

The door was instantly shut, a couple of men stood against it, and the youth was a prisoner. With a flash in his eyes he turned toward the rumseller.

The latter had come out from behind the bar, and now stood expanding his chest and looking fierce, in front of his fastidious customer.

"I intend to know why you came in here and called for my beer, and then refused to drink it?" he inquired aggressively.

"I think he saw a fly in it and it sickened him," interposed Temple, anxious ₤to avoid trouble.

"Is that so?" asked Pfaff.

"No," answered Chamberlain.

"Well, what was it?"

"Tell what it was then," echoed the loungers.

"I had always supposed that a man had a right to enter any sort of store and examine the goods, and that he could purchase or not as he wished," was the reply.

"Well, he can't do it here," replied the other. "I don't care for the price of the beer, but I don't intend that any man shall stick up his nose at it; you just drink that glass, or give me a good reason for not doing it, or I'll wipe up the floor with you."

Chamberlain was young and fiery; a threat was to him like a whip to an untamed horse; his pride was roused; he despised bar-room rows, but he could not allow a bully to insult him thus. His friend whispered, "take your beer, don't be a fool." The loungers drew nearer to see the young upstart punished for his insolence.

At this stage of affairs, a door back of the bar opened and Sam Putman came in.

"Holloa! what's this?" he inquired, his eyes lighting up with interest.

"Why," said Jacob, "this young fellow says my beer ain't fit for swill, and he's got me to draw it, and now is goin' off without drinkin' it."

"Did he pay for it?" asked Sam, throwing one leg over the bar.

"Yes."

"Well, it's his then, ain't it?"

"Yes; but —— "

"Then I don't see as it's any of your business what he does with it," was the cool reply.

"But I intend to make it some of my business," replied Pfaff, excitedly. "I don't allow

no man to throw mud on me and then rub
it in this sort of way."

"If you touch that young fellow," said Sam,
measuring his words slowly, "I'll throw you out
of the window into the river."

"Well, let him get his beer off my counter,
and out of my glass," sputtered the other;
but Gaffney had attended to that, having quietly
finished the troublesome liquor.

As Chamberlain continued his walk with his
friend, the latter began to question him as to
the cause of his sudden aversion to the glass
of liquor. At first the young man's replies
were unsatisfactory; he gave no reason for his
strange conduct, but on being pressed he said, —

"Did you hear Gaffney speak to me?"

"Yes."

"Well, he said when he saw me with a glass
of liquor in my hand, 'now I know you are one of
us'; that is what the trouble was. 'One
of us'; what did that mean? It didn't mean
that I was one of the workmen who could
hold his own at the forge, or on a grind-stone
or over the furnace. It meant that I was one
of the drinkers; one of the men who go on
a spree every Saturday night, who can't live
from one week's end to the other without
drink; **who are a curse to themselves and**

their families. That was what it meant; I saw it all in a flash, and I could no more sign such a compact, by drinking that glass, than I could commit murder."

"You are excited," said his companion in a queer muffled tone.

"Perhaps so; but if I am, I am sure of this, that I will never taste another drop of liquor in my life. I see clearly now; there are but two sides: those who drink and those who do not; the drunken and the sober."

"You are right," replied the other in a low voice, "keep your resolve. You have no appetite to fight; never allow it to waken."

"I am not so sure about not having any appetite; I have always been accustomed to wines, and at times stronger liquors, and I doubt not I shall have a fight of it, but I have tasted my last drop." .

"Would to God, I could say as much," acknowleged Temple, with a groan, and at once Chamberlain, who had been engrossed with his own resolve, awoke to the struggles of another.

"Come up to my room," he said, drawing the other's arm through his. Reaching the tiny apartment, he threw open the blinds so that the evening breeze came in and cooled their heated brows.

"Were you in earnest in what you said?" he asked.

"Yes, but it is of no use. I am made of weaker stuff than most men. Over and over again have I resolved to stop drinking, but I can't do it," was the reply.

"Why don't you sign the pledge?" asked the young man.

"I have several times."

"Do it again; make up your mind and stick to it."

"No use," was the reply.

To the best of his ability, his friend cheered him up; trying hard to give him more faith in his own power of resistance. Finally Temple said, —

"There is but one thing that can save me, the religion of Christ. I was well taught when I was young; I know the way, but strange though it may seem to you, I am not willing to give up to it."

What could Chamberlain say? Could he advise others to flee from the wrath to come while he stood still and braved it? Surely not. Yet his heart was stirred by this man's trouble; he longed to help him. It was like watching a man drown without stretching out a hand to save him.

When his visitor had departed, Chamberlain did not go down to supper. Instead, he sat alone and communed long with himself.

Finally, as the town-clock struck eleven, he arose, went down stairs, and out into the night. A short walk brought him to the lodgings of his friend. He found that he had not yet retired. His message, whatever it was, brought the tears to the other's eyes, and soon two earnest souls were kneeling side by side, entreating forgiveness, and cleansing at the throne of grace.

That night Tom Chamberlain and John Temple began life anew. The glorious surrender had been made. Two hearts had been won; two who had, but a few hours before, been identified with the sin and misery of Steep Street, of whom the drunkards could say, "you are of us," had crossed the line, and were rejoicing in the love of a new and all-powerful Master. With great joy in their hearts they communed one with the other, knowing that they would be "epistles known and read of all" in the factory and out. The test of true and right living would be most rigidly applied to them. It must be a whole consecration or none at all. Without discussing the question, Temple swept the pipes and tobacco from his shelf and threw them out of the window.

Not noting the flight of time, the two friends sat and planned for the future. The fields were white with harvest, and they were the laborers. It was a responsibility to which too few young men awaken. They felt their own weakness, — their own inability to cope with the powers of darkness so stoutly entrenched in the valley below, — yet to them was the promise, "Lo, I am with you alway."

The first gray tinge of morning was showing itself in the east when Chamberlain went back to his room. As the day broke, he sat at the open window — very happy, very peaceful. He felt that the knowledge of his sin, the burden that he had carried about ever since he awakened to the condition of Steep Street, was now gone. Like a runner freed from a load, he had such freedom as only Christ can give. As yet he had sent no word to his friend in the far-away city home. Perhaps it had been in part because there was nothing to tell but what he was bound not to divulge. Now, however, he had news that he knew would make Marshall happier than any other message that he could send, so he sat down and wrote, in a few simple sentences, of his decision, of his great joy, and of the friend who had at the same time been born into the Kingdom with him. In conclusion he earnestly asked him to remember them both in his prayers, as they sorely needed wisdom. This was enclosed in a letter to Doctor Ponsonby, and mailed at once.

"Good land! Have you had a fortune fall to you?" asked Mrs. Bowman, as he came into the kitchen with a very happy look.

"I guess so; a fortune that you can have too, if you wish," was the reply.

"Well, if there is anything good that's free, I'd like to know it, for I'm right there," said the landlady energetically shaking the fire.

"Salvation's free," said the young man.

"Look here young man, I ain't much on religion, and I spose you know it, but I don't never allow anybody to make fun of it in my presence. Joke just as much as you please in the right way, and I'll enjoy it when I have time; but don't make fun of things that some folks respect."

"God forbid that I should do anything of the kind. I was in earnest, for last night I gave my heart to the Lord, and I believe he has washed away my sins," replied Chamberlain earnestly.

"Do you mean to say that you have honestly and truly experienced religion?" was the astounded query.

"Yes."

"Well, I never. I hope it will last; it's dreadful to be a back-slider; that's what I am. You never get no comfort out of life while your a back-slider. I ain't been a happy Christian for a good many years, not since Rob was born; and I'm sure I've suffered enough on account of my short-comings. I've got so hardened that I durst not pray; but Mr. Chamberlain, won't you pray for Rob?"

There was a pathos, an entreaty in the voice that went to the young convert's heart. Poor, erring Rob? The only son of the widow Bowman. Easily led, full of good resolutions, abounding in broken promises; the tool of the smarter loungers in the village.

"We can both pray," said he, and they knelt on the kitchen floor and prayed. First, Chamberlain offered a faltering petition for the erring son, and the strong muscular woman by his side sobbed like a child, and added a few words of her own at the close.

"Be you a Methodist, Mr. Chamberlain?" she enquired, wiping her eyes on her apron.

"Why, I don't know; I had hardly thought."

"I thought 'cause you kneeled down maybe you was a Methodist; you know the Congregationalists always stand up when they pray."

Not feeling like discussing the different customs of denominations just then, Chamberlain
was silent, and breakfast being ready, they sat
down to eat, after which the lateness of the hour
compelled him to hurry away to the mill.

VI.

A. Favor.

ON an elevated plateau overlooking the factory street was an old-fashioned mansion,
surrounded by ample, well-kept grounds. The
general atmosphere of the place was that of
respectable old age. A departed generation built
the house, laid out the grounds, planted the
trees, sowed the hollyhocks, and no modernism
had re-arranged their works. Between the estate
and the straggling line of tenements a high board
fence, capped with spikes, was erected, as a "thus
far and no farther" to the juvenile apple-hunters
of the village below.

The estate was owned and occupied by a
maiden lady, Miss Louisa Whittier. Like it, she
belonged to the past. The last of the Whittiers,
she held scrupulously to the faded customs of
the race, as she did to the rusty silks and bom-
bazines that filled her attic trunks. None of the
Steep Street people knew her, and few of the

dwellers in the upper town were at all intimate, although her wealth and blue blood entitled her to more than usual consideration. She attended the North Church, of which Mr. Lamson was deacon. She was not, however, a member of the "Ladies' Charitable Society," "The Woman's Temperance Club," or "The Home Missionary Bureau." She was therefore, to many of the good ladies, a comparative stranger. Nevertheless, in spite of her negative qualities, Miss Whittier gave largely to the charities above named, and was regularly at church.

It was with a knowledge of most of these facts that Chamberlain lifted the brass dragon's-head knocker on the front door of the Whittier mansion, and dropped it with a clang that smote upon the quiet interior like an alarm of fire. There was a bustle within, a glimmer, as if a lamp were lighted to banish the fast-gathering shadows, a rustle, the door opened, and the lady of the house stood before the young man.

She was tall, with lovely white hair, a plain, shrewd face, and gray eyes that had the least glint of suspicion in them.

Raising his hat, he said, —

"Is this Miss Whittier?"

"It is."

"Can I see you for a few moments?"

The lady gave him a quick, keen glance. He had used the usual introductory phrase of the book agent.

"Pardon me, but have you anything to sell?" she said.

"No, madam," replied he, quietly, although with a flush.

The lady saw it, and said, —

"I am sure you will excuse my question when I tell you that almost every stranger who calls here has something to dispose of. Some of them are positively insulting in their pertinacity. It is they who have made me suspicious, and perhaps inhospitable. Will you walk in, sir?"

Chamberlain followed her into a square, stiffly-furnished parlor, and accepted a chair, his hostess seating herself on a sofa opposite him. At his left a door opened into a second parlor in which there was no light. By a window at the further end he could just discern a white-clad figure. From the graceful curves and careless posture, he decided that it was a young girl. She seemed not aware of his presence. Meanwhile Miss Whittier was regarding him with a courteous what-is-it,-sir? look that required him to speak.

"I will state the object of my visit as briefly as possible," he said, in response to her mute interrogation. "I am in the employ of the File Company."

"Indeed," said Miss Whittier's eyes, "you had better have been a peddler," but her lips remained shut.

"Since coming here I have seen the wretchedness of Steep Street till it seems as if I could stand it no longer. I believe I know the whole story of the misery that hangs like a cloud over the settlement, — I know every rum-hole."

"Undoubtedly," said the eyes.

"And I think I know of a way to alleviate these evils. I must, however, ask your assistance in carrying out my scheme."

"I think," was the cold answer, "that I have all the charities on hand that I care to encourage; yet, if you will show that your plan is a good one, I will contribute five dollars."

"You misunderstand me. I ask for no money. Let me explain. The mill people, many of them, drink beer, cider, ale, and stronger liquors, because there is nothing else to drink on the street. The wells furnish poison. The people dare not drink it. There is, and has been, absolute suffering on this account. I have been here several months, and all I have tasted has been rain-water from a hogshead cistern. Now, my proposal is to furnish good water for the mill people, and wash the taste for poisonous liquors out of their mouths."

"I doubt if it can be done. And even if it can be, is it not the duty of the File Company to do it?" replied the lady.

"The Company will do nothing; of that I am assured, and unless others do it, this suffering must continue," was the quick reply.

"Can it be done?"

"I think so," said Chamberlain, earnestly, "for this reason: The ridge upon which your place is situated extends to the next village, where the formation of land is nearly the same as here. In that village is a driven well that flows hundreds of gallons of pure water daily. Were such a well at the head of this street, it would amply furnish all the tenements."

"What is your proposition?" asked Miss Whittier, trying to hide her interest.

"I thought," said he, hesitating a little, "that if you would sell, for a reasonable price, a spot in the lower part of your garden, large enough for the well, that I should like to buy it, and try the experiment."

"Young man," interrupted the lady, suddenly, "did the File Company commission you to talk this up to me?"

"They did not; nor has any one in the company the faintest idea that it is thought of," was the prompt reply.

"You knew, perhaps, that the tenements were built close up to the line of our estate to gratify a grudge that the Company held against my father?"

"I did not."

Miss Whittier mused a few moments.

"How much would the well cost?" she said, finally.

"The man whom I consulted, offered to do it for one thousand dollars, and take the risk,"

"That is considerable money."

"It is with regard to the money that I wished to ask a favor of you."

There was a movement in the next room, and the visitor wondered, uneasily, how much of an audience the darkness contained.

"I wish to put the money in your hands, and have you close the bargain and pay the bills," continued he.

"That is a very extraordinary request. Pray why do you wish it? Have you yet collected the money?"

"The money to be used was left me by my father. I shall collect from no one; and I ask you to pay the bills that I may not be suspected of doing it."

"Really, I don't understand it. Why do you wish to hide the deed?" inquired Miss Whittier.

"I am, as I said, in the employ of the File Company, if they know that I do this, the consequences will be unpleasant,—that is the reason. Now will you grant me the favor, and keep my secret?"

Instead of answering, she called into the next room,—

"Miriam!"

"Yes, auntie."

"Will you come here a moment?"

The occupant of the lounging-chair at the further end of the second parlor, rose and came forward into the light.

"Have you been listening to our conversation, my dear?"

"Parts of it," was the languid reply.

"What do you think of it?"

"I don't see why you should care; you can put the money into the hands of your lawyer, and let him pay the bills."

"Perhaps you are right," was the answer.

During the short conversation, Chamberlain had been closely observing the young girl. When he heard the name Miriam, it sent his blood with a bound to his heart. At once he felt that the fair girl whom he had so awkwardly spattered with mud in the grinding-room, was about to appear again; nor was he mistaken. She stood in the doorway, looking fairer than when he had for the first time acknowledged the power of her beauty. She bestowed upon him a well-bred glance of indifference, and then turned her attention to her aunt, as if he were not present. The same anger that had possessed him before, when she had rated him as a file-grinder, for an instant came over him, and then, with a firm setting of his teeth together, he crushed it.

She glanced again at him, as the determined look so plainly stamped itself upon his face. It interested her, and following the new impulse, she said, —

"Will you introduce me, auntie?"

Miss Whittier complied with no little astonishment, after discovering afresh what the surname of the young man was.

The young girl sank into a huge chair, and said to him, with a witching glance, —

"Is it not very dangerous working in the file-factory, Mr. Chamberlain?"

"In some parts it is," he replied.

"I visited the works recently and saw all the departments. Some rooms were dreadful, — full of steam and heat, — and others had terrible machines in them. It seemed hardly possible that men could work there every day for years."

"There are some very powerful men there," answered Chamberlain.

"They all drink, do they not? Mr. Lamson said the works brutalized them so that in a few years they were little better than beasts."

"That is entirely untrue. Many of the men love their families, are honest, and upright."

"Yet, Mr. Lamson should know about this," she said.

"He does know," was the reply, with unmistakable emphasis.

The expression of mischief that had lighted the young lady's eyes when the conversation began, was replaced by one of offended dignity. Rising, she said to the other lady,—

"Will you excuse me, auntie?" and swept from the room.

The caller also rose to go; as he did so, Miss Whittier, looking him full in the eyes, said,—

"Mr. Chamberlain, will you tell me honestly your motive in trying to help this wretched people on Steep Street?"

With a blush, and voice trembling, Tom witnessed the confession so new to him; and how hard it was, only those who have fought the battle and conquered, can ever know.

"Because, madam, I have started out to serve the Lord Jesus Christ. I am but young in the service, and perhaps not over-wise; but it seemed that this sin-stricken street needed help, and such help as I can I shall give," he said.

The lady held out her hand and gave his a warm grasp.

"I am glad you told me. Your secret shall be safe. But do not try to hide your profession. Do you attend church here?" said she.

He mentioned having attended the North Church; and as he left, the lady again shook hands and cordially invited him to call, and also to sit in her pew whenever he attended church.

In passing out, he saw Miss Whitney in a hammock that swung by the path. In the darkness he could not tell whether or not she acknowledged his bow. Feeling much as if he had again thrown mud at her by his eager awkwardness, he walked slowly down to his lodgings.

Full of his project, and anxious to impart to his friend the successful termination of his negotiations, Chamberlain hurried to Temple's boarding-place. The latter listened in silence until he had finished, then said, —

"Don't you think you are putting out your money rather freely for a laboring man?"

Chamberlain colored. It had never occurred

to him that his friend might consider his action at all Quixotic.

"I believe this to be a practical and safe investment," he replied.

"I don't know about that. That amount of money put into a store would pay you interest if nothing else; but this well, which I should fear will never furnish much water, seems to me a visionary undertaking."

"I believe it can be successfully made. The man who bored that in the village below is sure of it."

"Of course he is; it will be a couple of hundred dollars in his pocket to have that conviction. But really, it does not seem to me that it is actually necessary. There are wells on the street."

How much these remarks discouraged Chamberlain would be difficult to tell. The thought would obtrude itself that he might be wrong, and that the Steep Streeters perhaps neglected water from choice, rather than from necessity. It would be possible even now to gracefully retire from the whole undertaking. The co-operation of the conservative Miss Whittier had been most grateful to him. Yet, he was enough of a man to refrain from carrying a project through for mere pride's sake.

"I will tell you," said his friend, noting the disappointment expressed on his mobile face "we will investigate this matter. I may not be a judge. I rarely drink water; never did even before I acquired a taste for the stronger liquors. We know where most of the wells are. Let's test the water by taking a drink from each."

"I need no further conviction as to the badness of the water, but am very willing to convince you. We will do it," agreed the other.

The succeeding day, as they came home to dinner, Forsyth's well, at the foot of the street, was visited. A tin pail, weighted by a stone attached to a clothes line, was the only means of drawing the water.

"You fellers lost something down there?" inquired the owner from his seat on the doorstep.

"Oh, no; we are going to have a drink," answered Temple.

"A drink! a drink! Has Pfaff failed? or are you going to commit suicide? Here, hold on, till I get the bottle and sweeten it for you."

"No, thank you; we wish to try it and see how bad it is."

"Well, it's as good as any about, but it's rank poison for all that. I believe, on my word,

that there is more typhoid fever to the glass
in that water than in any other in the country.
Help yourselves; the more you take, the less
there is left."

"Smells rather rank, does n't it?" remarked
Temple, sniffing at the yellowish-colored liquid.

"Drink away; smells go for nothing on Steep
Street," was the reply.

Most conscientiously the investigator took a
few sips and then poured the rest away, remark-
ing as he did so:—

"I think this well is poisoned by the drains
that have soaked the ground full of their filth.
Let us go further up the street and find a
place where there is no such accessory, and I
believe the water will be pure and sweet."

"Why is it not good in the works?"

"I think it is. Most of the men prefer beer
or something stronger. Few know how the
water does taste; I must confess I do not.
You remember the day you were so thirsty,
when we went into 'Hole in the Wall?' even
that day I did not touch a drop of water."

A short walk brought them to the head of
·the street, and abreast the Bowman cottage.
Passing through the narrow lane that separated
it from the adjoining tenements, they approached
one of the rear dwellings. Mrs. Hidden's door

standing wide open, emboldened them to enter.

"Can we have a drink of water?"

"Indeed you can," was the widow's hearty response, pouring out a glassful and handing it to him.

Chamberlain passed it to Temple, who raised it to his lips. As he did so, a burning flush swept over his face, and seemingly by a violent effort, he set it down, saying in an unsteady voice, —

"There is liquor in it, is there not?"

"To be sure; it would give you the cramp without. That won't hurt ye; the children drink it every day."

"I wants a d'ink," lisped a little one, toddling up and receiving a liberal portion of the doubly poisoned dose.

"Is James Hidden your son?" inquired Chamberlain, a thought suddenly coming to him.

"He is that, although it's ashamed I am to own him, the dirty, little drunkard! What would his father — God rest his soul — say if he knew what his boy had come to?"

"I don't see what else you could expect. You probably fed him on this liquor and water, until he got an appetite."

"Of course I let him drink it. Sure, he would

have died of the cholera if I had n't. What else could I do?"

"Whatever else I did, I would not bring up my children to be drunkards. That little one there loves it already, and in a few years will be as bad as Jimmie," said Temple, still severely smarting from his own temptation.

"We can't die of thirst, whatever comes. If there was decent water in the village there would be no need for us to take the whiskey. The mill folks could give us good water if they chose. When my man first came here, he had a plan all made for using the big engine in the file-shops to pump water from the river into a reservoir upon the top of the hill, and to do it nights; and they would n't hear to it, on account of the cost. It's them that makes us drunkards; and it's little they care, either, as long as the dividends are regular."

"Then your husband was a temperance man?"

"My husband never tasted liquor till he came here. The village we lived in before was a good, healthy place, and the boss took some interest in the people. He would n't allow a drop inside of his fences. The work-folks there were decent and respectable, and went to bed nights instead of howling about and breaking each other's heads.

We would n't have staid here if my man had n't been killed by the machinery."

"You seem to be discontented, but your neighbors are well enough satisfied," remarked Chamberlain.

"Satisfied!" almost screamed the woman; "that's all you know about it. There's more broken hearts among the women-folks of this street than there are broken heads among the drunken husbands, and that's saying a deal. The worse a person is, the worse they feel. There are many of them that have tried, time and time again, to get out of this, but they can't do it. People made a great noise about the poor, black slaves down South, and let the white slaves up North alone. Lamson is the slave-owner of this village, and Pfaff is his overseer."

"But one can leave,"

"Can one leave? Who will hire him when they know he comes from this village? You young men think you are free, but just try to spread your wings a little and see how soon they are clipped."

The "warning whistle" had already announced that it was time to start for the factory, and the two were obliged to hurry back without dinner.

"Are you satisfied as to the need of pure water here?" inquired the younger man.

"I am, and more. I am appalled at the danger the children are in. How blind I have been. How can godly people rest nights when close to their homes are scores of little ones being trained up to fill drunkards' graves. Put the well through, and God speed you! Would I had something to add to it. But stay; only a few are to get the benefit of this after all."

"Why?"

"Those at the foot of the hill won't go clear to the head of Steep Street for water."

"No, but the water will willingly come down to them," was the laughing reply, and without further explanation he entered the factory and began his afternoon's work.

VII.

Kerosene·as·a·Beverage.

CHAMBERLAIN spent the day following his call upon Miss Louisa in planning. While busy with his work his mind was teeming with schemes for the welfare of the mill folk. Many of the measures suggested by his fertile brain were visionary. The future was painted with the bright colors that youth, health, and imagination, untutored by failure, are wont to portray. Had he watched his friend Temple, he would have seen that he also was deep in day-dreams.

When the visions grew less real, and the two awoke to the life that was pulsing about them, a strong desire came over each to take the other into his confidence, and as the whistle blew, announcing the end of the day's work, Temple hurried over to Chamberlain and said, —

"Wait for me; I have something to tell you."

Leaving the works a little behind the herd

of supper-seeking operatives, they walked slowly homeward.

"I have been thinking," said Temple, eagerly, "that Pfaff has had things his own way long enough."

"Yes."

"You see he controls the trade of the file-hands. Not only in liquors, but in almost every line. That little variety-store of his contains about all the people use, except meat and fish. His prices are very high, and his goods second rate. He is king of the village, and some say that Lamson gets a share of his profits. I can't swear to that, but I do know that every other store-keeper in the settlement has in some way been crowded out a few weeks after starting, and to my mind Lamson did it."

"It's a shame," said Chamberlain, hotly.

"I have been contriving all day how to over-come this state of affairs, and I think if I had a little capital I could fix things so that a second store could be maintained in spite of Lamson."

"How would you do it?"

"Well, to begin right, I should leave my job, file-grinding. Every one so far who has started a store has been obliged to work in the factory during the day, and keep open evenings, and just as soon as they were fairly under way,

Lamson would dismiss them for some pretended offense. Then their rent would be raised, and some of Pfaff's friends would run up big bills and refuse to pay them. Windows would be broken and goods stolen, till the parties gave up and moved away, after which Pfaff would flourish as before."

"What a rascally piece of business. I should think the authorities in the upper town would stop it."

"They don't care what is done," replied Temple, "and besides, Lamson is a big man up there, and what his hands do is referred to him. He makes a show of indignation, promises investigation, and that is the end of it."

"Now about your plan?"

"It is this: I would lease one end of "Bug Palace" for two years, without telling Lamson what I wanted it for, — that would prevent any raise on the rent. Then I would stock the lower room with such goods as are most salable here. I understand that part perfectly, as I was clerk in a country store for years before I took to drinking. I should put out some money on shutters that would n't be easily broken. I should sell for cash to doubtful customers, and give credit only to those whom I knew were willing to pay. Finally, to total-abstinence families I would sell goods at cost."

"Pay people to be temperate?" was the sur-prised exclamation.

"Yes; pay them to let liquor alone, if need be," replied Temple.

"I don't know about the wisdom of that. By the way, how much money would you need to start a store?"

"I can tell after a very little figuring. It would not be a very large sum, but, small as it is, I can never hope to handle it. O, if I had the money that I have paid for poison, it would be doubly sufficient."

Some time after this conversation a freight-wagon stopped before one of the doors of "Bug Palace," and, unloading a heavy blue cask, drove away. It was directed to Temple, and was rolled by him into the room that he had selected for a store. Of the stock that he had purchased, this barrel was the first arrival. For several weeks the gossips of Steep Street had puzzled over Temple's strange behavior. The rumors of the manner in which he was changing the filthy room into an apartment redolent with paint and whitewash had been circulated, repeated, and en-larged upon. It was generally believed that a billiard and liquor-saloon was to be opened. Pfaff smiled at the idea. Not that he doubted the opening of such a place, but he was assured from the beginning of its failure. When the gamins reported that a cask of some kind of liquor had been rolled into the place, all doubt was laid aside; and those whose scores were heaviest at the old stand, determined to favor the new dealer with their patronage.

Among them was Gaffney, whose persistent thirst, even on Steep Street, provoked many a rough joke. During the day mysterious boxes arrived and were deposited in the new store. The whole settlement was on the *qui vive.* Gaffney, urged by his one mastering passion, determined to be the first to "christen" the saloon, and taking a quart bottle, started up the street. The other topers, with the curious etiquette that holds among them, decided to stay away until the "opening."

Temple was within, unpacking a case of goods, when a heavy knock fell on the door. He opened it and confronted Gaffney.

"Good evenin' and good luck; so you're starting a store?" said the latter heartily.

"Yes; but I am not ready to sell anything."

"Oh, that's all right," said his caller jovially, pushing his way in and seating himself on an empty box. "Houly Moses, but you've got the room as clean as a biled-shirt! Wouldn't ye like me to help ye a bit, now?"

"Thank you, I guess not," was the reply.

"Aha! ye don't trust me," said the other with a laugh, "but ye do me wrong; I've reformed, I have. I have left off drinking, and I'm goin' to live honest and pay me bills; what have ye in the bar'l?"

"Kerosene," replied Temple.

"Kerosene," shouted Gaffney with a huge laugh "Well, by the houly poker, but you're a cute one. Kerosene—I s'pose they call it that because it makes men light-headed?"

Temple laughed; not that he comprehended the other's insinuations, but from sheer good nature

"So you have actually reformed?" he inquired.

"I have that," was the prompt reply. "Now you may not believe it, but I emptied the liquor out of this bottle, and was going to the store to have it filled with kerosene for the old woman."

"Indeed," was the suspicious reply.

"Yes, sir," said Gaffney earnestly. "The old woman and I would be very glad to try your kerosene as long as you have a fresh bar'l. Maybe it would give you good luck to have us for your first customers. We spend lots of money in the course of a year."

"Gaffney," said Temple, taking the quart bot-

tle and going behind the counter, "you understand that this is kerosene?"

"Why, bless your heart, man dear, certainly
I do," was the delighted reply; "and any man
that tries to make me believe it's anything
else, will have a tough job of it. You may
trust me."

As he was his first customer, Temple did not
accept the coin that was ostentatiously fumbled
for, and the purchaser went away with his heart
full of gratitude.

A number of Gaffney's boon companions saw
him come out of the new saloon with something
under his coat, which they were sure was a
bottle, so they at once joined him.

"Did he treat?" was the inquiry.

"He did that, and right generous."

"Pass it 'round," was the general suggestion.

"He made me promise that I'd drink his
good health myself, afore I give any one else
a sup of it," said Gaffney, backing up against a
building. "So here goes; here's to the new
saloon and its owner; may he live long and
prosper! When Pfaff kicks us out we'll trade
with Temple, and when he fires us, we'll go
back to our first love."

Throwing back his head, and raising the bottle to his lips, he took a draught.

An instant later the bottle lay broken in the gutter, and the drinker, coughing, spitting, and swearing, was making his way rapidly toward the doctor's, followed by a hooting crowd.

As one result of his visit to Temple, he went to bed sober for the first time in a month; although vowing dire vengeance upon the villain who had "pizened him."

When Temple's project was fully under way, and the people really knew what the policy of the new store was to be, it provoked much comment. There was no dearth of customers, most of whom, in these first purchases, paid cash. One and all loudly denounced the rum-selling grocer, and vowed their unalterable intention of patronizing the "Temperance-store." A large number of those who made this resolve, and who often reiterated it, loaded the air with fumes that strangely belied their words, and that caused the new grocer strongly to suspect them of being tools of his rivals. He accordingly kept so close a watch that none of his goods were missing, although much unnecessary handling was indulged. All things considered, he had reason to be gratified with the success that had already been attained in the few hours of the store's existence. Aware of the close surveillance to which all in the village were sub-

jected, Temple knew that Lamson must be in
formed of his enterprise. Much to his surprise,
the agent had asked no questions, and raised
no objections when he had given notice of his
intention to leave the works. Neither had he in
any way attempted to check him in his enterprise. As sanguine as most men, the new
grocer imagined that things had been so well
planned as to cause him to feel that there was
no use in combating him.

About the time he reached this wise conclusion, the lawyer was sitting in his private
office, talking earnestly with the village constable, a man who was elected through his influence, and was one of his tools.

"A seizure is the thing now; only it must be
well devised, and kept quiet until all is ripe,"
said Lamson.

"You are not in earnest about raiding Pfaff,
too?" asked the man, with a ring of incredulity
in his voice.

"I am. First, you will go to Temple's and
discover the jugs and bottles; then you may
take the other place, and get what you can.
Then give young Averill all the points for a
half-column article. Let him talk pretty strong
on my efforts to crush the infamous traffic, etc.;
you understand?"

"Yes, sir; but why not let Pfaff off? I am afraid he will get angry and raise a row."

"No, he won't. He will be given the wink, and his fine will be paid; but this Temple will have to stand his, and if I am not mistaken, it will disgust his few good customers, and perhaps discourage him. By the way, do you know who backs him in this?"

"Can't find out for the life of me. I tried to pump that young Chamberlain last Saturday, but he didn't help me out any. He's an innocent, that feller. He asked me if I didn't suppose you was backing Temple. He thought it would be just like a good, benevolent deacon to do some such thing."

At a loss to interpret the wrathful expression on his employer's face, the constable paused in dismay.

"Did he say anything else?" asked Lamson, in a choked voice.

"No, sir; just then Temple came along, and I gave him the wink to be quiet, and he understood, and began to talk about the work."

"Well, be sure and keep all knowledge of this raid from Chamberlain; and don't talk much with him anyway," commanded the lawyer.

"All right, sir; but I'm sure of him. I've got him solid. Anything that he knows, I can find out, and that will be quite an advantage, considering how intimate he is with Temple. I put him on to the fact that we wanted to know whether anybody 'in the upper town furnished the cash for the 'temperance store,' and offered him a five if he would find out. You never see a feller so tickled —— "

"You——" began Lamson, fairly foaming with rage, and utterly unable to express his wrath.

"What's the matter with that?" asked the man, beginning also to be angry that his keenness should be questioned. "Didn't you tell me to pick out some young feller that I could trust, and put him on this thing? I tell you, this young Chamberlain can be of use to us. The men like him first-class. He is a good workman, and never drinks. Unless you do get him on your side, he will be likely to be against you."

"Yes, but — there is something in this matter that you don't know, — something that I can't explain; but remember this: don't tell Chamberlain *anything*. Watch him all you please. Talk with him, but don't give him another atom of information. If a hundred dollars would recall what you have already said to him, I would gladly pay it."

Amazed that his employer should be so stirred by what had been said to one of the common

laborers, the man left, and proceeded to carry
out the plans already laid for the breaking up
of the new store.

The day for the seizure came, and everything
worked well. Temple was taken by surprise, and
in conscious innocence, was more than willing
to have his store searched. What was his amazement, therefore, when the searchers discovered
in a tiny closet at the rear of the shop, a number of jugs and bottles filled with liquors. He
was at a loss to know how they came there, until a careful examination showed that the clap-
boards had been removed from the outside, a
board sawn through, affording access to the
closet-shelves.

"Pretty ingenious place you had rigged," said
the constable, with a sneer.

"Me!" gasped Temple.

"Yes, you! I knew you were a fraud, from
the first."

The other store was also raided, and the two
cases came to trial together. The few words
with which the constable reported the affair to
Lamson, may describe the success of the plot:—

"You see, I selected the jugs and bottles and
had them marked one night down in Pfaff's cellar, jest as you advised," he said; "then young
Henley took them over to the engine-house and

stored them under the floor until all was ready. When it was time, he took them up back of the store and slipped them through the opening, and we stepped in the front way and seized them."

"Yes."

" We *knew* what was in them jugs, and Temple never disputed it; he jest wilted. Well, then in the court-room, Pfaff's jugs set in one place, and were examined, and he was fined; and then they came to Temple's, and they was examined, — Temple all the while looking white as a sheet, — and hanged if his'n war n't all filled with *water !* "

" Water ? "

" Yes, sir, — water ! The jedge tasted it, and I tasted it, and the witnesses tasted it. 'T was some of that miserable Steep Street water, that's enough to make a hoss sick —— "

" Now," said Lamson, interrupting the voluble executor of the law, " what you must do, is to find out who did this. There is a traitor some- where. You must hunt him out."

" O, there ain't no traitor; it was just a joke of young Chamberlain's."

" What did he have to do with it ? " was the savage inquiry.

" Well, he was down to the engine-house when Henley came in with the bottles."

"What was he there for?"

"He was there to show Forsyth how to rig the flag-halliards so they would work better. He knows, 'cause he has been aboard a yacht."

"Well?"

"He was showing of him when in came Henley, quiet-like, and hid these things under the floor, and then went out and got some more, and then came in, and then went out three times. When he went away the last time, Chamberlain and Forsyth, who had been laying low in the room above, and watching through the floor-grate, went down to investigate, and found the bottles and jugs. They were sure he must have stole it, and put it there to drink on the sly, and Chamberlain thought it would be a good joke to empt' out the liquors and put in water; so they did it, although it 'most broke Forsyth's heart to pour away good stuff like that was, — but he 'd do 'most anything for a joke. Then they kept dark, and no one else knowed it till it come into court."

VIII.

Conquered.

ROBERT FLINT, although a thorough **man of** business, and deeply in love with dollars and cents, had, during his lifetime, surrounded his mansion with beautiful grounds. They were, to be sure, shut in by lofty fences and walls, but the interior had been seen by occasional guests, by venturesome boys, by midnight fruit-gatherers, and one and all proclaimed the gardens and groves unrivalled. When the close-fisted owner had breathed his last, more than one thought turned to the flowers that blossomed and fruit that ripened only to fade and decay, with the hope that at last these bounties of Nature might do good to somebody. But as far as the factory hands were concerned, the wish remained as far from fulfilment as before.

The gardener remained in charge of the place, and was greatly feared by trespassers. Instead of serving out the dainties of his garden to the

villagers, he kept stricter guard than ever,—locking the front gates and posting notices on all
the walls, threatening intruders with the rigors
of the law. In addition to this he purchased a
huge mastiff, which patrolled the premises with
unceasing vigilance. The only outsider that had
access to the grand house and its well-kept
grounds, as far as the public knew, was Mr. Lamson, who, as chief executor of the estate, had, as
a matter of course, full sway.

In getting acquainted with the town and its
surroundings, Chamberlain had as yet kept aloof
from his uncle's former residence. Having never
visited it, nor even glimpsed the lofty turrets of
the old castle-mansion, it was natural that, remembering the extreme penuriousness of his relative, he should unconsciously relegate it to a
position among the disagreeables of life, and
have little interest in it. When, however, one
or two of the workmen spoke of it as outshining
all of the estates in the upper town, he resolved
to see for himself.

It accordingly happened that one bright afternoon he found himself walking slowly in the direction of the Flint homestead. His first thought
had been to procure the keys from Lamson and
go all over the house, but a second had told him
that this would hardly be in keeping with the

" file-grinder character " that he had assumed;
moreover, he disliked to ask any favor of the
agent. A deep-rooted antipathy toward this man
had taken so strong a hold on his mind, that
he avoided him as much as possible. He therefore was about to explore the Flint estate on
the same footing that one of his companions in
the mill would, — that of a trespasser.

Passing along the main street, he reached the
front entrance, which was secured with a heavy
padlock. Through the trees he saw for the first
time the outlines of the stately mansion, looking
far away, cool, and inviting. Above the high
granite wall the tops of heavily-loaded fruit-trees
were visible, while summer-houses, graperies, stat-
uary, and rare flowering trees, shrubs, and vines
could be seen from an adjacent elevation.

The explorer wandered along the street front-
ing this walled oasis, and saw with a feeling of
rebellion the notices that shut out the world,
himself included. Reaching the limit of the
estate, he entered an open field, and still skirt-
ing the mossy wall continued his walk. Ere long
the wall was replaced by a high fence. This he
followed, half tempted to climb, even at the risk
of his neck, when he suddenly discovered a
broken slat, and an instant later stood within
the jealously-guarded enclosure.

Although aware that he of all others had a right to tread this exclusive domain, he felt like an intruder. It was as if the spirit of the owner had expressed itself in the forbidding fences and breathed out an omnipresent "No admittance."

The care on all sides shown by the thrifty trees and plants, the graveled walks and close-cut turf, the rustic seats and shady arbors, gave the place an inhabited air, which only the silent mansion contradicted. The gardener must be a wonder, thought the young man, as he delightedly took in the beautiful details of the grounds. Roaming cautiously through the ample domain, sampling the luscious fruits that ripened only to waste, plucking an occasional blossom, Chamberlain passed the most enjoyable hour that he had known since his arrival in Steelville. Grown bolder by his success, he promised himself many another visit to his relative's estate.

In the course of his wanderings he came quite near the mansion. An eager desire possessed him to visit it. He pictured himself swinging in a hammock over the wide veranda in the deep shade of the elms, or playing tennis on the level lawn in front of the house. It was like a look back into his own life. As he pondered he did not forget that, had he so chosen, instead of toiling through the heat of summer, he might have been lounging at the mountains, or vegetating at the seashore. And even now, thought he, it is not too late; I can obtain leave of absence, don a yachting-suit, and join my former chums in a month's frolic. But the vision of Steep Street, sweltering through the summer heat, with the added discomforts that poverty and sin bring, caused him to resolve with extra vim and firmness that he would stick to his post.

A deep growl awoke him from his reverie. Glancing quickly in the direction from whence it came, he saw the great watch-dog that was the terror of the villagers, advancing toward him, his lips drawn back, showing glistening teeth, and his eyes flaming with ferocity. It was too late to flee back through the garden. Before half the distance was accomplished the mastiff would overtake him. There was no weapon at hand with which defence could be made, and a glance at the bristling back of the advancing foe showed that pacific measures could not avail. The only means of escape was by climbing a tree. The fruit-trees were most of them too small to assure safety. Not far away, however, was a large apple-tree, against which leaned a ladder. Instantly deciding, Chamberlain ran for this, a hoarse bark from the dog showing that

he was pursued. Reaching the ladder he sprang
up its rounds with an agility that months in a
city gymnasium had given him. A half-second
later the mastiff was leaping frantically at the
foot of the tree, baffled and furious. The ladder, instead of resting against a branch, as the
young man had at first supposed, led to a small
platform built across the limbs, forming a cosy
summer-house, and to his utter astonishment and
confusion, on one of the rustic seats sat Miss
Whitney, gazing at him with a *hauteur* that was
unmistakable.

"I beg your pardon," said he, coloring deeply,
"for disturbing you, but the dog hurried
me."

She bowed rather coldly, but said nothing.

"I suppose I shall have to wait till the gardener appears," he resumed, after a pause, seating himself on a bench opposite her.

Miriam Whitney was in reality much vexed at
what she considered an unwarranted intrusion.
To be sure she could not blame the young man
for springing up the ladder out of reach of the
dog, but she was angry at his being on the
premises, and after a short attempt at reading,
shut her book and advancing to the ladder,
started to descend. The dog, seeming to confuse
her with the stranger who had escaped up the

same way, sprang towards her with so fierce an aspect that she recoiled in terror.

"He thinks us both trespassers," said Chamberlain, with a touch of enjoyment in his voice.

"You are mistaken, sir," she said, "the dog knows me well."

Then with a determined air she again attempted to go down, calling to the furious dog in a voice that should have soothed him had he any ear for music. But with strange obstinacy the creature with flashing eyes continued to leap halfway up the ladder, almost overturning it in his eagerness.

"Had you not better wait until the dog's owner comes?"

"I wish to go now," she said.

"If there is no other way I will go down and attempt to drive the dog away," replied Chamberlain, his mettle rising, "but he is only doing his duty, and I dislike to hurt him."

Miss Whitney considered this speech a mere piece of bravado, but when the youth wrenched a leg from one of the seats, and taking off his coat wrapped it around his left arm, she saw that he was thoroughly in earnest. She made a movement as if to deter him, but pride kept her lips shut.

Armed as described, he slowly descended the

ladder, the young lady with white face watching his every move. At first sight it seemed as if it were to be a most unequal battle. The sinewy form of the youth did not balance the deep chest and heavy jaws of the mastiff. Chamberlain, however, knew something of dogs. He was aware that the fiercest can be subdued by proper means. More than once he had seen professional trainers completely cow some of the most savage of the canine tribe. It was therefore with a definite plan of operations in his mind that he entered the lists.

Already the animal was leaping up and snapping at his feet. With a quick spring he was on the ground at one side, facing the brute. He heard an exclamation of alarm as the dog bounded toward him and knew it was from Miss Whitney. In the brief second that he had to think, he rejoiced that she should care. The next instant the dog was worrying the coat-shield on his left arm. When the creature had his jaws fully set in the coat, with a quick motion Chamberlain slipped the bench-leg through the brass-studded collar. Then dropping the coat, he twisted on the improvised lever till the creature in spite of frantic struggles lay on the grass with the young man's knee under his fore-shoulder, almost choked to death. It would have been easy

work to finish the matter and kill the dog,
but this he did not wish to do.

"Are you hurt, Mr. Chamberlain?" said an
anxious, almost tearful voice at his elbow, and
the victor, panting and flushed with victory,
looked up and saw his late partner of the
arbor standing by his side. The proud air had
entirely vanished.

"Not a bit," said he heartily, "nor is the
dog. We are only a little out of breath."

Still holding the potent lever, he pulled the
exhausted mastiff to the kennel, which was not
far distant, and chained him. Then he returned
to the tree, where stood Miss Whitney, holding his coat and leaning against the ladder,
still white with fright.

"I am afraid you are ill," said the young
man, really concerned.

"No, I am not, but I feel a little faint. I
think I will go home. Our place adjoins this,"
she replied.

With a quick return of color she accepted
the proffered arm. Together they crossed the
grounds in a direction opposite to that by which
the young man entered. After going a few
hundred yards a low wall, the only one in the
Flint estate, was reached. Stopping at a turn-
stile, Miss Whitney held out her hand, —

"Mr. Chamberlain," she said, "I am ashamed and sorry that my rudeness forced you into that dreadful battle with the dog. Will you forget it?"

"Never," replied he with a smile, "for that most fortunate fracas has really introduced me to Miss Whitney."

"Won't you come in," she said, with a graceful gesture toward her home.

"No, thank you, I must go and see how the dog fares."

"Do you know the gardener?" she enquired.

"No."

"He is very severe with all intruders," she said, adding hurriedly. "Since I was a child I have had access to the grounds because we were neighbors."

"I think I can pacify him if I meet him," was the assured reply.

The fair girl standing at the turn-stile struggled with herself for an instant, and then said,—

"I should be pleased to have you call, Mr. Chamberlain."

"Thank you," was the vague reply, and they parted. He striding toward the silent Flint mansion, she going a few steps, and then turning to watch his vigorous figure till he passed out of sight.

"I wonder what the girls will say if he does call?" she soliloquized. "A file-grinder; a factory-hand; an ungrammatical — but he is n't ungrammatical, he uses splendid English, and is a gentleman; a perfect gentleman, and no coward either. I wonder how many of the young men in our set would have faced that dog and conquered him? I wonder if he will turn out like the rest of them and call at the first opportunity?"

Returning to the dog-kennel, Chamberlain examined the mastiff. He found him lying at full length, breathing heavily, and still much exhausted. With a heart full of pity, he went to the garden-pump near by, drew some water, and allowed the dog to lap it, which he did greedily. After that he seemed better, and raised himself up, constantly turning his great, intelligent eyes up to his conqueror's face, as if to beg his mercy. The young man noticed that the dog had greeted him this time with no growl, and when he patted his head, there came a faint wag of the tail. Poor, old, faithful fellow, he was much puzzled by this young stranger, who had so roughly handled him; yet, he was willing, when mastered, to pay allegiance, so he wagged his tail and tried to lay his head against his knee.

Meanwhile, Chamberlain had been expecting the arrival of the gardener, of whose sternness he had often heard. How he had better meet the old man, he could not fully decide. He was a trespasser, but so was Miss Whitney. The thought came that under cover of her name he might gracefully retreat, but he at once dismissed it. Some distance away he could see the outlines of a cottage, that he surmised must belong to the gardener. Had he known what to say, it is possible that he might have made his way thither; but the fact that his identity must be kept a secret deterred him, and he at last reluctantly started to retrace his steps, and steal out as he came in. He had gone but a short distance when he heard the chains rattle, and turning, saw the dog trying to follow. There was nothing hostile in the motion; on the contrary, every motion expressed the utmost friendliness. Obeying his first impulse, he went back, unchained him, and again started to traverse the ground, the mastiff trotting sedately at his heels. When the fence was reached the dog paused, his eloquent eyes entreating permission to accompany his new master; but that could not be, so he was told to remain. When the end of the picket fence was gained, the young man turned and looked back. The dog was earnestly watching · him, as if hoping that the decision might be revoked. It was with a real regret that Chamberlain passed out of sight, feeling as if he had left a true friend, and vowing if he could do so, to purchase the noble animal to which, in an afternoon, he had be·come so strongly attached.

IX.

The·Tigers·Number·One.

ALL the young and live masculine members of the mill settlement, as soon as they were old enough to be addressed as Mister, joined the engine company. Their machine, the Tiger Number One, was an old-fashioned hand-engine, that required about forty men on the brakes. This company of "fire-fighters" were notoriously hard drinkers. Liquor was always to be found in their assembly-room. The avowed purpose of the association was to have a good time. When there was a fire they attended it, recklessly perilled life and limb, after which all hands had a grand carousal. The Tigers were an aggressive company; so much so that their trips to neighboring factory villages were usually attended by fistic exploits that decorated their members, as well as their opponents, with bulged cheeks and black eyes, the possession of which was deemed no disgrace.

Sam Putnam was foreman of this company, and although he was far from being a bully, his weaker and more cowardly companions managed, if possible, to entangle him in their fights, so that he had quite a local reputation. He had no desire to quarrel, and when sober could not be induced to do so; but when excited by liquor he lost his cool poise, and the dry humor that was the delight of the men, and took a hand in almost anything that turned up.

The Rev. Charles Snow, the pastor of the aristocratic up-town church, became acquainted with Sam. Admiring his splendid proportions and finding him talkative and courteous, the good man fancied that here was one who was not far from the Kingdom. The minister was an extremely stiff man, slow of speech, awkward of gait, yet a scholar and a powerful preacher. It was, as he often acknowledged, the greatest trial of his life to face an individual in private and ask about his soul's welfare. He could thunder from the pulpit, could answer questions, but to broach the subject personally seemed well-nigh impossible. Most of his congregation were aware of his failings in this particular, and as they were a conservative people, thought it of little consequence, as long as his discourses were scholarly

In talking with the foreman of the engine

company, more than ever before in his life had the minister wished to introduce the subject of subjects. Sam appeared quite willing to concede almost anything, and the opportunity was ripe; but the deep-rooted, morbid bashfulness, if that was it, kept the inquiry back, and they separated without any religious conversation. One statement, however, that the giant made clung to the gentleman.

They had been talking of drunkenness, suggested by the sight of a well-known Steep-street sot.

"I hope that none of the employés in your department drink," said the minister, stiffly, ignorant of what every boy in his congregation knew, that nearly all drank.

"Certainly not," was the grave reply. "Deacon Lamson would never allow it."

"Ah," said the minister, "I am gratified to hear it. Deacon Lamson is certainly an excellent man, — altogether different from Mr. Flint, the former owner of the steel-works."

"I never had any fault to find with Flint. He was no hypocrite, at all events," said Sam, with a gleam in his eye.

"No," was the awkward reply, "undoubtedly not. Don't you think, my friend, — er — that — a —some sort of an association for the promotion of temperance would be a benefit to this village?"

"A kind of Reform Club?"

"Yes; something of the kind. A society that should gather say once a week, or even oftener, to put down liquor."

"We have one already. Our engine company, the Tigers Number One, are engaged in that sort of work," said Sam, solemnly.

"Indeed; I am glad to hear it. How many members have you?"

"Forty-three."

"I should be glad to come down and address the men on the subject. What nights do you assemble?" said the clergyman, his heart warming at the thought.

"Wednesdays and Saturdays at half-past eight in the evening. Glad to have you come, I'm sure. You'll find us in earnest about putting liquor down."

The words of the leader of the company had been the subject of much thought and prayer on the part of the worthy man of God. He believed that a strong under-current of temperance was already setting in the mill-village, although his parishioners would have scouted the very idea. He determined to fulfill his promise, lend them a helping hand, and if possible, sow some Gospel seed that should ripen into precious fruit.

As for Sam, he had passed through so many experiences with ministers and missionaries, that he forgot all about it, never dreaming that the proposed visit would be carried out.

One evening about twenty of the men were gathered in the assembly-room of the engine-house, playing cards and dominoes, smoking and drinking, when a new comer, stepping up to Sam, said, with a grin, —

"Parson Snow is down-stairs, inquiring for you."

Sam jumped to his feet in dismay. He had told the men, in his inimitable way, of his answer to the minister, about "putting down liquor," and in their glee they had nearly brought down the house; and now the man himself was here!

"Ask him up, Sam; we'll get him drunk," said one or two.

"That's so; ask him up," said half-a-dozen, ripe for a lark.

"Boys," said Sam, speaking rapidly, "put all the bottles and glasses out of sight. Open the windows and let as much smoke out as possible. Quietly now; no noise. This is my game; I am going to manage it."

By the time he reappeared with the clergy-man, the room had undergone a wonderful change. No sign of bottle, glass, or jug, was to be seen.

The spittoons were pushed under the tables out of sight. The heavy cloud of smoke that had filled the room, was rapidly disappearing through the open windows. One or two of the members, who were feeling sleepy, were bolstered up in corners where they would not be conspicuous.

Sam and his guest passed down the length of the room, and took possession of the very diminutive platform that was built for the chairman.

"Gentleman of the company," said Sam, "some time since I invited this gentleman to visit us and speak in one of our meetings. Here he is Now let's all listen to what he's got to say. You all know who he is without my introducing him. He is Minister Snow, from up above."

"Amen," said Gaffney from the corner, where he was propped up in a state of collapse.

The applause that greeted Sam's speech, and Gaffney's response, was tremendous, and the minister thought he had rarely seen so enthusiastic an audience.

"My friends," began the speaker.

"Amen," said Gaffney.

"Thank you; let us hope that we shall all be friends in the fullest sense of the word," said the minister heartily.

"A——" began the voice, but somebody near by put a broad palm over his mouth, and stopped the word on the first syllable.

"I have been a fireman," continued the speaker, "although never belonging to an engine company——"

"Men," said Gaffney, finishing his word as the hand was for an instant withdrawn. It was not specially noticeable, however, as another storm of applause succeeded.

The clergyman continued his speech; and as he became interested in his subject, the eloquence that he actually possessed came to his aid, and ere long the laugh in every face had disappeared, and the men were eagerly listening.

Sam, who at first had been manifestly uneasy, grew cooler, and listened with attention. The temptation to extravagant applause, which had beset the men at first, was entirely quelled; even Gaffney subsided.

The address, which was brief, but full of information and power, made itself felt. The firemen expected to hear a milk-and-water appeal that would convulse them with laughter. On the contrary, they heard liquor-drinking and liquor-selling arraigned with such power, that they were dumbfounded. The shambling, awkward minister, whose manners even they could criticise, stood before them the most eloquent man they had ever heard. They drank in his words with eager attention, and forgot the secret purposes that they had cherished.

When the speech was finished, Sam called for a vote of thanks, which they gave. He then abruptly closed, alleging a private business-meeting of the engine company to follow directly. After which he hurried the minister away, down the stairs, and out into the night, going part of the way home with him.

When he returned the men were still there, although remarkably quiet.

"Don't do that again, Sam, you 'll break us up entirely," said one of them.

"Hump," was the testy reply, "you must be a fool if you can't stand it to hear both sides of a question."

"That parson ain't no slouch, fur all he toes-out so," said another. "He laid it right down in fine shape. Still I wish you had n't done it, Sam. It 's jest took all the taste outen my beer."

"Nonsense, what could I do? War n't I sweating for fear some of you fellers would give him some lip and show him what a fool I had made of myself in inviting him? You would have insulted him if he had n't been too smart for you. You are wrong in thinking all ministers fools. As a rule they are smarter than any of us; but that is no reason that we should get down on our knees when they tell us to. I 'm going home," responded the leader.

Sam went, and the meeting adjourned; but thereafter the engine company were dubbed the "Reform Club," much to their disgust.

Thrilled with a great exultation over his reception at the engine-house, Mr. Snow had gone home to tell his wife of his hopes, and to pray earnestly that more light might come to those whom he considered seekers after it. That these prayers were not heard and answered, in spite of the minister's mistaken ideas of the "Reform Club," cannot for an instant be claimed.

When next he saw his deacon, Mr. Lamson, for whose energy and consecration he had sincere respect, he hailed him with a joyous ring in his voice.

"I have good news for you, my brother," he said, shaking him heartily by the hand, and forgetting for the once his bashful frigidity.

"Very glad to hear it," was the suave reply. "What is it, — another hundred thousand given to missions?"

"This is something right at home; a chance for rejoicing in your own mill village."

"Indeed," said Lamson, with less enthusiasm.

He was not at all anxious to discuss the affairs of his operatives, even with his pastor, and was heartily regretting that it was not some missionary donation.

"I addressed a large meeting of the mill-men, last evening, and was most pleasantly received. I honestly believe that many of those men are not far from the Kingdom."

"Where did you hold the meeting; open air?"

"No; in the engine-house, by special invitation. Mr. Putnam secured me, and the enthusiasm was very great. The men seemed deeply interested in the few facts that I was able to bring them, relative to liquor-drinking. I took occasion, also, to arraign both the liquor-dealer and all who were accomplices in selling the deadly stuff; and, by the way they listened, I am sure it was a revelation to them."

"It must have been," was the mechanical reply.

"By the way, your action in arresting the liquor-selling in your village, pleased me exceedingly. Pfaff has long been a curse to the place; can you not drive him out entirely?"

"Not as yet; I have been watching for the

opportunity, that occurred last week, for a very long time. When things of which I have not a right to speak are at last settled, I can do as I would like to do now," was the vague reply.

"I am sure you will; the Lord bless you, my brother," was the earnest response, as they parted, the pastor to write a glowing letter to a brother minister, on the indications of an approaching revival, in which he was wiser than he knew; and Lamson, to hurry down to the mill and summon Sam.

"Did you invite Mr. Snow to come to the engine-house?" he demanded.

"I guess I did," was the slow reply.

"What for? Arn't we bothered enough now by outsiders, without having him around; what has come over you?"

"It was a mistake — a joke," answered Sam, more humbly than he had spoken for some time.

"Let's know just how it happened," demanded the lawyer; and Sam told the whole story.

"Now, what about the young upstart; does he still get on well?" said the agent.

"The men like him better every day; I like him myself. He has got the make-up of a man."

"Never mind that; is he going through it all;
the puddling, and all, mind?"

"I think he is, and if he don't *know* all
there is to be known in the mill before his
time is up, my name is n't Putnam."

"Nonsense," was the impatient reply. "I am
not afraid of so much as you think. There are
things he can never know, unless your admira·
tion for him leads you to tell him."

"I ain't a traitor," was the short reply.

"Well, what is to be done with him? Can
you think of any scheme that shall lead him to
get disgusted with the whole business, and
throw it up?"

"No, I can't. His habits·are perfectly good;
he has no vices, and is cool and level-headed.
Such a man is iron-clad."

"Man! He is but a boy," said Lamson.

"Yet he has beaten you at every move, so
far,—kinder rough for you to be beaten by a
boy, when all of the advantage is on your side,
too."

The other bit his lips wrathfully, but said
nothing, and Putnam continued.

"I tell you, there is no hold to be got on
this young feller, because he don't drink, nor
gamble, nor care a snap for any kind of dissipation. If he had one vice, you could ruin him,

and would, I suppose. I would n't help do that; but as it is, he can't be touched by you."

"I will euchre him yet," said the agent.

"I doubt it; you are cunning, but he's what is better, — he is shrewd. My idea is, that he has got the whole situation in his grasp, and can read us all like books. When he pulled Temple out of drunkenness and set him on his feet, he secured the friendship of one of the most level-headed men in the mill; and when he — when he —"

"When he what?"

"When he pulled my little Molly out of the river, he gained my friendship; and whatever may come to me or you, I won't ruin him."

"That's a good sentiment; stick to it," said Lamson, with an inscrutable expression. "I have it now. He is a generous fellow, — a good fellow. As soon as it can be arranged so that he will not suspect too sudden a move, we will seek his friendship."

"No more treachery with him," was the warning.

"Bless you, no! I have been harsh with him because it looked like ruin o me, if I did not use such measures; but I see a better way. Let me do all the acting hereafter; you just keep quiet, and wait for orders."

X.

Recognized.

AN old man, gray, wrinkled, but vigorous, was walking rapidly down the main street of the upper town of Steelville. In front of him trotted a fine mastiff. Both man and dog had a characteristic dignity that led people to step out of their way. The man, noticing no one, went into the post-office, looked on the list, and as there was no letter for him, turned to depart. As he did so Tom Chamberlain entered through the single door. The dog pricked up his ears, wagged his tail, and made straight for him with extravagant expressions of joy. The young man patted his head, and the dog kissed his hand affectionately.

"Be careful," warned the old man, seeing the motion. "Turk dislikes strangers."

The mastiff's actions, however, contradicted the statement, for he continued to show his delight.

"How did you make friends with him, Mr.

Chamberlain?" asked the postmaster, who was looking on with interest.

"Oh, we are old acquaintances," was the reply.

Leaving the office he started up the street for a walk, and had gone but a short distance when he noticed that Turk was following contentedly. Turning to send him back, he encountered the old gentleman.

"Did I understand your name to be Chamberlain, sir?" he asked, courteously.

"Yes, sir."

"You remind me of a gentleman whom I once knew of the same name, — George Chamberlain. He married a sister of Robert Flint. Perhaps you knew him."

"I have heard of him," said the other, his color rising at the sound of the familiar name, "but do not remember ever to have seen him."

"He was a fine young man, and Miss Alice, his wife, was a lovely lady. They are dead now."

"You knew them both, you say?" asked Chamberlain, wiping the perspiration from his forehead.

"Many a time have I carried Miss Alice in my arms all over the garden when it was damp, that she might see the flowers. She was very fond and proud of my garden. And her husband I knew as well as if he had been a relative."

"And do I appear like him?" said the poor fellow, with brimming eyes, in spite of his efforts at self-control.

The old man adjusted his glasses and looked searchingly at his companion.

"Are you George Chamberlain's boy?" he said, sharply.

"Let us go inside, and I will tell you," was the answer, for they were already at the high gate that opened into the Flint grounds. When they had entered, the gardener eagerly put the question again.

"Yes, I am his son," was the reply.

"I knew it! I knew it! You are little Tom," throwing his arms about him in excess of joy. "You look like him, you speak like him, you have his whole bearing. You are Miss Alice's boy. Did she never tell you of old Allan?"

"She died a year after father. I was barely three years old, and can remember but little about her."

"To be sure! to be sure!" said the other, wiping his eyes. "And then you were placed under a guardian to be educated. Oh, but my lad, I'm right glad to see you. It does my heart good!"

"I didn't intend at first to tell of my relationship, but when you spoke of my father and mother, I could not bear to go away without hearing more of them."

"You are not in any trouble that you are — forgive me, Master Tom, but you are not hiding for any reason?" asked the gardener, anxiously.

"No, indeed, nothing of the kind. I will tell you in part what I am doing. Only, what I say must not be repeated till I give you permission. It is quite important that it should be kept secret."

"Very well, sir," was the respectful reply.

"I am in the file-works as a common laborer. Every one in town, who thinks of it, supposes that I am like all the rest of the hands there, and that is just what I wish."

"No word of mine shall undeceive them, sir," said Allan.

"When I was at school," continued he, after a pause, "all the other fellows had fathers and mothers who were often writing and sending them things,—little things they were many times; but I would have given all my pocket money for the love that accompanied them. Doctor Ponsonby was kind, but he never knew how I longed for some real flesh-and-blood relatives."

"It must have been hard. My woman and I used often to wonder how Miss Alice's boy fared. But we heard little or nothing from you.

Master Robert had some sort of feeling against your father, and would not talk about any of you. Now, Master Thomas, won't you come to our cottage and let the old woman have a sight at you? She is n't very well, and it will be better than medicine for her."

There was such entreaty in the tone, and hospitality had been so frugally bestowed since he had been in Steelville, that Tom accepted and crossed the grounds toward the vine-covered cottage. As they passed the apple-tree containing the rustic seat, Chamberlain halted and told the gardener of his adventure, and how he had made friends with Turk.

"Ah, that is why he was so glad to see you. He was conquered, and was willing to own it. These mastiffs never forget. I don't suppose any power on earth could make him attack you again," said Allan.

The dog seemed to know that they were talking about him, for he looked from one to the other, then pushed his cold nose into the young man's hand, as an oath of fealty, and trotted ahead toward the cottage. At the door stood a wee, bent figure, — faded and wrinkled, but still kindly and beaming.

"Who, think you, this gentleman is?" asked Allan.

"I 'm sure I cannot tell, with these last glasses ye brought me, Allan, dear; but whoever he may be, he is welcome."

"This is Miss Alice's boy," said he, with a tremble in his voice.

"The Lord be praised!" ejaculated the old lady. "How I have longed to see you, dear lad! Come in, come in. You may not feel acquainted with Allan and me, but we know you. Your mother and father have spent many pleasant hours in this little house."

So deeply was Chamberlain stirred by the simple-hearted hospitality, that it brought a big lump in his throat, which he tried in vain to swallow. He had in his loneliness longed for the home element that other boys were so rich in. They had brothers, and sisters, and parents, but he had none. It was not wonderful that he had become reticent, and was in the habit of looking on both sides of a question before he became enthusiastic over it. His friendship for Will Marshall was the only real affection he had as yet felt for any one, beside the vague feeling that haunted him when he tried to recall the face that had once leaned over him in his cradle, and had soothed his baby troubles. The misty memory-picture had grown so faint as to be almost obliterated, and of late years had become blended with a miniature of his mother that he possessed. He strove to keep the two separate, for he felt that when they blended he should lose the last real look of the mother he so longed for.

The old couple, in their quaint little home, telling him of his mother, seemed to bring the past nearer. At last he had found friends who could talk sympathetically of his parents. It seemed to him, in his thankfulness, as if he would not exchange their simple, heartfelt affection for anything on earth.

Old Allan told his wife about his employment in the works, and she was filled with kindly concern.

"I fear you will never stand it. Do you feel well, dear?" she said.

"Yes, indeed; it is toughening me. I am a great deal stronger than I was when I entered."

"Where do you board? At the hotel?" she inquired.

He told the name of his humble boarding place, and Allan's wife lifted her hands in astonishment.

"Do they cook to suit you?" she asked.

"I have had better meals," was the laughing reply; "but they do the best they can. The food is plain and wholesome. It is such as the rest get, and possibly a trifle better. I can stand it."

"I have been thinking, Allan, dear, that we have a spare room, and could have him with us, — if you would be willing to come here," she said, turning to the visitor.

He saw the eagerness in her eyes, and the pleased look in her husband's face, and he thought how delightful it would be. There would be the whole range of the garden; he could enter the mansion, unseen by prying eyes, and have access to the library. These possible enjoyments flashed over him at once, but he put them aside.

"Thank you," he said, sorrowfully; "I wish I could come, but it is impossible. I am performing a difficult mission, and my place for the present is among the operatives; working as they work, living as they live."

"But you will come often to see us?" said Allan and his wife in a breath.

"I will, you may be sure; if only to get some of these buns," he answered, with a jolly laugh.

The old couple laughed joyously with him.

"That is a family taste. I never knew one of your kin who did not like them, and they always said that Martha's were the best ever made," said Allan.

"I don't know, Allan, dear, but mayhap the lad would like to go over the house and see his mother's room and the family portraits," said Martha, in a hesitating manner.

"Indeed I would, if it would not make Lamson angry with you," was the eager reply.

"Mr. Lamson is not my master," said the old man, with an expressive nod. "He issues many commands, but they do not overturn the regular order of things. I know my business, and attend to it. He is only an executor."

After a little delay, Allan secured a large bunch of keys, and followed by the whole company, including Turk, made his way to the mansion. The great doors swung open, and the son, with beating heart, entered the house that for years had been his mother's home. From the hall with its marble floor, which sent the echoes of their footsteps ringing through the empty apartments, they passed up the broad stairs to a pretty alcoved room, the hangings and decorations of which were so warm and pleasant as to entirely banish the deserted feeling that had oppressed the young man when first he entered the house.

"Miss Alice's room," said old Martha, in a tone of loving reverence; and he felt as if at last he stood in the presence of his mother.

With true tact, the gardener and his wife slipped away, and he entered alone, and standing in the middle of the apartment looked about him. In one of the alcoved windows was a rocking-chair, before which stood a quaint, little work-table with some unfinished work still on it. Scissors, thimble, and thread lay as if in use but a moment before. As the son looked, the form that he could but mistily remember grew again, and seemed to occupy the accustomed seat. The dear mother-face that had soothed his baby dreams was again almost real, — almost tangible. He sank on his knees by the chair and blindly reached out for a hand-clasp — a touch.

"O, my mother!" he whispered, "my mother!"

Kneeling thus in this atmosphere made holy by mother-love, a great peace came over him. He had long been aware that the prayers of tha mother had many times ascended for her only son; and now that they were answered, and tha' he had become a follower of his mother's Saviour, the blessedness of such a relation filled him with joy inexpressible. The sweet poetry of the Psalmist, — "I am Thy servant and the son of Thy handmaid," — ran again and again through his mind. As he arose from his knees, after a silent, heartfelt prayer for guidance, that he might so live as one day to meet that mother

in Heaven, his eye caught a tiny gold ring sus-
pended by a blue ribbon from a part of the
chandelier. Upon taking it down he found in it
the initials A. E. F. — his mother's before mar-
riage. Accepting this as a precious memento of
this visit, which perhaps could not be repeated
until his period of probation was over, Chamberlain hung it on his watch-chain and rejoined his
friends in the hall. In obedience to his request,
they now proceeded to the family picture gal-
lery, where hung portraits of the Flints for
generations. Among them all he at once recognized the sweet, girlish face that had so long
been with him; that was his ideal of perfect
loveliness. He tarried long before this picture of
his mother, impressing its every feature on his
mind, until he was called away by old Allan.

"I thought perhaps you might be interested
to see the picture of your uncle. The light is
going very fast," he said, apologetically.

It was with no little interest that the nephew
halted before the portrait of him whose letter
he had read and re-read, and whose request had
changed the whole thread of his life. As he
expected, the face was full of stern lines, — full
of firm resolve and haughty pride. There was
in the keen eye a look of constant pain and un-
rest, that the artist must have faithfully copied, so

well did it tally with the rest of the face. The aquiline nose, the thin lips, betokened the acquisitive cast of the mind; while the lofty, dome-shaped forehead, from which the hair was brushed carelessly away, indicated intellectual ability.

"Poor master Robert," said Allan; "he was crossed in love when but a young man, and never got over it. The pain was always with him. He tried to drown it by money-making and by study, but the picture tells how he succeeded. He was a strange man, and grew bitter as he grew older; yet, he did many kind acts unbeknown, and I shall never forget his goodness to me."

"Did he study much?"

"All night long sometimes. He never rested well nights, and he could only forget his troubles by hard work. I know he said to me one day, in his quick, nervous way: 'Allan, they call labor a curse; to me it is a blessing, — the only blessing I enjoy.' His library contains books in many outlandish tongues, and he could read them all. When he could n't study on account of his head, he used to work over the fruit-trees and the flowers; and good gardener as I then claimed to be, it was all I could do to keep pace with him."

After a glance at the library, that **was far**

too brief to satisfy him, and a general survey
of the different rooms, enlivened by the remi-
niscences of the aged couple, Chamberlain again
stood on the gravelled walk. As twilight was
already fast turning into dark, he bade them
good evening, and escorted to the gate by Turk
started for home.

XI.

In · Remembrance · of · Me.

A SWEET Sabbath hush had settled over Steelville. The wide-throated chimneys of the file-works had ceased to belch forth smoke, — the throbbing engines and crashing trip-hammers were at rest. The only sounds that broke the quiet were the far-off shouts of the quoit-throwers, and even they, softened by distance, served to intensify the stillness.

In the upper settlement the noise of the world seemed entirely shut away. The bells had ceased to clang, and even the gentle vibrant tolling of the North Church bell had gone lingeringly over the distant hills, and was lost in the brooding silence.

Within the church were gathered the worshipers; it was Communion Sabbath. The beautiful audience-room, with its mellow light, its reverent congregation, its absorbing quiet, seemed the abiding place of holy thought, of penitent resolve.

Among the communicants sat Chamberlain and Temple. Before God and men they solemnly covenanted to follow in the footsteps of the Master. Into their full hearts flowed a sweet and healing peace. Softened, purified, they rejoiced in acknowledging before the world their belief. Very happy were they as they bowed before the Lord, full of real purpose to preach Christ and Him crucified, by word and act, for the rest of their lives.

"This is the House of God; this is the gate of Heaven," murmured Chamberlain, his hand seeking Temple's.

Miss Whittier, in whose pew the young men sat, watched them with gratified interest. Conservative she was, as were most of the North Church people; yet her heart warmed toward the two youthful soldiers, so zealous for the Lord. There were others among the congregation, who awakened by the sight of two men from the file-works among them, as worshipers, rejoiced, and forgetting their inbred stiffness, warmly welcomed them.

The Rev. Mr. Snow, thankful above all others that a movement was begun in the lower village, prayed and praised with fire and eloquence that a direct answer of prayer alone can inspire. He prayed openly, earnestly, for the mill settlement, pleading its wretchedness and misery, till even Lamson, really touched, wiped his eyes. Few hearts are so hardened that the Spirit can not strive with them. Foolish, blind Lamson; plotting to defraud Steep Street,—to rob God! Listen to the voice in your heart; it is the Lord's! He pleads with you! Even you who have for years robbed Him; even you, hypocrite, falsifier, and you, as ever before, harden your heart and reject him. Alas! what are the few dollars you gain compared with the worth of your soul?

"This is my body broken for you," trembled the voice of the pastor, and the thought of the great atonement pervaded the room like a living presence.

"Eat ye all of it."

With love and reverence, with broken, con-trite hearts, the new disciples ate, remembering Him who, on Calvary, died that their sins might be no more.

"This is my blood of the New Testament shed for you," read the thrilling voice.

How precious that blood, the starting tear, the quivering lip, the heart-leap of love, could ill testify. Gethsemane and the cross rose be-fore them. The agony that no tongue could paint, no words express, the boundless love

that wrested even from the biting pangs of
death the glorious victory, swept over them in
its wonderful beauty, its power, its God-likeness.

"Drink ye all of it."

Bearing the symbol of the precious blood,
the deacons served with reverence. From scores
of hearts rose earnest prayer and fresh resolve.
Then came the plaintive hymn, sung without
organ or choir, the hymn that brought to mind
the "upper chamber," where were gathered "the
few."

"After they had sung a hymn they went out."

As Chamberlain and Temple walked toward
home, the heart of the former fairly overflowed
with joy.

"I am so happy," he said, "I wish I could
see Will Marshall. How he longed for my conversion; how happy he would be! I must
write him."

"Who is Marshall?" asked Temple, in a
strange, hoarse voice.

The other looked at him in surprise.

"He is my friend," he said; "you have heard
me speak of him."

"Oh, yes," was the absent reply, "I believe
I have."

"He is a splendid fellow. Some day I hope we
both may see him; he would be such a help

to us If ever a man loved and served the Lord Jesus, that man is Will Marshall. I always honored him, but now I love him for it."

Temple was silent.

"Why do you hurry so?" asked Chamberlain finally. "Won't people wonder at our walking at this rate?"

"I must get home," said Temple, a bright flush burning in his cheek. "Don't hinder me; don't do it! I must be alone!"

With increasing surprise Chamberlain allowed himself to be hurried along toward the mill village. Fortunately for his feelings, few went that way, and their rapid pace was not noticed.

Reaching his boarding place, Temple hastened in, hardly saying good-bye. His companion, in his great happiness, attributed it to overpowering emotion. Full of peace, he went home with a heart-hunger to share his gladness with some one, — any one.

He met Gaffney, and was going by with the usual nod, when the thought came, "Why not share with him?"

"Nonsense, he would laugh at me," was the mental reply.

"What of that? Preach the gospel to *every* creature," came the answer, and with much misgiving, he said, —

"Gaffney, where are you bound?"

"After some one who has the price of a drink to lend," was the answer. "Does that happen to be yourself?"

"Come up to my room and let us talk it over."

The bloated sot followed the young man up the winding stairway and seated himself in one of the two chairs that the room contained.

Chamberlain could not but notice the broad shoulders and good proportions of the drunkard, disfigured though he was by the liquor. They seemed more noticeable in the room than they did out of doors.

"Gaffney, you must have been a powerful man once," he said.

"That I was, boy, that I was; next to Sam Putnam, I was. Few men in this village or the next cared to meddle with me."

"And now —"

"Now the little kids on the street 'square off' at me and call me names; but that's none of your business," said Gaffney suddenly, waxing angry. "You will never be half the man I was."

"Gaffney," said Chamberlain, "the Lord Jesus Christ at this moment looks into your heart, and sees that you hate rum, and would be free from it. He will help you. He can set you free."

"It 's a lie!" said the other, the tears starting to his eyes and running down his face. "It 's
a lie ; no power can save me! Have n't I sworn
that I would break off, and failed? Have n't I
tried everything ? "

"*He* can save you."

" I 'm a Catholic," said Gaffney. " I don't
train in your crowd. I tell you, nothing can be
done."

"Catholic or Protestant, the Lord has the
power, and only waits for you to ask him. Will
you do it ? "

"I would if I could believe it," answered the
wretched man, "but what is the use? Now, there
is Deacon Lamson —— "

"Never mind him. He must some day answer
for himself. Let us look only at our own disease," was the steady reply.

"If this is so, why don't some one try it ? "

"Hundreds have, and have been saved. Men
who loved liquor as well, and perhaps better than
you do, have been freed from it. There is Temple. He has asked for this help and received it.
Before doing so he failed in every single resolve
he made."

"Don't Temple drink nothing now ? " asked
Gaffney, impressed.

"Not a drop! I never saw such a change in

a man. He prayed and was helped. Come over to his room and let him talk to us about it."

A three-minutes' walk brought them to the house. Entering, they ascended to Temple's room. The door was locked. The young man knocked.

"Who is there?" said a hoarse voice.

"Chamberlain."

A volley of imprecations followed, accompanied by a crash of glass, as though a tumbler had been hurled at the door. The fierce fumes of Steep-street whiskey penetrated even to the hall.

Gaffney laughed, a despairing, horrible laugh, and said, —

"That's it! He is drunk as a fiddler! He prayed and got help! Just the kind of help I am looking for! Just the help they all get! What a fool I was to think that I could be free!"

With an oath Gaffney started to go down stairs, but Chamberlain, his whole energies absorbed by an earnest desire to save the soul that had acknowledged an interest, and resolutely crowding aside his doubts, threw himself upon his knees in the passage-way and begged the Lord, for his name's sake, to heal this soul,

— not to allow the fall of another to keep him out of the Kingdom. At first the man laid a rough hand on his shoulder and attempted to pass him, but as the earnest petition arose he paused, and soon his hand fell, and he staggered back and leaned against the wall.

"Stop, boy, stop," he whispered huskily. "It's mocking to pray for me; I ain't worth it."

"O Lord, heal this soul. Give him faith; give him light; keep him safe. O Lord, make him thy servant even now."

"Don't, lad; spare me. I hate it all now, but in an hour I'll be just as bad as ever. Don't let me take the holy name on my lips and then desecrate it; let me go."

"Draw him nearer to Thee. Let him see Thee as Thou art. Give him true repentance. Guard him from this moment as Thine own. O Lord, thou hast promised though one's sins be as scarlet, they shall be white as snow; though they be red like crimson, they shall be white as wool. It is so with this man; his sins have been many."

"Yes, yes; mountains!" groaned the drunkard.

"He acknowledges them, — he repents; and now he pleads Thy promises. Thy blood was shed for the forgiveness of his sins, and through Thy great loving kindness he now claims it."

"Yes, Lord," sobbed Gaffney, utterly broken down, and at length upon his knees; "I've tried everything else, and although I've known it in my heart that you could help me, I have been too cranky to give you a show; but if you'll forget it, O Lord, and forgive my sin, I'll pitch in and serve ye my level best. I'm a poor, miserable, shucks of a man, but I mean what I say, — I mean business every time."

It was a rough prayer, but it went straight up to the Great White Throne, and the drunkard rose to his feet forgiven.

During the petition a great silence had fallen upon the group. No more oaths came from the room where Temple was; and if he heard, he made no sign. At length Chamberlain knocked again and listened for reply. All was still. He softly and lovingly called his friend's name, determined, if possible, to win him back to righteousness, even if this fall — which had inexpressibly shocked him — should tempt him to abandon all hope. He felt that the Lord had shown him great mercy in bringing Gaffney to himself; and wonderfully encouraged, he resolved, if need be, to stay all night before his friend's door, lest he should come out desperate and drown remembrance in carousing. With a hearty grip of the hand, and a warm "God bless you,"

Gaffney had gone home to impart the glad news to his drunken wife.

As Chamberlain stood softly knocking, the landlady came up the stairs, a bunch of keys in her hand.

"Here," she said, "I can let you in. Try this key."

Inserting the skeleton key that she presented, he carefully pushed the other out, and then, with an apology on his lips, unlocked the door and entered the room. It was empty. An open window showed the manner of Temple's exit, and the broken glass and empty bottle spoke only too eloquently of his frightful debauch. With a heavy heart he stood in the middle of the small apartment and looked around. There was the Bible, a present from Miss Whittier, stained and torn, swept to the floor by a drunken hand. He picked it up and laid it gently in its accustomed place, praying the while that the day might come, and speedily, that John Temple, clothed and in his right mind, might again value it as before, and again try to live up to its teaching.

Mechanically he locked the door, after leaving a note on the open Bible, begging his friend to try again, and whatever his resolution, to come and see him before going away. With a

faint hope that this might, through God's bless‑
ing, be the means of arresting his downward
course, the young man went sorrowfully to his
lodgings. How much he had leaned upon his
friend he now knew, for he felt so sadly alone
that he was well-nigh discouraged. He dreaded
the coming week, when all the men would be
scoffing at the fallen convert; and above all he
feared for the influence it would have upon
them. That the Lord could and did keep those
who trusted fully in Him, he did not doubt;
but would not the file-grinders question it?
There was Gaffney, to be sure, who seemed to
be really converted, but there was every chance
for him to slip. A drunken wife, a set of
rioting, drinking neighbors, and but a slight
knowledge of the "way of life." The Lord
could teach him; but Chamberlain trembled as
he thought of the self-confidence of the man,
even when he was in the gutter. No doubt he
meant to do right, and would for a time; — but
was it lack of faith on Chamberlain's part, or
a knowledge of men, that led him to distrust?
Perhaps it was both; yet the young man prayed:
"O Lord, for the sake of poor, down-trodden
Steep Street, let not this man fall."

So pressed was he by the burden that rested up‑
on him, that two hours later, just in the edge of

the evening, he strolled down the street, to see if Gaffney was in any of his usual haunts. At first his search was unsuccessful. One place after another was visited, and no signs of the burly figure were to be seen. Becoming a little more cheerful, at not readily finding the object of his search, he went on, determined to convince himself that his doubts were unfounded. The last place on his list was the engine-house, and on the steps he found him, in a deep, drunken sleep. With a groan he turned away and hurried home.

Passing one of the "loafing corners," he tarried an instant to hear the last of a story that one of the young roughs was relating.

"After he got through with his sermon, and was sitting as independent as you please, refusing to touch a drop of anything, one of the fellers slips up behind him and holds his arms, and another chucks the nose of a bottle right into his mouth. At first he struggled like a good one, but all of a sudden he stopped, and drank till they had to pull it away, and now he's drunk as a trooper."

Completely discouraged, feeling as if the Powers of Darkness were too strongly entrenched in Steep Street for even a soul to be saved, he passed along. The knowledge that men could deliberately force another to drink, and rejoice in a downfall that would probably mean the loss of a soul, was to him inexplicable. Why should not the most depraved be glad if any one had the grace given him to climb up out of the miry pit?

XII.

Tam's·Secret.

IT was midnight. Chamberlain, unable to sleep after the scenes of the afternoon, quietly dressed and started for a walk, hoping the fresh air would calm his throbbing brain Without thinking as to where he might go, he passed through the village, over the road tha* he traveled four times a day. No lights were burning except in the engine-house, where a glimmer through the close-drawn shutters showed that some of the company were still prolonging their Sunday spree. Going rapidly through the settlement, he reached the great enclosure in which stood the buildings of the file-works. All was so silent that it seemed not the same place that it did in the glare of the daylight, with the machinery making hideous din. A feeling of awe came into his mind as the buildings loomed up before him like masses of shadow.

As he strode on, the remembrance of Temple as he had appeared at his best, when he was trying so hard to serve the Lord, came again and again to the young man. It could not be possible that he had been deceived as to his own real desire for a new life, and the thought that it had all been a sham from the first, which many would bring forward, was, he felt assured, entirely groundless. The suddenness with which Temple had fallen, and the shock that it produced in connection with the impressive communion service, would certainly do harm.

Over and over again he had recalled even the minutest details of speech and action. The awful problem as to why his friend had been suffered to slip back to living death when just rescued, was more than he could solve. He knew that Temple must have been converted, must have loved the Lord, must have been accepted and forgiven. Had this not been so, could he ever have kept from liquor as he had for months before the dreadful Sunday? As he recalled that Sabbath, the strange feverishness of his companion after the service, his frantic haste to reach home, his incoherence, all combined to perplex the young man. Shuddering at the thought of his fearful fall,— praying that even now there might

be hope for him, yet ignorant as to the cause
of his relapse, Chamberlain sped on.

At length he became wearied and turned toward home. His heated blood had cooled, and
he felt that he could leave the matter
to the Lord, assured that it would all come
out right. By the time the file-works were
reached on the way back, he was weary enough
to take a "short cut," and leaving the main
road he entered a path that ran along in the
shadow of the lofty board fence in the rear of
the mill-enclosure. This path was used by the
operatives alone, and led to the river, where a
narrow foot-bridge connected it with the Steep-street
settlement. He hurried on in the uncertain light,
sometimes splashing in little pools of rain-water,
at others stepping carefully over some queer
shadow. The night, partly cloudy, partly bright,
and the strangeness of the situation, were not
without their effect; an uncanny feeling which the
loneliness and the piercing cries of the whip-
poor-wills served to intensify, came over him.
About one-half the length of the seemingly in-
terminable board fence had been passed, when
close by sounded a human voice. As he had
been walking softly and doubted if the speaker
had either seen or heard him, he instantly
stood still and listened, and after an instant's

silence it came again,—this time distinctly, a man's voice, sad and querulous, not loud, but clear as a bell.

"I'm verra, verra weary," it said, "verra weary."

Chamberlain's first thought had been that it was some one belated like himself, and traversing the same path; but to his astonishment he now discovered that the voice came from the mill-yard. The portion nearest him was crowded with buildings not in use, and made available as a sort of storage yard. He had been in it but once, and could summon a dim vision of two or three rusty boilers, heaps of building material, an acre or two of cases, and a few stone-cutters' shanties; the last named built up against the lofty fence. As nearly as he could tell, the voice came from one of these sheds.

"I saw George Chamberlain the other day in the works. Aye, but he's a fine lad. I have a mind to tell him about that cheating Lamson. Robert Flint will never believe but what he is a' right, but don't I ken him?"

Startled and astounded, Chamberlain stood rooted to the spot. The plaintive Scotch voice had mentioned his father's name as well as that of his uncle, and had condemned Lamson. Who was this stranger who spent the night in the yard where only the watchman had a right? And how came he by his knowledge even of the names he used?

"Ah, Tam! Tam! ye have no head for villanies," continued the voice, "Why could ye no accept Lamson's proposal and meck yeer fortune? Has yeer conscience paid? Robert Flint dinna' believe ye, and George Chamberlain went awa' so that ye could na' tell him. Ye think he's back, but dinna be sure. It does na' luke just like him. It may be one who has his appearing."

Crowding close to the fence, he was drinking in every word. At first, when the unseen speaker had apostrophized Tam, he had thought that he was spoken to, but the tone and the subsequent words convinced him that the speaker's name was Tam. He wondered who he might be. The name was totally unfamiliar.

"Ye would na' make the crucibles into polish in secret, would ye, Tam, because ye kenned it wad be thieving from the company, but what gained ye by yeer conscience? Only the hate o' Lamson. Had not the Loord raised up Sam Putnam, wad ye no been kilt? Aye, that ye would, Tam. Thank the Loord, auld lad, for Sam and thank him that ye kept yeer conscience — amen."

The speaker ceased, and there was again the
deep night-silence.   For a long time Chamberlain stood waiting to hear more, but the strange
Scotchman spoke no other word.   Chamberlain,
longing for a sight of him, looked wistfully at
the high fence with its row of sharp spikes,
but could see that any attempt to scale it would
be useless.

At last, unable to leave without an effort toward better acquaintance, he knocked softly on
the fence.

There was a rustle on the other side, as if
one had roused up to a sitting posture to listen.

Again he knocked.

"What is that rappin'?" said the sad voice
with a startled tremor.

"A friend,"

"What friend?"

"Chamberlain."

"It's a lee, Chamberlain's dead.   Who are ye
that's been listening to a puir demented mon?
Go yeer way, ye canna fule me."

A sound came as if a rickety door were pushed
aside.

"Don't go!" called Chamberlain, "I have
something to say to you."

"Tal it to the trees, whisper it to the chimneys, sing it to the empty buildings.   They all

have ears,—they can hear,—they have voices,—they can answer."

"Don't go, Tam," he called.

"Eh! Hoo do ye ken my name, eavesdropper? Ye should be hanged by the ears!" returned the voice, and the sound of hasty footsteps echoed through the yard, and quiet again reigned.

Feeling that it was of no use to stay longer, Chamberlain went his way, and ere long reached home. He had little time before daybreak to get even a nap, had he been in sleeping trim; but the exciting events of the night, coupled with the sad occurrence of the day preceding, made him feel as if he should never be able to sleep again, although he was mortally weary. Partaking of a light breakfast, he went to the mill, where he found that the story of Temple's disgrace had gone the rounds. Most of the men assured all who spoke of it, and some who did not, that it was "just what they knew would come." Chamberlain fancied that even on the countenance of the agent, there was an "I-told-you-so" expression. But the latter said nothing; indeed of late, he had avoided even the morning nod with which he had formerly greeted the unwelcome novice.

As for Chamberlain, the comments of the men fell on ears deadened by extreme fatigue, yet

even with the weariness came the painful feeling, that there were those who would perhaps
never again "take stock in any sort of reform."

With the energy which had become a part of
his being, he determined that very noon to explore the part of the factory adjoining the
stone-cutters' sheds, and discover, if possible, who
the sad Scotchman was. The monologue in which
had figured names that few of the men in the
factory used, gave an added mystery to the whole
affair. Had the young man a superstitious
nature, he might have supposed that a garrulous
ghost had been voicing the thoughts of the
past in some favorite retreat, and have considered investigation in daylight to be useless
from the outset. Such a thought never occurred
to him, and he ate the lunch that Mrs. Bowman had, under protest, substituted for a warm
dinner, and started for the deserted rear yards.
The surroundings of the works were of much
greater magnitude than a casual observer would
suppose. Our anxious explorer began to be aware
of this, as after passing the long reaches of coal,
in the great coal yards, he came to a second
series of yards, where stood scores of empty
freight cars, on tracks weed-grown and rails red
with rust. Here and there, lounging in the
shade of the cars, playing "forty-five," in quiet

nooks, were his fellow-workmen. He received
many a kindly nod, many a hearty invitation to
join the various groups. Somehow the kindli-
ness of his companions on this particular day
specially touched him. It drove the loneliness out
of his heart, in a measure, to know that the
men respected and liked him. How much he
could rely on this popularity in time of trouble,
or how little it would take to turn these friendly
ones into bitter enemies, was not the question.
They liked him now, and that was a comfort.
When he had reached the furthest limit of the
freight yard he found himself shut away from
further search by an extension of the same lofty
spike-capped fence that held him off on the preceding night. By what means access was gained
to the special yard that he now desired to
visit, he was not able exactly to recall. This
was not in the least to be wondered at, as his
first and only visit had taken place when he
was but a novice in the manufactory, and so
overcrowded with new sights and strange surroundings that distinct impressions of each were
more than an ordinary mind could receive.
With a faint recollection of entering a long
building, which served as a gateway for this enclosure, he turned his attention to the sheds and
houses in the vicinity. From the top of a box-

car he was able to survey the chimneys of at least a dozen buildings on a line with the fence. Some of them he was familar with, while others were entirely strange. He was able finally to decide with tolerable certainty upon one that was probably the "gate-house" to the secluded yard. With some difficulty he found this great barn-like structure, and was about to enter it and explore, when the "warning whistle" sounded, and he was forced to forego his intention for that day, and return to his work.

The next noon he renewed the attempt, and was on the spot ten minutes after the "speed" had shut down. The main door of the building was locked, an unusual thing, by the way, in the "empty yards," where nothing of value was stored, and Chamberlain was forced to use his ingenuity to gain entrance. Briefly surveying the doors and windows, he saw that one of the latter was fastened by a stick braced against the bottom sash in close proximity to a broken pane of glass. This not only afforded him a chance to get in, but it also gave him some information, for the stick that acted as fastening was soiled in the centre, its most convenient grasping place, and the sides of the sash were stained as if by grimy hands; there were also boot-heel marks on the sill, as if some more clumsy climbers had, with difficulty, entered in this way. The depth of the stains and the many heel-marks testified to the frequency with which this means of ingress and egress were used.

Unseen by any of his fellows, Chamberlain climbed into the great empty structure, and stood taking his bearings. The absence of stored goods or stock greatly facilitated a rapid survey of the one apartment. At first, even with this help, he could not see what communication could be had with the further yard, but a closer inspection revealed a door which must have been open when he was there before. This yielded easily to his touch, and he found himself nearing the goal of his hopes. Once on the ground, the sights even when he was a novice—which, by the way, explained his admittance to a portion of the works from which most of the old hands were debarred,—came back to him. Here and there through the weeds that had grown up in wild luxuriance, ran paths that appeared to end nowhere in particular, and to be of no definite use.

An air of desolation and decay was imparted to the whole place, by vines clambering over piles of rust-clad castings, forcing themselves through the spokes of broken cog-wheels as if to bind them forever to the earth, or clinging to the weather-worn buildings as though they would add even their feeble strength to the efforts of wind and weather to pull them down. A number of buildings, of stone and wood, stood in this yard, and as Chamberlain debated which first to examine, a step sounded on the pathway behind him, and turning quickly he was confronted by the watchman of that section.

"Look here, young feller! What do you want in this part of the works?" he inquired roughly.

"Oh, I am just looking around," was the quiet reply.

"Well, get right out. Orders is strict not to let nobody in here; been enough stealing done by you 'piece hands'."

"I did n't see anything to steal except a rusty boiler or two," said Chamberlain, good-humoredly.

"Well, orders is orders, so git."

"By the way, is Tam round here to-day?" enquired Chamberlain, in a very ordinary voice.

"Tam who?" was the query, without a trace of the consternation that was expected.

"Why, Tam, the Scotchman."

"He ain't been in here, whoever he is. You are the only one who has been here for weeks, and what possessed you I don't see.   I should never have known you were here, either, if you hadn't left that window open."

Chamberlain mentally reproached himself for such carelessness, even while studying the expression of the man's face. It appeared to be perfectly honest, and he came to the con-clusion that the watchman knew nothing about the little Scotchman.

"Don't let any of the fellers know that you've been in here," said the man in parting. "Because if the boss gets wind of it he will bounce me."

"All right, I won't mention it."

XIII.

What·the·Church·Did·About·It.

IT was Wednesday evening. "Prayer-meeting night," the elderly folk were wont to call it. The regular attendants, a few saintly mothers, one or two deacons, several elderly brethren, and half-a-score of sisters had already gathered in the vestry. On this particular occasion there were in addition numbers of others, whose faces were seldom seen in the house of God during the midweek. Their presence was due to the report that had gone forth, that there would be a "lively time" at this meeting, and they had gathered to enjoy it. When the bell ceased tolling, the pastor read the Scriptures, offered prayer and gave out a hymn. During the latter exercise, the clock in the rear of the room struck the hour with painful distinctness, interrupting, as it always did, at the usual place. After singing, during which the cabinet organ lost its breath and was compelled to stop, the pastor made a few remarks. The meeting was then thrown open to the brethren.

Brother Closson offered his every-meeting petition, that they "all might be burnin' and shinin' lights."

"Jes' so" Johnson spoke of the work among the Telegoos, and of the encouragement that it should he to all who were "in the service."

Miss Ferguson began a verse, became confused, lost her reckoning, and her sister finished it.

Deacon Wilson spoke briefly and pointedly upon the subject contained in the chapter with which the meeting was opened.

Everything had gone on as usual. Even the hymns were carefully started too high, and broken down on in the stereotyped way.

All the dryness of an ordinary, dull meeting was present, yet a deep interest pervaded the room which had not been touched by exhortation or prayer. It lay outside of the accustomed speeches, and when the benediction was pronounced, and all members of the church had been requested to remain, it began to manifest itself.

With reluctance and sorrow Mr. Snow began upon the subject. In a voice tremulous with suppressed emotion, he went over the brief

career of John Temple since he had come under
the notice of the church. He spoke of the
young man's apparent sincerity, of his humility,
and his dependence on a Higher Power. He
was aware, he said, that many in the congregation wondered that one who promised so well
should, on the very afternoon of his admission
to the Church of Christ, have gone back to his
sins. It was a calamity, not alone to the
sufferer, but also to every Christian there. It
would cause the enemies of Christ to rejoice,
and would discourage the weaker Christians.
Many of the unsaved, who had watched with a
ray of hope the progress of the convert, would
believe that it was all a sham,— that there was
no salvation from the power of drink.

"In this emergency," continued the pastor,
"it behooves the church to do something. It
is her duty to remove the stumbling-block by
which this man, our brother, fell. And lest
there be misunderstanding, let me relate exactly
how his fall came about. He believed, with
the rest of us, that he was saved from a most
terrible appetite for strong drink. Since his
conversion, no drop had passed his lips. His
taste for liquor was not taken away, but the
Lord gave him grace to overcome it. He felt
his own weakness, and by constant prayer and

careful avoidance of places of temptation, he was kept from falling. This church, through its most sacred ordinance, that of communion, placed the temptation in the hands of the unhappy man. We served him with the alcohol for which he had the horrible thirst, and when once it was tasted all strength for resistance was gone. We are guilty,—ignorantly, without doubt, but guilty. At the table of the Lord we have furnished *poison*. We have caused a brother to fall, to plunge into a whirlpool of excess, to flee away, in a mad debauch, where, none knows but the All-pitying One. How shall we atone?"

The pastor ceased speaking, and for several moments a hush reigned in the room. At length Deacon Wilson rose. He was known as a thorough, perhaps a fanatical, temperance man.

"It seems to me," he said, with feeling, "that this lesson from the Lord should be a profit to us. Other churches have been awake on this subject. Several, to my knowledge, have adopted non-alcoholic wine at their communion service. Why should not we at once do the same?"

"This meeting has been called as a regular church business meeting, and the question can be settled here and now," said the pastor. "We await a motion."

"I would move that non-intoxicating wine be hereafter used at our church communion," said Deacon Wilson.

"Second the motion," said one of the sisters.

At this juncture a handsome, portly gentleman of fifty or over, who had been sitting quietly in the rear of the room, rose and went forward, taking a position where the audience could see his every motion. It was customary there for speakers to address the congregation from whatever part of the room they had been sitting. This movement, therefore, arrested the attention of all. In a deep, mellow voice, in accents that showed culture, he began. He said he believed that a church that followed closely in the footsteps of the Master could not fall far short of its whole duty. With tender reverence he described the last supper, the eating of bread, the drinking of the cup.

"Now," said he, in conclusion, "I deplore deeply the sad event that has occurred, but let us not charge ourselves with it, for in this case we are blameless. We have done as Christ commanded. The young man fell, not because of the communion service, but because he did not use the will that God gave him.

Would not our action in substituting some other liquid for the divinely ordered wine be a criticism upon the action of the Master? Would not, also, the beauty and completeness of the service be sacrificed, were we to lay rude hands upon it?"

The gentleman sat down, and there was no reply to his words. Even Deacon Wilson appeared loth to enter into controversy with him, and it looked as if, as is the case in many places, the mere presence of a great man was going to shut the mouths of all who did not exactly agree with him. Chamberlain, however, with all his sorrow for Temple, and an unavoidable sense of humiliation when he knew that many would put him into the same category, felt the old spirit of debate taking possession of him, and noting the weak points in the other's address, rose.

There was a rustle of interest and a subsequent hush as his first words fell on the ears of the listeners.

"Mr. Temple was my friend," he said slowly. "I was with him the evening he gave his heart to the Saviour. It was that night that I, also, was born into the kingdom. The hopes and the fears, the honest, earnest love for the Saviour, the consuming desire to lead others to

Him, that Temple possessed, were not hid from
me. I knew of them all, and rejoiced in them.
I remember that several times my friend came
to me and said, with an inexpressible thrill of
joy in his voice, 'I am so happy. What a
wonderful, glorious Saviour, to have forgiven me.'
The men in the file-works knew of his former
drinking habits, of his previous efforts at reform,
and of his failures, and were watching him with
interest. It will be a great disappointment to
some of them, for there are, I believe, hearts
there that are dimly yearning for salvation.
There is but one power that can hinder this
from being a great damage to them. That it
will be overruled, I believe.

"If, however, we know the cause of the sad
fall; if, as our pastor says, it was due to the
alcohol in the communion wine, it seems as if
it had been given directly to this church for a
lesson. Paul said he would eat no more meat
while the world stood, if the eating of meat
caused his brother to stumble. And is not that
the spirit of the Gospel from beginning to end?
Our brother thinks we should follow literally
every move of the Master at the last supper.
Should we not, then, *always* gather in an upper
room? Should we not partake of *unleavened*
bread? Should not those who break the bread

and pour the cup, be also girded with towels, and wash the disciples' feet? Perhaps I am wrong, but I believe the *spirit* of the ordinance is what the Lord wishes, and not the letter. 'In remembrance of Him.' Would it not be a closer, more loving remembrance of Him, than we could possibly arrive at otherwise, if we substituted for the alcoholic wine, the pure juice of the grape, and in that way removed cause for stumbling from the path of the weak? In doing this let us not think that we are stooping to help Steep Street and the mill folk, and that we are above such temptation, for I recall another such case, coming to the honored head of a wealthy family in New York. Any one who has dallied with this fearful temptation is in danger, and those who most scornfully scout the idea are most in peril."

Before this speech was finished the gentleman took out his watch, looked at it, closed it with a snap, rose slowly, and passed out. When the door had closed behind him, and Chamberlain had seated himself, the pastor put the question, and, thanks to the sisters present, who all voted on the right side, the victory was won. The North Church would no more put temptation to the lips of her children. The pastor overtook Chamberlain as he was going home.

"I want you to join me in prayer for Temple," he said. "I cannot believe that he will be lost. I think this church is guilty, and, as her pastor, I feel the burden of this guilt resting very heavily upon me. The Lord has said: 'If two of you are agreed as touching any thing, it shall be done.' Now I most heartily believe that, and I propose that you and I test it, — that we prove the Lord."

Kneeling by the roadside, they prayed, and rose with a feeling that their prayers were heard, and an assurance that they would be answered.

"There is another burden that I am bearing before the Lord," said Mr. Snow, with some hesitation, "and one that I wish you might share. It is the case of the gentleman who rose and left the room while you were speaking; perhaps you noticed him?"

"I did; who was he?"

"Mr. Whitney," was the reply, and Chamberlain knew that his opponent in the evening's debate was the father of Miriam.

"Why did he leave the room so abruptly? Was it because he saw that the case was going against him?"

"I do not think so; I am aware that it looked much like it, but he has many business cares, and attended this meeting when he could really ill afford the time. That I know. The people of this congregation are somewhat in fear of him, as he has a remarkable insight into character, and does not hesitate to condemn fraud wherever seen. He is the soul of independence, thinks and acts for himself, and asks no one's advice. What he said in the meeting was his honest opinion. If he ever changes, he will just as honestly acknowledge it."

"I am glad to know that. He is a noble-looking man, and it troubled me to think that his action might be caused by a petty chagrin," said Chamberlain.

"And now, my brother, what is the feeling in the mill toward the great question? What think the men of Christ? You are near to their hearts. It is said that you are popular among them. If so, you should be able to put your finger on their religious pulse and tell just how it beats. Brother Lamson tells me they are totally indifferent. He does not appear to be as sanguine in seeing opportunities to do these people good as I could wish, but he is cumbered with many worldly cares. What do you think of the outlook for a religious awakening in the mill village?"

"I think that while the men have such an

example as Deacon Lamson daily before them, they will be exceedingly slow to embrace his religion," was the hot reply.

"The unfaithfulness of one man does not in any way do away with the question of one's personal responsibility before God," was the solemn reply.

"Of course not."

"Without doubt, Lamson is worldly. How many of us are entirely free from it? He is also stern and dignified toward those in his employ. I could wish that he took a deeper interest in the young men under his care, but his probity is unquestioned, and he lives up to the letter of his profession. Do you not think so?"

"I should be exceedingly glad it if were so," replied Chamberlain.

"Now my dear young friend," said the pastor, "remember it is a very serious thing in any way to pass judgment on a fellow laborer in the Lord's vineyard, and I would caution you to examine your own heart carefully before God, and see if this dislike does not in some way spring from some earthly or worldly desire in yourself."

"I don't know how it could. What I have seen in no way touches me individually," was the surprised reply.

"Let us suppose a case. A young man, bright and intelligent, through stress of circumstances is forced to enter a factory to earn his livelihood. He is superior in birth and education to his companions and is aware of it, although he is not conceited. He expects to be rapidly advanced, especially as he is very faithful in the performance of his duties. In addition to this, he joins a church, the same in which the owner of the factory is a leading member. He has no thought that this will in any way advance him temporally, yet the coldness with which the owner, his brother in Christ, treats him, leads him, in a measure, to misjudge and dislike him. Now I will not defend the mill owner in his coldness and his failure to recognize true merit, but is the young man fitted to calmly pass judgment on him as a man and a Christian? Will there not be a little of envy and disappointment intermixed with his estimate of that man?"

Chamberlain laughed a hearty, jolly laugh, and the pastor joined him.

"Am I not right?" he said delightedly, "does not the cap fit, my brother? Come you are too honest a man to deny it when you are fairly caught."

"You have n't hit it," was the reply, with a very broad smile. "There is no advancement that Lamson can give me that I covet. I have ambitions but he cannot help them on. If I could tell them to any one, it would be to you. But seriously and honestly, I never expected, never wished, and would not accept the best place Lamson could give me."

"Would you not accept more remunerative employment?" asked the pastor, with an air of deep disappointment.

"No, decidedly not." Was the positive reply.

"I am sorry. I thought I had the key to the whole problem, and had made up my mind to influence Brother Lamson to accept you as a protegé."

"Pray do nothing of the kind. I am aware it is a strange statement to make for a 'piece hand,' a day laborer, but I am perfectly satisfied, and by being allowed to go my own way, will sooner accomplish my ambitions than any other way."

"Is the Lord Jesus Christ with you in these ambitions?" Asked Mr. Snow with a piercing look,

"He is," was the reverent reply.

"Then I am satisfied. Yet I am loth to give up my wish to serve you; young men are far too apt to underrate the advantages that may accrue to them through the influence of friends."

"There are others in the mill who deserve promotion, and when you become acquainted with them they will be delighted beyond measure to have their merits recognized. I am very grateful, but it is out of the question for me to wish for any advancement that Mr. Lamson could proffer."

The good man stood for a few minutes in deep thought, while Chamberlain waited respectfully for him to wholly ease his mind of the cares and plans for the mill folks and himself. At length he said,

"Speaking of Brother Lamson, although you have made no specific charges against him, I can see that you feel that he is not in the right place, or to put it more frankly, that he is a hypocrite. In that, I am certain you are mistaken. As your pastor, as well as his, I want to ask you after prayer for guidance, to go to him and have an honest, earnest talk with him. Whatever you may have against him state fully and clearly, provided it be any thing in which he is at fault and that touches you. If there is any thing that after careful weighing you find is any of your business, go and talk with him, and I am sure he will meet you kindly and willingly, and rectify whatever wrong he may intentionally or unintentionally have done."

"You are still of the opinion that a part of my dislike springs from wounded personal vanity?" inquired Chamberlain.

"My brother," was the reply, "I have known many men, and been able to settle many differences among members of my church, and few there are of the best, but have full as much personal pride as their profession will bear."

When the good-nights had been said and Chamberlain had started for home, he found that he had promised to call upon the lawyer and talk with him. Looking at the whole affair from the pastor's stand-point, he wondered that such a course should have been advised, for the latter supposed him to be but a workman. Just what his feelings toward the agent might be at that moment, he could hardly tell. There was a bare possibility that the man might be misunderstood by the people of the village. He had known of cases where an aristocrat of the strictest probity and unimpeachable character had been hated and maligned by the menials in his employ, till some of the falsehoods were actually believed and were widely circulated. Lamson had in many ways striven to hinder him, but that might be from a mere petty jealousy which was very far removed from real criminality. Even now the man might be ashamed of it. The case did not look quite so black from this manner of viewing it as it did from the other, and Chamberlain resolved at all **events to give him a chance to clear himself.**

XIV.

Tom's·Request.

"CAN I see Mr. Lamson?"

"What name, sir?" asked the servant.

"Chamberlain," was the reply.

"I will see."

Sitting in the elegantly furnished parlor of the Lamson house, the visitor looked about with some curiosity. He had an idea that a bachelor was likely when furnishing his apartments, in a measure to express his own individuality. Yet nothing Lamsonian appeared in this room. There was no hint at vulgarity, no approach to coarseness; on the contrary it was furnished with care and delicate taste. He marveled a trifle at this, till he remembered having heard of the mother of the lawyer, a quiet, silver-haired, sweet-faced lady, whom all loved. This was quite a relief, and the remembrance, rescued with difficulty from oblivion, became a positive recollection. "Lamson's mother!" The more he reflected, the more he wondered if she, with the usual mother-blindness, adored her son. It was strange what an influence the knowledge that this man had a mother, had upon Chamberlain. His animosity seemed to lose its edge. The fact that one person loved Lamson, even though he might be unworthy, placed him in a new light, and raised him to a higher grade. Just then his name was spoken, and the subject of his thoughts stood before him.

"Glad to see you, Chamberlain," he said cordially. "Have you at last decided to allow yourself an evening's relaxation? I verily believe you are the hardest worker in the shops."

"Oh, no, there are many who do more than I. My self-denial, in the way of society pleasures, has been forced, as you must acknowledge. I enjoy such life too well to be without it otherwise."

"I hear good reports of you from the workmen," continued the agent. "With one voice, they say that you are one of the best men we have yet had, and that your mastery of the different processes of file-making, is rapid and accurate."

"Thank you," was the reply; a flush of pleasure stealing into the brown cheeks. "I am glad that they think so. Their praise is to be valued."

"It is, indeed," was the hearty reply.

"My errand here, this evening," said Chamberlain, was with reference to Temple."

"Oh," said Lamson, with an impenetrable look.

"He, as you know, perhaps, leased a room on Steep Street, and started a small store."

"Yes."

"It was to be a temperance grocery store, where, all who wished, could purchase goods without having liquors thrust under their noses. Of course this would be an injury to Pfaff, but every Christian I have yet met has thus far acknowledged that he is a nuisance. The fact is, the time has come when that liquor shop in the lower village ought to be closed."

"Mr. Chamberlain," said Lamson, with an appearance of sincerity, "you have spoken of something that has long worried me. Pfaff *is* a nuisance. His rum-shop ought to be shut up, and, were it possible, should be. But my hands are tied."

Surprised at the unequivocal condemnation of the man whom he was said secretly to uphold, Chamberlain was silent, and Lamson went on.

"Your uncle, Robert Flint, was, in many respects, a strange man. Whatever he did, he never *would* undo. Whatever he said, he stuck to. Pfaff saved his life, when he was in some desperate danger in the mill, long years ago, and he never forgot it. He promised the man any thing, almost, that he might ask, and, like a wily fellow that he was, the German asked for a life-lease of the building in which his business is situated, and to be allowed to sell liquor as long as he wished."

"And it was given him?"

"Certainly. And not only that, but Mr. Flint made me promise in no way to restrict him in the full use of his privileges. You can see how I am placed. I cannot, and will not, break my word. It will be impossible for any one to dislodge him, for, as I have said, he holds a life-lease. He it is who has been, and is, dragging Steep Street down to bitter and lasting wretchedness. What can be done is more than I can tell. Can you solve this problem?"

Chamberlain pondered. The facts cited by the agent, if they were facts, put things in an entirely new light. Might not his, and, indeed, the general, impression of Lamson be wrong? Those who did not know of the life-lease, and the promise, would be likely to condemn the agent for the sin that he was, apparently, party to. People in the upper settlement trusted and honored him. He had been chosen deacon. Was not the vulgar prejudice a mistaken one? Lamson waited, and allowed the leaven of his words to work in the young man's mind.

"Mr. Lamson," said he, finally, "I wish to beg your pardon for having doubted you. We are both members of the same church. We are disciples of the same Master. I have wronged you in my thoughts, on this subject, which you would have explained, had I asked you. Will you pardon me?"

"Do not speak of it," was the hearty response. "You were right in condemning me, if, as you thought, I could have dislodged Pfaff. Let us forget it. I have vindicated myself, and we at last understand one another."

"You were asking," continued Chamberlain, "what could be done to solve this problem. I have studied it, and two things are suggested to me. One is, to give the people of the street good drinking water, and the other is, to establish a rival store that shall draw as much trade as possible away from the liquor-shop."

"Very good, if they were practicable, but I fear neither is," was the reply, with an intonation of regret.

"I do not agree with you. They both are

feasible. For instance, good water can be struck on the plateau just above the street," returned the young man, warming up to a defense of his plans.

"All the land there is owned by parties who are at enmity with the file-company. Miss Whittier would sooner burn her house than sell a foot of her land. Besides, the water there would have the same impregnation that all the wells in the vicinity possess."

"I am sure you will be glad to know you are wrong. A driven well is already finished on the other side of Miss Whittier's fence, and flows pure, cold water enough to supply all Steep Street, and the mill also," was the quick reply.

Lamson's face darkened. Chamberlain did not notice it, but went on to describe the advantages that would ensue from such a well, assured that the agent, although conservative, was with him.

"How is the water to be got to them?" he asked.

"By pipes running into each house. It would cost but a trifling sum, and what a blessing it would be!"

Lamson shook his head as if in deep thought.

"Just now," he said slowly, "I am afraid we cannot afford to put out any money on piping.

I wish we might.   The project is a good one.
It is yours, I suppose?"

"Yes," said Chamberlain, with genuine pride,
which displayed itself in his voice, and was
noticed by Lamson.

"It is a noble thought, and no doubt cost you
considerable, or did Miss Whittier assume the
expense," he continued.

"I did it."

Again the face of the agent assumed its
cloud.   Chamberlain, seeing it, laid it to deep
thought, and mentally rejoiced that at last he
had found Lamson so willing to plan for the
prosperity of Steep Street.

"I believe I can see your hand in the new
store, also," said the agent, with a sharp glance.

"That was Temple's thought.   I only furnished
the money."

Lamson shaded his face and sat for a few
moments in deep thought.

"I suppose," he said, "you would like to have
that continued?"

"I should."

"Have you any one in mind to run it?"

"I have not," was the reply.

"I believe I know a man who would be just
the one wanted," averred Lamson.   "He lives in
a neighboring town.   I will drop him a line,

and, if you wish, he will call and see you within a day or two. Until then, if I were you, I should keep the place shut."

"Thank you," said Chamberlain, greatly re lieved. "I have been puzzled to know whom to put there. Your help will come in just the right time."

Swayed by the candid confessions of the lawyer, Chamberlain went away sure that the general impression among the help, that Lamson was a rascal and a hypocrite, was without foundation. As it happened, something occurred that very evening that led him further to believe in his innocence as regarded all such charges. Across the river, just on the edge of the mill-dam, leading from the factory-yard to the Steep-street side, ran a foot-bridge. It was a frail structure, and but little used, except by the "water-gate tender" in his trips to raise or lower the "flash-boards." In his determination to become acquainted with all parts of the vast mill estate, Chamberlain had often passed over this foot-bridge. The factory-buildings adjacent to it were most of them windowless, while the ample yards were shut in by lofty fences, making it possible for one standing on this bridge to be as much alone as if miles away from human habitation. The waterfall, upon the edge of which the

bridge clung, tumbled down over a series of
rough granite steps, throwing the spray high in
the air, and wetting the branches of the maples
and elms that grew, not alone on either side,
but also on a narrow island strip in mid-stream,
extending close up to the dam.   This rocky
island, its sides constantly fretted by the surging
waters, its phalanx of trees, ever narrowing, till
they stood almost in single file at the foot of
the dam, was, to Chamberlain's eyes, a spot of
rare beauty.   When the mill was not running
the waters thundered over the dam, sometimes
sweeping over the island, bending down the
underbrush, loosening the boulders, and causing
even the sturdy trees to quiver and shake.
During work-hours, the side-canals drew off the
surplus water, and only narrow threads of silver
splashed over and ran across the rapidly-drying
rocks.

On the evening in question the young man
had wandered to this spot and stood now in his
favorite attitude, leaning against the railing and
looking down into the empty river-bed.   Absorbed in thought, he did not notice that the
railing, pressed by his weight, was slowly yield-
ing.   When at length, it suddenly snapped and
broke, ere he could recover himself, he was
precipitated into the mass of tree-tops that

reached up toward him from the little island. Fortunate for him it was, that they were bound together by luxuriant grape-vines, that the branches were green and thrifty, and that so much intervened to break the fall. As it was, dizzy, bewildered, stunned, he reached the ground without serious injury. Upon attempting to rise he found himself in a curious predicament. The great oak, into whose friendly arms he had fallen, had as its neighbor a thrifty young beech. Wedged between the two, his ankle firmly caught in a rock-crevice, Chamberlain found he could not get up unassisted. The distance between the two trees was enough to admit of his moving freely, yet held him too tightly to allow him to release his prisoned foot. In vain he writhed and squirmed, using his strength, skill, ingenuity. All were alike useless.

With no little difficulty, he looked at his watch, which was still running, in spite of the shaking up it had received, and discovered that it wanted but five minutes of whistle-time. At six, the canal-gates would be shut, and the water would again thunder over the dam. The very place where he lay, had been for the past few days swept by an angry torrent, swelled by recent rains. There was little probability that the water had lowered enough to make it safe.

The dampness of the ground and the tree-trunks proved that during the brief noon-hour, the place where he lay had been water-swept. The steady roar of the machinery would soon give place to the thunder of the waterfall, and neither would allow his voice to be heard. The case looked serious. There was a bare possibility that the water-gate man might cross the bridge and might rescue him, but it was a chance in a thousand. One-half the time had already gone swift-winged, and he was listening with nervous apprehension for the clanking of the gate-chains, when looking up he saw a man walking leisurely across the foot-bridge. How his heart beat with hope and fear! Nearer came the stranger, and he raised his voice and cried, "Help! help!" But the clattering and clanging and roaring of the mills drove the sound away from the friendly ears. Again he cried, and again with the same result. The gentleman walked quietly on, and was passing the place of the accident, when he noticed the broken rail. With a gesture of surprise, he peered down into the river-bed, and at once saw Chamberlain looking up to him with all the eloquence of appeal that a youth threatened with a horrible death could express in a look.

When Chamberlain saw who it was, as he did

in a second glance, his heart sank within him,
foi he encountered the steel-blue eyes of Lam
son. Why should he have been so disappointed
that it was not some rough workman, or even
some enemy, instead of the polite lawyer? Perhaps this was because he thought that, were he
ever so anxious, he would not possess the faculty
for a quick rescue, or possibly he had not yet
laid aside his deep-rooted distrust. At all events
it was a most shocking disappointment when he
discovered that his only hope of help lay in this
man in faultless broadcloth. Even in the greatest extremity one is impressed by the most
trivial things, and as Chamberlain looked up and
saw the broad expanse of spotless linen, and the
rays of the summer-sun struck full on the dia-
mond shirt-stud, he was almost in despair. But
Lamson did not stand idly regarding him. He
called down some sentence which might have
been encouraging or otherwise, so mangled were
the words by the din of the trip-hammers, and
then darted back to the factory. That he could
run, the young man had never imagined, for the
pompous walk had ever seemed a part of his
personality. Soon Lamson reappeared with a long
rope, which, with almost incredible deftness, he
made fast to the planks of the foot-bridge and ,
then threw down. So sure was the cast that the

young man laid hold of it, but was even then not able to extricate himself.

"Send down one of the men," he called after a violent effort. But Lamson had no such thought. Already the clanking of the gate-chains had ceased, and a great silence fallen over the river-valley. From the street on the further side of the factory now came the shouts and laughter of the thronging operatives, striking with a startling distinctness on the ear of the imprisoned man at the foot of the fall. With so much of help so near, and yet to be unable to take any advantage of it, was like starving in the midst of plenty. Already the brimming pond had begun to overflow, and where there had a moment before been but a few small jets of water, were now constantly growing streams. A few minutes' delay would serve to settle the matter.

Bound down as he was, Chamberlain knew that he could not, by any possibility, keep his head above even a shallow stream. Meanwhile, in a sort of doubting stupor, he beheld Lamson strip off coat and vest and shoes, and swing himself over the edge of the dam. Not until after a quick, agile scramble over the slimy rocks, and he stood by his side, did he comprehend that he would actually risk so much

for any one. Yet now he stood over him, his
face flushed with the unusual exertion, the
knees of his pants green with rock-slime, his
stockings wet and torn. Without a word he set
at work to loosen the cloven rock that held the
ankle captive, and after a little prying and
pounding, it gave way and rolled into the turgid
stream that had already wet the foot through
and through. With the assistance of the strong
hand, — its firmness and strength impressed the
rescued man with great surprise, — he arose.

"We must be quick unless we wish to climb
these trees and stay all night," said the agent.
"Are you hurt? Think with a little help you
can go up the rope?"

"Yes, indeed! Go ahead, and I'll follow,"
said Chamberlain, again grasping the outstretched
hand.

"Oh, no," was the laughing reply. "I came
down here after you. I am strong and well.
You may be badly hurt without knowing it. It
is wiser for you to go first."

Recognizing the good sense in this, Chamberlain acquiesced, and in the face of a fine sheet
of water, with a broad stream falling on each
side, the two men began the ascent. The rocks,
grown more slippery than ever, afforded a most
insecure footing, and the air seemed full of fall-

ing water. In an instant they were drenched. Chamberlain, still dizzy from his fall, several times swung off from his feet, but the strong arm of the agent helped him back. As they neared the edge of the fall, the stream of water grew denser, and now fell steadily over them, and seemed to have the weight of hundreds of pounds. When, at last, they stood on the narrow foot-bridge, Lamson shook the water from himself like a shaggy water-dog, and said, jovially, —

"This makes me ten years younger. I declare, shower - baths agree with me first-rate."

"I wish I could express my gratitude. You have saved my life. I shall not soon forget it," said the rescued man with feeling.

"Nonsense! Do the same for me when I get in a similar fix, and it will be all right," was the careless answer. "Now, you must hurry home. I am sorry that I can't go with you, but I think as long as your ankle does not appear to be sprained, and you have no broken bones, the exercise of walking will not hurt you. Good luck, and don't try to emulate Sam Patch any more, by jumping over falls."

With a quick step and a parting wave of the hand, the agent walked rapidly away, and Cham-

berlain started in the opposite direction, his
warm heart overflowing with gratitude toward
his deliverer, and a strong resolution never again
to doubt a man who could show himself at once
so brave and so capable.

XV.

Tennis·and·Temperance.

"I AM sure, Master Tom, they would be very glad to have you join them," said old Allan, earnestly.

"It would do me good to have a game, but file-grinders are not apt to be up in such arts."

"They will never suspect. How should they? Has not any young man in this country a right to excel in any game? Let me introduce you to them."

"No," was the decided reply. "It was foolish for me to think of such a thing. I will not intrude. They are having a jolly time; why should it be marred by the presence of a laborer? I know how they feel."

The old gardener did not reply, but the expression on his face said plainly that no one could, for an instant, think Miss Alice's boy an intruder.

The two speakers were in the garden, behind a half-hedge of hollyhocks, looking over at the beautiful lawn in front of the Flint mansion There, three persons were playing tennis. On. of them was Miss Whitney; the other two, a young lady and a gentleman, were strangers. They had obtained permission from Lamson to use the grounds, and now were enjoying their liberty to the utmost. At length Miss Whitney dropped her racquet and strolled away through the garden. The other two, who were evidently lovers, seemed not at all loth to have her depart, for they at once seated themselves on a rustic bench and engaged in earnest conversation.

From behind the hollyhocks, Chamberlain watched the fair girl, as she slowly approached. With unconscious grace she moved over the close-cropped grass, toward the spot where stood the gardener. The old man had, as usual, begun to prune and pet his plants, and, in so doing, had stepped from behind the screen of plants and now was in plain sight.

"Oh, Allan," she said, with the freedom of an old acquaintance, "why are n't you a young man? A nice-looking, agreeable young man? I need one this afternoon."

The gardener's eyes twinkled.

"You want one to play tennis with?" he asked.

"Yes. Cousin Harvey and Kate are so awfully dull. They do such bare-faced cheating in favor of one another that it is impossible to beat them. Can you not change one of these hollyhocks into a youth, tall and fair, who shall be my partner and help me win a game?"

"Master Tom," said Allan, turning toward him, "fortune favors you."

Somewhat embarrassed, Chamberlain stepped forward, hat in hand, and made a polite bow.

"Pray consider me a transformed hollyhock," he said.

A wave of crimson swept over the young lady's face.

"I beg pardon," she said, with just a tinge of iciness; "I had no idea that any one, besides the gardener, was present."

"Master Tom is just the one to fill out the game; he is a crack player," remarked Allan.

"Do you play tennis, Mr. Chamberlain?" asked Miriam, with some surprise.

"I have played," was his modest reply.

Miss Whitney hesitated a moment, then said, —

"I should be very glad to have you join us in a game, and, oh!" she continued, gaining enthusiasm, "do let us beat Harvey and Kate!"

Crossing the lawn, he was introduced, and the game began. Harvey was no poor player, and when he found that Chamberlain was not a novice, a new interest lighted his eyes, and he dropped his listlessness and entered into the game in the heartiest way imaginable. With the stimulus of Miriam Whitney's energetic admonition to "be sure and beat," he played well, perhaps better than he ever had before; so well, that at the end of the game, his partner was clapping her hands at the rueful looks of Harvey and Kate, for they were badly worsted.

"You play elegantly, Mr. Chamberlain; better than any young man in town. What couldn't you do at tennis, if only you practised!" she exclaimed.

The impersonal way in which she spoke this, the enthusiasm over the game that made her forget all in rejoicing, pleased him greatly. He liked sincerity, and the pleasure expressed by Miss Whitney was genuine. For the time being he felt proud and happy, and determined, if they played again, to do even better than before.

Harvey, Chamberlain's opponent in the game, was a fine young fellow, fresh from West Point, and with all the taking ways of a genuine cadet. He was frank and boyish, and, at the same time, dignified.

"Are you summering here?" asked Harvey.

"No, I work in the file-shops," replied Chamberlain.

"Oh," said Harvey, with a surprised air.

"Bookkeeping?" asked the young man, after a pause.

"Oh, no; I am just now in the foundry-room."

"Pretty hard work, isn't it?" asked Harvey.

"Yes, it is; but I think it a very healthful life. There is no class of men that I am acquainted with, who are so universally strong and free from sickness, as are the foundry-men."

"Awful hard drinkers," returned the cadet.

"Some of them."

"What sticks me is, why a laborer can't drink without making a beast of himself. Now you can pick out dozens of gentlemen, who drink for a life-time, and never lose their balance."

"My experience has been, that liquor demoralizes a gentleman even more than a laborer," replied Chamberlain.

"Why, hang it all, excuse me, but I mean the real, blue-blooded gentlemen, and — you know

— perhaps you may not have had a chance to be with them much."

Harvey blurted this out, growing very red, and trusting to the sincerity and good-heartedness with which it was spoken, to ward off offense.

" Possibly not," replied the other, with an assured smile; " but let us take a case in hand. You would call our Senator M—— a blue-blooded gentleman ? "

" Yes."

" I saw him three years ago last winter, in Washington, carried to his room by two porters, drunk. He certainly looked more demoralized than a red-shirted workman would have appeared in the same case. His tall hat was muddy and jammed ; his gold eye-glasses were broken, and his gray hair crusted with mud and blood. He is a princely man, but he had made a beast of himself. I must confess that the sight was to me a surprise, at that time, because I believed as you do. Since then, having taken some pains to look into the subject, I actually find the liquor-curse everywhere the same ; in the homes of wealth and culture, as well as in the workman's cottage."

At first the young men had been talking alone, but the girls had drawn near, and now stood listening to Tom's earnest words.

"Really, you are quite an apostle of temperance, Mr. Chamberlain," said Kate, with a slight tone of sarcasm; "but I think you overestimate its influence upon the educated. It is my belief that wine is a gift of God; that we are to use it moderately, wisely; if we find ourselves growing too fond of it, we should combat it, as we would any other temptation."

"If you could ask the gentlemen-drunkards through the world, what had brought them to their desperate case, I think they would all agree that it was that creed," was Chamberlain's reply.

"There are those that can take wine daily, and never show it in the least; good, honest, Christian gentlemen. Now, there is my uncle, Mr. Whitney. He is a good example of what I call the blue-blooded, self-controlled gentleman. He takes wine at dinner always, and I will defy any one to say that it affects him," said Harvey.

Chamberlain glanced involuntarily at Miriam, and was startled at the look of pallor that her face assumed, when this statement was made with so much confidence. She was unaware of his quick look, and after a brief discussion, during which neither side appeared to gain any decided advantage, each, on the contrary, becoming more firmly established in their own way of thinking, the subject was dropped.

Another game of tennis followed, in which Chamberlain and his fair partner earned more laurels; then, excusing himself, he went to say good-bye to old Allan and Martha, before going back to Steep Street.

On the evening after this pleasant discussion, Chamberlain found himself at the North Church, enjoying the regular Wednesday-evening prayer-meeting, and a soul-stirring gathering it was. Testimonies, exhortations, and prayers were filled with the fervor that betokens the presence of the Holy Spirit. Nearly all present had spoken, even though it was but a word. A spirit of prayerful anxiety for the unsaved pervaded the gathering. The conviction had at last found its way into the minds of the comfortable Christians of the upper settlement, that there were souls to be saved in the mill village. For years it had been quietly conceded that nothing could be done for this class. Mention was often made in conference-meetings of the sad state of affairs among this floating, fighting population, as well as the exceptional goodness of the upper settlement, but nothing further was done. Now, however, the interest in the mill folk, instead of being of the former general nature, was coming nearer to practical, individual labor. Chamberlain entered the church, not as a drone, but as a worker, and was welcomed, assisted, and encouraged. He was thought to be a common workman, and, at first, was relegated to the place for laborers, a back seat and silent corner, but he did not long remain there. A natural speaker, before he had taken part in many meetings his every word attracted attention. Speaking, as he often did, of the factory folk, he was considered an authority, and was consulted whenever a new plan was brought up for their welfare. Many were broached, now that people were fairly awake, and many a fervent prayer arose for help for Steep Street.

The mission-school in the room that had once been a store was, from the first, well supplied with teachers from the North Church. Chamberlain was chosen superintendent, in spite of his urgent wish to remain in the background. The people whom this school was designed to reach seemed proud that one of their number, as they regarded him, should be considered the best man to run "the Sabbath-school." It was strange to hear profane, irreligious file-workers congratulating themselves that Steep Street could turn out "just as good Gospel-slingers as could be found."

In a manner, the workmen were proud of Chamberlain. They liked to listen to his straight-forward testimonies. What he said was always listened to, and, as yet, in the midst of any of his talks, there had been no rising and tramp-ing-out of a restless half-dozen. Most of the speakers were subject to this annoyance; even Pastor Snow was not exempt. A very impor-tant result of the evening meetings and the Sabbath services was the gradual breaking-down of the barrier between the people of the upper village and the mill folk. Little by little, the bitter hate that had been entertained against the North Church people was dying out. As fast as it was seen that the indifference and contempt of the church-goers either did not exist, or had been laid aside, the villagers became cordial. Many of the men on Steep Street at-tended the meetings, and more would, when they were assured that it was to be popular. One among them, however, could not be induced to come near the room, and that was Sam Putnam. He refused Chamberlain, with a snappishness in his tones that the latter had never before heard. And yet, in his ordinary conversation that day, he was more affable than usual.

He would not come to the meetings, and his satellites did as he did. There were those among the workers who believed that Sam would yet be a follower of the Master. One of the special subjects of prayer in the new school was this scoffing giant, who held most of the male population of the village under his control. Night after night they prayed, and night after night Sam went the rounds, drank, rioted, and caroused, ignoring the fact that the soldiers of Prince Immanuel were preparing for war upon the sin and misery of Steep Street.

But to return to the prayer-meeting in the vestry of the North Church. When the people gathered, the weather was clear and beautiful, but while the meeting was in session an array of black clouds came over the sky, and soon a peal of thunder announced the presence of a storm. The church was, perhaps, the most unsafe place in Steelville in which to be during a thunder-storm. Situated on high ground, having no trees, nor buildings of any height, about it, and sending a spire two hundred feet into the air, it was a noted lightning-attractor. Four times, during severe storms, had it been struck.

While the people did not reproach or blame the Creator, they never had faith enough to stay in the building during a shower. So it happened that when the first peal came, they began to rise and go out. The pastor, with

great forethought, at once dismissed the congregation, and all surged toward the doors. The
most fearful started at once for home, through
the pouring. rain, rather than run the risk of
being struck by lightning. The fright did not,
by any means, confine itself to the sisters, as
many of the brethren were splashing away from
the · point of danger as fast as their dignity
would permit.

When the crowd had thinned considerably,
the calmer remnant, standing in the ample porch
had opportunity to observe one another. Chamberlain had discovered, some time before, that
Miriam Whitney was one of those without an
umbrella. She was also one who had not tied
a handkerchief over her bonnet, gathered up her
skirts, and fled from the perilous spot.

"This is a very dangerous place, Mr. Chamberlain," she observed, with a bewitching smile.
" Aren't you afraid ? "

" I ought to be," answered he. " But, being
somewhat of a stranger, I have yet to learn
just when to be frightened and when to be
brave. I am most unfortunate in not having
brought an umbrella. I could then have relieved
you from any fears that you may have; but as
it is I am powerless. If you intend to stay here
for a few minutes, I will go out and borrow one."

"I know of a better scheme than that," she returned, drawing nearer, and lowering her voice. "In the furnace-room, where the sexton puts his things, there is a green-silk umbrella. We can have that, if only we can get it. The sexton is away, or I should have borrowed it of him."

Chamberlain seized upon the idea, and went at once to explore that part of the church in which the furnace-room was situated. He was not long in finding it, and in discovering further that the door was locked. The only possible mode of entrance was by means of a ventilator over the door. Swinging himself through this, with no little difficulty, he alighted in an unfinished room. On one side were piles of kindling, reaching to the ceiling; on another, a long table, stained with kerosene, on which stood in a row the church-lamps with the chimneys tipped back and wicks turned up ready for lighting. Boxes and barrels, shovels and hods, filled the centre of the room. Remembering how umbrellas gravitate toward corners, he began his search. There were hosts of things, in the worst possible confusion, leaning in all the corners, and it was no pleasant task to tip them all forward and look behind for the green-silk protector. At length, however, his search was successful, and it was unearthed.

It was of huge dimensions, and its spread, when open, was tent-like. Climbing out, after passing it to Miss Whitney, Chamberlain again stood in the porch, but this time armed with an umbrella that was calculated to command respect, if not awe. All of the feminine part of the congregation had gone, when they stepped out into the rain. Only a few of the brethren who concluded to "resk it," now remained in the churchporch. They watched the young couple as they sallied forth, exchanging a mild joke or two with regard to there "being room for one more."

The mammoth umbrella, held low, sheltered them wonderfully. There was a sense of nearness and companionship, as they struggled together against the storm, under one tent, shut away from the rest of the world. What a thrill of strength and pride the youth felt, as his fair companion clung to his arm! Is there ever, in young manhood, a more supreme content and self-exaltation, than exist when he breasts a storm, be it ever so mild, with the knowledge that the one by his side is borne along by his strength, and depends upon him for guidance and protection?

During the walk Miriam talked pleasantly, and Chamberlain enjoyed himself rarely. When first he knew Miss Whitney, he felt at times that she introduced varied topics, that she might know the extent of his information. So well was this done, if indeed it were not all imagination, that he had no opportunity to be at all provoked. Of late, however, not in the slightest degree had this been apparent. With instinctive pride he had not done himself injustice, nor had he attempted to air his knowledge. A weaker man would have done this. A self-educated file-grinder, unless a miracle of modesty, would have exhibited, in panoramic succession, his views on such subjects as he had on hand, and that would have ended the entertainment; but Chamberlain, with the instincts of a true gentleman, refrained from all "splurge," and consequently secured the respect and confidence of the acknowleged belle of Steelville. How much he valued these charily bestowed gifts, it would be hard to express.

In the course of their conversation, Miss Whitney mentioned that her father was ill, and also that Jim, the hostler, was away that evening, otherwise he would have come for her. Chamberlain expressed his gratitude for these favoring circumstances, and with a light half-banter, they chatted till the gateway was reached. Passing up the broad, gravelled walk, he left his fair charge on the veranda and started away. He

had gone but a few steps when he was hailed
in a rough tone, and turning, saw Mr. Whitney advancing round the side of the house, lantern in hand. He had no hat on, and looked
flushed and excited. As he came forward he
lurched from side to side, taking almost all of
the wide pathway. He looked very angry about
something.

"Here, you Jim, why don't you get to the
stable and water the horse? He has n't had a
drink for a fortnight! He is perishing of thirst.
How many times must I tell you to water him
three times a day?" he called.

In some bewilderment, Chamberlain glanced
about for Jim. No one was in sight. Even
Miriam had disappeared. Then it flashed over
him that the gentleman mistook him for the
delinquent hostler. Reflecting that it was too
bad for the animal not to have water if he was
thirsty, he took the lantern and started for the
barn, Mr. Whitney following and abusing him
roundly for his negligence. He had, when in
the barn, some little trouble in finding the pail
and the pump. The horse fortunately made
known his abiding place by a gentle whinneying.
Keeping the lantern swinging as much as possible, and turning away from the gentleman as
much as he could, Chamberlain drew the water

and gave the animal all he wanted. Then following the fault-finding directions, he arranged the bedding a little differently, loosened the "throat-latch" of the halter, and did a half-dozen little chores that seemed to trouble the owner. Bustling round, lurching against the stable-walls, hunting up all kinds of faults, Mr. Whitney was so busy that he did not look at the face of the hostler. Even when he abused him, he was examining what was wrong rather than the appearance of the wrong-doer. As Chamberlain glanced up to the top of the stairs that led from the kitchen of the mansion down to the stable, he saw a white-faced figure standing in the shadow and was sure it was Miriam. Sorry that she should witness the scene, he hurried through with his tasks, and after a parting salute from Mr. Whitney, slipped away. Returning to the front path, he recovered the umbrella from behind the shrub where he had dropped it, and started for home. The rain had ceased, and the clouds in broken masses were rapidly rolling away.

"Mr. Chamberlain," said a voice at his elbow. He turned and saw Miriam. The moon broke through the clouds and showed the face white and tear-stained.

"Mr Chamberlain, will you pray for my

father?" she said. "You know my fears, you know this terrible secret, and you are the only one. You said on the tennis ground, that you believed the Lord would hear prayer for relatives who were in danger, if only we had faith to utter them. Will . you pray for my father?"

"We will both pray that his eyes may be opened to his danger. At nine this evening I shall be in my room and will pray. Will you, here at your home, join me in the prayer of your heart?"

"I will! I will! And, oh, I hope the Lord will hear."

"You may be sure of it," said Chamberlain with the emphasis of strong faith.

XVI.

The · Queer · Fisherman.

FOR an eighth of a mile along the river-
bank extended the buildings and yards of
the file-works. Above, on the opposite side, was
Steep Street. Below stretched dense thickets,
through which the cattle from the meadows had
forced narrow paths. On the mill side, the land
was level; on the other, shelving and hilly.
The higher bank was covered with a mixed
growth of birch, pine, and scrub oak, bound together with wild grapevines. So dense was this
young forest, that few penetrated it, even the
birds' nesters preferring to go where there was
better traveling. To Chamberlain, this stretch of
woodland had a peculiar charm. Several times
after work-hours, while the days were long, he had
gone into this labyrinth, startling the kingfishers
from their skeleton perches, and rousing the indignation of the red squirrels to its highest
pitch. During his rambles in this miniature wil-

derness, he had never met a soul, and therefore, little by little, had come to consider himself as its only explorer, and to feel a Crusoe-like ownership of the wild domain.

One day, as he was walking softly along a bed of forest-moss that stretched several rods and was as soft as if woven in Persian looms, he heard, coming from below at the water's edge, a clear, tremulous voice. For an instant, he was in doubt as to where he had heard those tones before, but a moment's reflection brought back the midnight scene in the rear of the file-works. There could be no mistake; the Scotch accent, the plaintive cadence, the mellow clearness, belonged to none but the voice of that night. It must be Tam.

"Oh, Lord, saund me a fish," said the voice.

Chamberlain, remembering the shyness shown on the former occasion, peered cautiously through the thick-standing trees, to catch a glimpse of him. At first he was unsuccessful, but soon he saw, bending over the water, a figure dressed in a workman's suit, holding a fishing-pole.

"Oh, Lord, remember poor Tam, and saund him a fish," he prayed.

Cautiously, step by step, Chamberlain stole near the fisherman. At last, he was as close as he could safely come, without being detected.

Not far from Tam, at the foot of a huge tree, burned a tiny fire in a fireplace of stones. Leaving his fish-pole, ever and anon, the little Scotchman replenished this fire, and then went back to pray the more earnestly for "a fish, just one wee fish." There was in the words, — in all the acts of the little old man, — an absolute, unwavering faith, that seemed sure of success. He would catch the fish, Chamberlain felt positive, even if it were the first and last that ever inhabited those waters. The young man longed to have a good look at the face of the fisherman, and soon the opportunity was given. A blue-jay lit in the tree behind which he was hidden, and began screaming its shrill alarm, till the woods rang. The Scotchman turned toward it, with his finger on his lips. "Peace," he said, "would ye tal the world that Tam is here?"

The jay flew off. Chamberlain, with a strange fascination, was gazing at the face that he now, for the first time, saw. It was seamed and scarred till it had almost lost the likeness of humanity. Only the great, sad eyes, dark and full, redeemed it from being hideous. The hands, too, he noticed, were warped and scarred in the same way. Some great calamity had befallen this man. What it was, he could not conjecture.

"Thank the Lord! He has saunt me a fish," said Tam, suddenly drawing the pole up fiom the water. On its end was a curious net, in which struggled a fine perch. With accustomed hand, the lonely fisherman dressed it, and soon had it cooking over the coals. Spell-bound by the strangeness of the scene, Chamberlain remained in his hiding place. According to custom, the little man discoursed to himself, of things that happened in the past, of affairs at the mill, using names that made the listener start with surprise. Much of what he said was incomprehensible, yet there were many sentences which, although without present meaning, were laid away in memory's storehouse, some day to be of use. When the simple meal was cooked, the Scotchman took off his cap and, reverently kneeling, prayed.

"O Lord," he said, "luke doon into these woods to poor Tam! From Thy Throne in the heavens bend doon and listen. Here is one, Lord, who has not bowed the knee to Lamson, nor consented to his iniquity. Here is one, who, that he might keep the word of Thy patience, refused to join hands with the ungouly, and is now an outcast because of it. 'Twas no' because I was better than many another, but rather because I one day expect to meet Thee, my Redeemer, face to face. I dare not do wrong when I think of this. I remember also, dear Lord, how Thou didst deliver me from mine appetite, how Thou didst rebuke the destroyer and set me free. I praise Thee for it. Keep me in Thy holy keeping and let me never stray from Thee. Amen!"

When he had finished his unique grace, the hermit drew some crackers from his pocket and made a hearty meal, finishing with a draught of river-water. He then carefully extinguished the fire, threw the stones into the water, and covered the blackened embers with earth and leaves. After this, he washed with scrupulous care. He then parted the bushes and vanished—so quietly and quickly, that Chamberlain was for a moment too much surprised to follow. Then remembering that this strange being was possessed of much valuable information about the mills, and that he mentioned many things that held a decided air of mystery, he attempted to go after him. Quickly and noiselessly, he stole down to the small, open space where the repast had been eaten, and glanced hastily about. Not seeing him, he plunged into the thicket that had, but a few seconds prior, hidden the slight form of the fisherman. Once in this dense growth, he was unable to make any progress. Not only were the trees growing close and in inextricable confusion, but the worst of all creepers, the squirrel-vine, with its armor of thorns, had bound and lashed the mass of living verdure so tightly together, that it seemed hardly possible that even a rabbit could find a pathway. After a short and fruitless struggle, Chamberlain retreated with scratched hands and torn clothes.

How the Scotchman had penetrated it, was a mystery. For an instant he pondered, and then started up the bank, and avoiding the most tangled portions of the forest, made his way rapidly in the direction of the mills. He was sure that some portion of the factory-yard was the destination of the Scotchman. The river was too wide to be crossed except at the bridges. A narrow foot-bridge led across the stream near the path that had been the scene of his former adventure with Tam, and it was here that he expected him to make his appearance. Hurrying forward, he reached this bridge and stationed himself where he could command a full view of it and the footpath that led from it. His assumption was well based, for a few moments later Tam came in sight, crossed stealthily to the further side, and hurried along in the direction of the deserted yards. When he was far enough ahead, Chamberlain followed, curious to know how he accomplished the seemingly impossible feat of surmounting the wall.

In the shadow of the fence, he followed the figure till almost opposite the spot where he had stood and listened so long on a former occasion. Here Tam paused, glanced in all directions to see if the coast was clear, then seized one of the fence boards by its lower end, slid it up several feet from the ground, and crept under, then pushed it into its place again. As soon as this was done Chamberlain came forward to note carefully the gateway that the little hermit had made use of. Reaching the place, his quick eye at once detected the very board that had been raised. It was slightly discolored at the lower end, and when carefully examined had the unstable air that things which are not solidly fastened are apt to have. Yet the casual observer would never have dreamed that it differed from the rest of the spike-capped boards of the fence. To be so sure of the location that he might know the place, even in the night, Chamberlain looked about for bearings. A stone or a stump close at hand would be all that he wished.

As he scanned the surface of the field for such a landmark, he saw by the narrow foot-path, exactly opposite the secret gateway, a stake of hard wood driven so deep into the ground as to be almost hidden. This, then, was some one's guide-post. It did not seem likely that it was used by Tam, for such characters never need land-marks. They invariably possess an instinct that is most reliable and above outside help. Aware of this fact, Chamberlain pondered the matter and wondered if others knew of that way of entering the proscribed precincts of the yard.

The many sentences dropped by the little Scotchman had awakened in him a growing dis-trust of the mill management. To be sure, Lamson's plausible explanation of Pfaff's presence and privileges in the mill settlement had so far overcome his former suspicion that he had frankly begged the agent's pardon. Yet here was this strange hermit fisherman,—this man who seemed perfectly well to have known not only his uncle Robert Flint, but his father as well — speaking of some deep plot that was de-priving the company of legitimate profits. That there was something back of all this, Chamber-lain could not but believe. Yet what it was remained a mystery. With all the acuteness that he naturally possessed, he found it impossible to get on the track of anything wrong in the file business. Most carefully had he watched places where it seemed to him fraud would most likely be practised, but no sign of anything wrong had he discovered.

As he recrossed the river on his way to Steep Street, a white, haggard face strained toward him out of the thick bushes. Chamberlain did not see it and went on unconsciously. When he had passed, its possessor rose and stood with an anguished, despairing look, gazing after him. It was John Temple.

That very evening, an hour later, an important errand called Chamberlain to the mill, and after it was accomplished, he started to pass around the building, attracted to the rear yard by the knowledge of its mysterious tenant.

"Going down the haunted path?" inquired one of the watchmen, who was standing, lantern in hand, near the corner.

"The what?"

"Why, the river-path. It's ha'nted, you know."

"What haunts it?" inquired Chamberlain, with interest.

"O, I dunno, ghosts or something. I believe there was a man murdered along there three years ago, and he has been seen walking up and down the path."

Tom started on without further question and had gone but a few paces, when the watchman again hailed him.

"Better come through the yard with me." he advised.

" I 'm not afraid."

"That don't count either way," said the other earnestly; "a young feller like you don't want to poke his nose into any ghost business. It 's mighty dangerous."

The more anxious he was to keep the young man away from the river-path, the more determined Chamberlain was to explore it. He therefore started down the path and was soon alone in the darkness. Although he had so carefully noted the tiny landmark, it took him some time to identify it. When at last it was discovered, and he stood again with his ear close to the hidden gateway, he was tempted. to explore the dark yard then and there. Whether or not he would have carried out his wish cannot be told, for so intently was he listening for Tam's tremulous voice, that he did not hear the soft step behind him, nor did he take alarm until strong arms were thrown around him and he found himself on the ground. He used all of his strength in attempting to free himself from his unseen antagonist, yet without avail; and in a short time, breathless and wearied, he lay conquered, his hands lashed firmly to his sides, a handkerchief bound tightly about his eyes. He uttered no cry, for the uselessness of it was apparent to him. None would come to his rescue on the "haunted path." A muscular arm raised him to his feet and turned him around and around till he was so dizzy that he almost fell down, and then before he could in any way recover the lost bearings, he was led away. For some minutes they kept to the path, then reached rough ground, where he was pulled over rocks and stumps in a most unceremonious manner. At length, after splashing through a shallow brook or pool, a building was entered, as Chamberlain knew by the difference in the air. Here a halt was made, and after a whispered consultation the bandage was taken from his eyes. With great curiosity he looked about and found himself in a large room, dimly lighted by two or three candles. The monstrous shadows and the vast emptiness of the place had a most weird effect, and no doubt our hero would have been frightened had he not recognized the place as the "gate-house" to the rear yard, explored by him one noon. His captors had left him in the middle of the apartment and were gone before he had seen them. On attempting to move, he found that the line securing his hands was made fast to an iron bar that stood up from the plank floor. Willing to test the strength of his fastenings and much reassured when he knew that he was in the mill, he began vigorously to struggle. As he did so an unearthly groan rang through the empty spaces of the great room.

"He struggles. Shall they be his lasht?" asked a hollow voice.

"Yea," responded a chorus, which Chamberlain estimated contained three voices, including the Hibernian interlocutor. As he had been in more than one college scrape of a nature similar to this, he felt at home, and was pondering the best course to pursue, when a happy thought struck him. He saw no one, but without doubt he was observed. If he appeared so overcome by fear as to faint, would they not show themselves?

"The executioner comes," said the sepulchral voice, with its ridiculous intonation and accent, and, with measured stride, a white-robed figure appeared and advanced.

"Oh! spare me! spare me! I'll never go near the haunted path again," shrieked Chamberlain, with an agony so startling that even the ghost jumped.

"Will you shware it?"

But no answer came. The captive had fainted and fallen in a heap upon the floor.

The ghost paused irresolutely, then advanced cautiously and raised the limp hand.

"Come out here, Mike," he said. "The lad has fainted dead away. Let's carry him out, and leave him by the road-side. He will never trouble us again."

"By the howly St. Pathrick, but that was well done," said the interlocutor, coming out of a shadowy corner. "Here, Jack, lend us a hand."

As they prepared to raise the prostrate figure, the passage-window, through which Chamberlain had entered on his first visit, was opened, and Sam Putnam swung himself in.

"What in thunder are you fellers up to?" he asked, in great astonishment.

"We have been givin' this bye a lesson on the dangerosity av inquisitiveness," replied Mike, with an abashed air.

"Who is it? Why, it's young Chamberlain! Who hit him? What's the matter?"

"He's only shcared. We showed him a ghost, and he fainted, that's all."

"Well, how did he come here?" asked the giant, with an angry ring in his voice.

Meekly Mike narrated the watchman's attempt to keep him away, his attitude of listening at the secret gate, and the method of capture. When he had finished, Sam said, abruptly, —

"Get back to your places, every one of you, and don't try any more risky work, whatever happens."

Obediently the three filed out, and left Putnam with the captive. Thinking it time to recover, the latter sighed heavily and opened his eyes.

"Get up," was the not-unkindly command.

"My hands are tied, and I don't think I can," was the reply.

With an expression of entire disgust, Putnam cut the cords and led the young man to the window. Both climbed out and stood in the yard.

"I suppose this foolish joke on the part of the 'night-puddlers' will be told all over the mill by you to-morrow?" enquired Sam, gloomily.

Surprised that he was not threatened, Chamberlain replied:

"There is no special need of my telling any one."

"I wish you would keep it quiet, then. They are good fellows, and were only on a lark."

"Why are they about this part of the mill, instead of being near the furnaces?" asked Chamberlain, but received no answer. Without further conversation the two walked to one of the side-gates, and the intruder was dismissed,

with a gruff "good-night."   As Sam went back
to the rear yard, he muttered to himself,—

"If that young feller has n't some object in
hanging around here, I am mistaken.   There
ain't a thing happens in the works, but he
knows.   I don't wonder the dekin hates him."

XVII.

Mrs. Bowman's Burgle.

MRS. BOWMAN'S husband had been a soldier; and, although not slain by a bullet, he came home to die a victim to the decanter. Whether he was a brave man or not does not appear, but were one to judge him by his only son, poor Rob, he must have been one of the most arrant cowards in existence. Mrs. Bowman, on the contrary, feared nothing. As muscular as a man, and possessed of an iron constitution, coupled with untiring energy, she was the exact opposite of her shiftless, easy-going boy.

Among the happenings that took place during the stay of Chamberlain, was the payment of quite a sum of money, "back-pay," that stood to her husband's credit with the government. The widow, fearing the banks, resolved to keep it in her own house, and, as she supposed, had no confidants in this decision. One night, not long after the sum had been received, the lady of the house was awakened by a noise on the lower floor. Thinking it must be some drunken man from the village, she stepped into her son's room and told him to go down and investigate. With horror unfeigned, he refused. He would go nowhere without company, and the idea of descending the stairs to meet a possible ghost, or midnight-assassin, was more than he would entertain. Mrs. Bowman, therefore, started down the stairs to wreak substantial vengeance upon the intruder, should he be found.

Her quest was more successful than she had supposed it would be, for, in the kitchen, trying to open the tiny medicine-closet over the fireplace was a man. She recognized Gaffney, as she supposed, and at once settled upon a plan for punishment that seemed suited to the offense. Near the chimney was a brick-lined coal-closet, with a door almost ponderous in strength. It was now empty, and she resolved to put him in it. The door stood slightly ajar, and she felt certain that, could she take him by surprise, she could hustle him in there before he had time to resist. Swiftly and noiselessly she advanced, and seized him by the collar, and in a twinkling he was a prisoner, and the door was securely bolted. Then, without a word, she returned to her room, and slept soundly till morning.

The first one up in the house, she was about to open the impromptu cell, and release the town drunkard, when she noticed, lying on the table, a valise, which, being partly open, displayed a set of tools such as she had never before seen. More from instinct than from any appreciation of possible danger, she called Chamberlain's attention to them, and he at once pronounced them burglar's tools. His statement was corroborated by two men, who happened to be passing at the time, and who, producing hand-cuffs, informed the astonished household that they were city officers, on the track of a notorious house-breaker. They felt extremely well over their luck, and, after a brief preparation, opened the door and secured their man.

"One thing I should like to know," he said, as the "wristers" were put on. "What man took me?"

"Man!" said Mrs. Bowman. "It was only me! Why, I could handle two of you, even if you be a buggler!"

"Well," said the house-breaker, as he departed, "you've done what few men could do. Slippery Jack caught by a woman! I'll go out of the business directly."

At once Mrs. Bowman was a heroine. Her name came out in the city papers. All praised her. But, as they lauded her exploit, they laughed at Rob, who was more dejected than ever. In a most melancholy state of mind, he sought Chamberlain, as he was doing some evening work in the mill, and confided to his muscular friend all of his trouble. The young man was greatly amused over the other's earnestness and honesty in confessing his cowardice, and asking advice as to its cure.

"Have you ever asked the Lord to make you brave?" said he, finally.

"No-o," replied Rob, slowly. "I did n't know as he would care to help a feller in that line."

"The next time you see any thing that frightens you, just pray as hard as you can, and go and examine it. You may be sure the Lord will take care of you."

Rob promised, and started for home, greatly cheered. Even in going the short distance between the mill and his house, he had a chance to test his new plan, for on the opposite side of the street stood a white, ghostly figure, raising its hands as if to warn him away. His first impulse was to run, but a second helped him to overcome it. Advancing toward it, he prayed :

"O! Lord help me! O! Lord help me!"

Closer and closer he came, and still it did not vanish. His prayer became almost frantic, and the sweat stood in drops on his forehead. As he reached the figure, with a shudder, he put out his hand, and felt, — a common stone-post with a shirt tied around it, the sleeves flapping in the wind. A spasm of joy almost choked him. The Lord had helped him. He had been brave for once; had taken the first step toward the self-command necessary to true manhood. He did not see two fun-loving file-workers slip away in the darkness, nor did he hear the surprised exclamation:

"I never believed the little feller had half as much pluck!"

Rob did not stop here, however; he continued to grow in courage. He surprised his mother by offering to institute family worship. He actually spoke in prayer-meeting shortly after, and did well, too. And better still, he called at the home of one of the worst men in the settlement one evening, in great fear and trembling, to be sure, but praying with all his might, and spoke words of such power that the worthless scapegrace owned the misery of the life he led, and his desire for a nobler one.

"I've found the secret of strength," he said

to Chamberlain. "It is to put it all on to the
Lord's shoulders. Why, two weeks ago I was
so weak that I could n't go by a beer shop
without yeilding to the desire for drink; and I
was so cowardly that I used to get mother to
go with me to the mill and come for me after-
wards. I never dared to go anywhere, unless
with a crowd. I s'pose every one despised me,
— I know they did, — but the Lord did n't. But
now when I get frightened, I just say, 'O Lord,
this is your world, don't let any thing in it
hurt me; and if I must be hurt, help me to
bear it like a Christian,' — and he is with me
every time."

Mrs. Bowman was not blind to the great change
that had come over her son. He no longer
drank, and for that she greatly rejoiced; yet
she was not satisfied. The utter dependence
that her boy had placed upon her, even when
he was led by evil companions, was exceedingly
sweet. She was only too glad to be brave for
him; to go to the mill; to meet him dark
nights; to help him in his chores; to protect
him. Now as he stood up and acted and lived
for himself, she could hardly bear it. The new-
found strength appeared to rob her of her child,
and the poor woman was wretched. It was not
jealousy that made her feel thus disappointed,

but a misguided, but tender, mother-love. She tried in many ways to get him back to the former state of dependence; she "wanted her baby again." It would have been a relief to her to have him get thoroughly frightened and claim her protection. She found that they were growing apart, and felt as if he were robbing her of one of her prerogatives in being brave. Yet she saw, with increasing joy, that Rob improved. One night, waking suddenly, she saw what looked like the figure of a man leaning over a chair as if to reach the bureau where their money was kept, and hoping Rob would claim her protection, she awoke him in pretended terror. Rising, he entered the room, laid his hand on the figure, and it resolved itself into a pile of clothing. This was almost too much for the woman to bear; she felt like crying over the failure.

It happened at this time that the upper town was excavating a reservoir not far from Mrs. Bowman's house. The water ran in so fast — as the ground was springy — that a pump must be kept going all night, the workman receiving double pay. Rob applied for and received the job. His mother remonstrated, coaxed, and drew frightful pictures of midnight darkness; and it must be confessed Rob trembled not a little, but did not change his mind. He was to pump from three in the afternoon till twelve at night, when he would be relieved. The foolish woman, racked with the thought that her boy was more and more lost to her, resolved that night to win him back if possible.

The situation of the reservoir was dismal enough. Only a few empty houses were near, and the road was little traveled in the night. Of course Rob had a touch of his old timidity; but he kept pumping and praying, and got over it after a while; and when the cold shivers ceased to chase each other up and down his back, he felt happy. The man who was to relieve him came at eleven, and fussing around, put up a shelter against possible rain, and settled down to work just as the clock struck twelve. Rob then went home through the silent streets, with his heart in his mouth, and a prayer crowding it down. Nothing evil happened. He unlocked the door, stepped in, closed and locked it again, went up stairs, read his chapter, retired, and was soon sound asleep. How long he had slept is uncertain, when suddenly awakening he listened. No sound but the beating of — crash! a sudden heavy fall in the wood-shed, followed by a long silence. Rob trembled as if in an ague fit, and lay still, hoping Chamberlain would be roused. Five min-

utes passed, — ten ; it must have been imagina
tion. Perhaps it was the cat knocking something
down ; there were lots of cats — bang ! came
another heavy fall, close to the kitchen door.
He was now praying for dear life, and strange
to say, was gaining courage. Soon he rose and
lighted a lamp, and before going further, read
a few verses from his Bible. He then quickly
dressed, took the Bible and the light, and started
for the wood-shed, praying as he went. Reaching
the kitchen door, with white cheeks and beating
heart, he drew the bolt and stepped into the
shed; as he did so, a ghastly, muddy, ragged
creature partly raised herself from the floor and
looked wildly at him.

But we must go back a little. Mrs. Bowman,
as has been stated, had determined to win Rob
back to her that night, or never. At about
quarter of eleven, with a sheet folded under her
arm, she started for the reservoir with the intention of giving him a good scare, and then
protecting him. As she came in sight of the
little lantern which threw a giant shadow of Rob
across the street, and grotesquely copied every
movement, she heard the clock strike eleven.
Her son stood with his back to the pit, pumping leisurely. A short ladder went down to the
pit's bottom, and rested upon a little platform

of earth. Supposing that Rob would have to come down there for something or other, she descended, wrapped herself in the sheet, and waited. Soon she heard voices.

"Take the ladder," shouted her son.

"What?" asked the other.

"Take the ladder."

"That man must be pretty deaf," thought Mrs. Bowman. "I wish he'd go away, and Rob would hurry up."

At that moment the ladder was drawn up, leaving her there without means of escape! Her first impulse was to call out, but pride held her back. They would undoubtedly put it down again, she argued. In this she was disappointed, as the possessor was building a shelter from a horse blanket, a pole, and the ladder.

Soon Rob said good-night, and left. Every thing grew quiet again, and there was no sound but the dull strokes of the pump. Chilled and disappointed, she waited a few minutes, and then spoke.

"Mister!" said she softly.

"Mister!" louder.

"Mister!" louder still.

"Mister!" shrieking.

Chunk—chunk—chunk, went the pump steadily and calmly.

" Fire ! Murder ! "

Chunk — chunk — chunk.

She threw stones. The first struck the wall of earth in front of her; the second nearly pulled her off of the little platform, and to keep from falling she put one foot down into the cold water that reached nearly to her knee; the third came down on her head. What should she do? It was very cold. She called again, tried to climb up the damp, earthy side, and slipped off into the water. She threw more stones, and finally prayed. Soon after, it occurred to her to pull up the hose and stop the pumping. A wet, slippery search revealed it after a while, and the pump coughed, strangled, and stopped. After an age of deliberation, the ladder was let slowly down into the pit, and the man started to follow it, when what appeared to be a monster from the depths of the earth, sprang up its welcome rounds and disappeared in the direction of Steep Street. The pumper fled in the opposite direction.

Reaching home, Mrs. Bowman entered the wood-shed through the window and started for the kitchen door. The saw-horse maliciously stood in the way, caught her dress with its rigid arms, and threw her headlong. Somewhat stunned, she arose, groped around for a while, and got lost ;

thought she saw a light, started eagerly toward it, met the saw-horse again, and was thrown into an empty coal-hod. The rake dropped across her back, a coal-sieve fell on her head, her foot caught in a crack in the floor and would n't come out, and to cap it all, Rob came with a lamp and ordered her off the premises! With difficulty, she recovered herself enough to make herself known, when Rob helped her up and into the kitchen. Then, like the kindly son that he was, he brought dry clothing, untied her soaking shoes, and was so good and tender that the widow actually broke down and cried, embracing him the while with such energy that it took his breath away.

"Where have you been, mother?" he finally asked, in wonder.

"O Rob, I'm a wicked woman. I went out a puppus to scare you, and the Lord punished me for it. I've been down in the reservoy."

"To scare me! Don't you want me to be a man?" asked the son, with a quiver on his lip.

"Yes, yes; but I want you to love me — to let me *do* for you. For years I've stood between you and every danger, and now you put me aside. I'm a fool, — I know I am, — but it's because I love you so."

Rob understood without any more explanation.

and kissed the faded cheek, and laughed a quiet little laugh.

"Don't you fret, my mother," he said, affectionately; "you'll never lose your grip on me; and as for my getting along without you, it could n't be done."

XVIII.

Pfaff's Picnic.

SATURDAY night was, with the Steep-street population, the grand carousal time of the week, and on Sunday they slept. Whether they respected the Sabbath enough to keep it free from their orgies, or whether they could not wait until that day, but must needs begin as soon as free from the week's labor, is an open question. Certain it is that Saturday night, — the whole of it, — was as noisy and turbulent as any inmate of. bedlam could wish. Possessors of clear consciences and good digestion slept during these hilarious times, but the nervous and dyspeptic were kept awake. Among the former class was Chamberlain. As a rule, little of Steep-street rioting did he hear, after the first week or two of his novitiate. Soundly and sweetly he slept, while drunken songs, oaths, yells, and a medley of hideous noises came up from the lower end of the settlement.

Perhaps, had he been more wakeful, he might have prevented Pfaff's picnic, but on second thought it was much better that sleep held him fast, for the rough, half-intoxicated men might have injured him. In order to describe the picnic, we must go back a little. Lamson had promised, with seeming sincerity, to provide the new store with a suitable manager. This he did, introducing a Mr. Drummond, who said he was acquainted with the business, and was moreover a strict temperance man. Lamson only knew of him by hearsay, but he produced a letter from the pastor of a church some miles away, that gave him a good character. As Chamberlain could not, by any possibility, run the store himself, he was very much relieved when this person presented himself, and the bargain was completed. For several days the business had gone on swimmingly, then came the picnic. It had been Pfaff's plan, and he had made most elaborate preparations. Nearly all of the engine company were invited, together with three or four outsiders, who were known to be hard drinkers and desperate rioters. Precisely what the programme was, none of the men knew, but that plenty of liquor would be provided and that some frolic was to be indulged in, all were aware. They gathered therefore in the rumseller's upper room, where pipes and liquors were at once liberally supplied.

"What is all this for?" asked one.

"For nothing! All free!" replied Pfaff.

"Yes, but what is the cause of this picnic? Had any good luck?"

"Oh," returned he, "this is my birthday; I am celebrating for that. I want all the boys to drink my good health."

There were few in that company who needed urging. Sam Putnam, with his usual self-poise, held off as long as any, but at last was prevailed upon to drink, and ere long was as wild and ready for "some fun" as any of the rest of them. When the company were ripe for the sport, Pfaff proposed it.

"Boys," he said, "this ain't only a picnic it's a surprise party."

"Who on?" some one asked.

"Do you remember the store that sold Gaffney kerosene and almost poisoned him?"

"I guess we do," was the reply.

"Don't I?" said Gaffney.

"Well, look here, I found the keys to it in the street this afternoon."

Pfaff held up the bunch of keys and looked around in triumph.

"What of that?"

"Well, we will give that store a surprise party. We will go in and have a circus, — a picnic. They say there never shall be a drop of liquor drank in that store. Let's make them lie; let's take a pail of liquor up there and drink it!"

The proposition was received with acclamation, and soon the whole party were on their way to the place.

Pfaff took the lead, and when the building was reached, unlocked the door and let his followers in. With suspicious readiness, he found lamps and lighted them, keeping the shutters closed, that there might not be too much display made to outsiders. Crackers, cheese, prunes, and dried currants were then handed out over the counter by the genial German, whose jokes at the expense of the unfortunate proprietor of the store were so exceedingly funny, that the men almost went into fits, laughing.

By degrees, the spirit of mischief grew stronger among the visitors. With malignant glee, they broke open barrels of flour, pulled the spigot out of the vinegar cask, smashed boxes of spices, and acted like a band of Apache Indians. In the two hours of rough sport in which they indulged, there was more damage inflicted than hundreds of dollars could replace. At last, when the work was about done to Pfaff's satisfaction, he proposed an adjournment to his own store for more liquor. He was the most sober man of the party, and therefore the leader. With noisy songs, by twos and threes, they straggled down toward the rumshop. Once there, the liquor-seller threw the keys into the river and with a sigh of relief, took a long drink. As a rule, he was not given to drinking. He was too mean to do much more than drain the glasses for which others paid. Yet he had in the years past awakened an appetite that would some day, and that not far distant, drag him to the lowest level, if it were possible to further debase anything so degraded. Now that his picnic was a success, he drank heavily.

Pfaff felt that he had triumphed. His two great enemies in the village, as he believed, were the temperance-store and the new water-works. He hated one as much as the other. Both favored temperance, both injured his business, and he felt that he must crush them together. The store had received its death blow. What a grand success it would be, could he, that very night, in some way, destroy the beautiful fountain that was playing at the head of the street! He had heard its waters praised by the people on the street till he was sick of the name of it. Now if he could spoil it, would

not that be the most joyful moment of his life?
He was just drunk enough to appreciate and
pity the intoxication of his companions. Stealing
away from them, he procured a hammer and
two or three keg bungs, and started up the
street. In his befogged intellect was the idea
that he could, with these things, plug the pipe
through which the water came. He argued that
once were the water stopped, the pressure ac-
cumulating in the pipe would burst it, and thus
forever do away with the possibility of the hated
"sweet water" ever again appearing at the surface at Steep Street.

Chuckling to himself at the thought of his own
bright views, he staggered up the street, stopping at the store to give the door a triumphant
kick. Then he made his way up to the little
plateau, where spouted the obnoxious fountain.
As yet the pipes had not been laid to conduct
water to the houses. Indeed although it had
already furnished water to almost all of the
water-drinkers below, it was in an unfinished
condition. A single inch-pipe, eighteen inches
long, rose from a rough platform of planks.
Through this the water flowed clear, cold, and
sweet. Falling on the planks, it ran off into an
improvised basin of rough stones, the overflow
forming a tiny brook, that ran down the Steep-

street gutters, cleansing them from the filth of the sink-drains.

Pfaff was slow and deliberate in his preparations to suppress the hated water, and his manner of treating his elusive enemy was original.

After gaining the top of the street, he stood with ponderous gravity, balancing himself by the side of the fence, gloating over his rare opportunity for revenge. At last he felt that he was in a position to crush this hated dispenser of pure water.

"No bishness here," he said, looking savagely at the pipe. "Spoilsh my trade   Inger the people.   No bishness here!"

The spirituous energy that he had felt, when first he started for the fountain, was somewhat abated. He began to feel sleepy, and doubtless would have lain down by the fence for a nap, had not his cherished purpose roused him to action. Drawing the wooden plugs from his pocket, he put the hammer on the ground, as if it were made of glass, — then hunted in his pockets for it, wondered where it was, stepped on it, and, with an air of great wisdom, picked it up again, and was ready for the attack.

Advancing with dignity and care, he knelt on the plank flooring, oblivious of the water that was wetting his knees. Getting in the proper position, he attempted to force one of the plugs into the open mouth of the pipe. For an instant it stopped the stream, and he removed his hand and raised the hammer to strike a heavy blow, when the gathered force blew the plug high in the air, and the fountain played on as before. The hammer fell on the top of the pipe, splashing the water full in the face of the vengeful rumseller. Still on his knees, he hunted for the other plug, and, after a long search, discovered it. With extra care, he placed it as before, and again raised the hammer, and the plug leaped into the air as before.

Pfaff was provoked. His plan for bursting the pipe had failed. He grew angry and threw the hammer away. A man of his inexorable pertinacity, even though drunk, would not give up a scheme unless forced to. So he looked around for something else with which to wreak his spite upon the spouting well. Far and near he hunted, picking up stones, and rejecting them, as unfit for his purpose, and growing drunker every minute.

At last he found a short piece of board, and, clasping it firmly, tottered back to the point of attack. Just how to use the board puzzled him. At first he placed it against the pipe, and strove to bend it, and perhaps break it off. Then he carefully put it down upon the top of the pipe, deflecting the stream from its perpendicular, and causing it to spout out from under the board at an angle. As the covering was so slanted that the stream was turned away from him, he imagined that he had succeeded in stopping it, and, in the excess of his zeal and joy, vowed to stay there all night and tire the thing out. For several minutes he held the board in that position, then he began to grow weary. The night breeze made him shiver. In his wet clothes, unused, as he was, to any sort of exposure, there was danger that he would catch cold. His arms also ached, from the effort required to hold the board.

His fertile brain finally hit upon an expedient by which the subjugation of his enemy could be accomplished, and, at the same time, his own comfort be secured. He would sit on the board. Carefully turning round, at the same time holding his improvised seat in its place, he gently lowered himself to it. The feat was almost accomplished, when one of those unaccountable lurches, by which drunken men are apt to upset their best-laid plans, overcame him. He lurched, the board slipped off on the further side of the pipe, and, losing his balance, he sat squarely

down, with his back against the pipe, closer
than was comfortable, for, so near did he come
to sitting on the pipe, that the round iron arm
forced its cold eighteen inches of length inside
of his short coat and vest, and now was playing
away in the back of his neck, as untamed and
free as ever.

With a gurgling cry, the water-logged rum-
seller attempted to break away, but the firm
iron held him fast. His coat and vest, most
unfortunately for his comfort, were of first-class
material. Both were buttoned, and, no matter
how much he tugged and pulled, he was held
tight. Although the water was rapidly sobering
him, it was also bringing on a terrible chill.
With all his might he struggled, trying to tear
himself away from the ceaseless shower-bath.
At first he was either too proud or too much
befogged to call for assistance, but as he began
to realize his desperate condition, he raised a
husky, wavering cry.

Boisterous Steep Street, accustomed to the
most unearthly sounds from throats of brass,
would never note that thick, choking wail. Perhaps the fact that he had caused so many
helpless ones to cry for aid, and had shown no
pity, would now, in some judicial way, hinder
his own rescue. Not that Pfaff entertained any

such thoughts.. He was simply grovelling in his fears, and lifting up his pitiful voice, hoping some one would come to his relief.

As we have said, Chamberlain was a sound sleeper. The noise of the street had not, during the whole night, disturbed him; but now, as morning was drawing near, he stirred and became wakeful. First, he heard the shrill voice of a barn-yard fowl, far over the hills, then a faint, quavering cry that sounded human. In his drowsy state, the two sounds were confusedly mingled. That they actually meant any thing, he did not realize. One was to him as meaningless as the other. Both came from the misty land of dreams, where the strangest occurrences awaken only calm surprise in the mind of the dreamer.

"Help! help!" came the faint voice. With the most dispassionate interest, Chamberlain wove this cry into his morning dreams, growing little by little more conscious, till at length he began to think that something was the matter. Suddenly rousing himself, he sat up and listened. The quavering wail that he now heard made him leap to the floor and throw up the window. He naturally looked toward the fountain, and in the moonlight saw a figure bound to the planks, but writhing and calling piteously.

Hastily donning his clothes, he ran down-
stairs and soon stood by the dripping man.
He disengaged him from the pipe, and drew
him from the steady-flowing water. From head
to foot the rum-seller was soaking wet. As soon
as fairly released, he rolled over in a faint, a
chill, or something ˙similar, straightening out as
stiff as a board. Realizing the preciousness of
time, if the man was to be brought out of it,
Chamberlain put forth all of his strength, and,
lifting him, bore him the short distance between
the fountain and his boarding-place. The German was a heavy man, and the feat was
no small one, but it was successfully accomplished. Chamberlain, panting with the violence
of his exertions, stood in the diminutive entry,
and, calling to his landlady, wakened the household.

"I can't have him here," said Mrs. Bowman,
when she learned who it was. "He has done
harm enough to me and mine, without my
helping him."

"You have no objection to my putting him
n my room till this faint is over?" asked
Chamberlain.

"Yes, I have."

"Mrs. Bowman," said Chamberlain, sternly, "a
few minutes' delay will cause the death of this

man. Are you prepared to assume this responsibility?"

The rigid form was laid on the bed, the soaking clothes were removed, and warm blankets were wrapped around the cold figure. It seemed impossible for warmth ever to return to the chilled and livid body. A doctor had arrived and was active in his directions for his resuscitation. At length the brisk rubbings, the ceaseless efforts, were rewarded. Pfaff opened his eyes and uttered a groan. Chamberlain, in his anxious thankfulness, could have cried for joy.

"Now I s'pose he can go?" said Mrs. Bowman.

The physician turned to her, a rebuke in his eyes.

"Has the man no money?" he said.

"Money! yes!" was the half-hysterical reply. "He is rich, but he could n't stay here if he was king. He is a murderer! He killed my husband by selling him rum. I begged him to stop, and he laughed at me. My nephew is in jail to-day because he sold him liquor and got him crazy drunk, and he did what he never would have done in his sober senses. No! I say he shall not stay under this roof, — not if he were dying!"

Pfaff opened his eyes and looked at the frantic woman, then shivered and turned away.

"I don't blame her," said the doctor. "Now that I recognize him, I see that it is the rum-seller down below. I don't blame the woman for hating the sight of him."

"But can he be moved?" asked Chamberlain.

"Certainly not. Her hysterics will wear themselves out in a few minutes, and then she will have to listen to reason. But, if I am any judge, this man will be in a high fever before the day ends."

XIX.

The·Night·Gang.

CHAMBERLAIN'S love of adventure would not long permit him to leave unexplored a place so interesting as the rear yard of the file-works. Often since he had "shadowed" Tam as far as the hidden gate, had he planned to visit the enclosure some night and find out for himself all it contained. He determined, also, to learn for what purpose some of the buildings in that section of the works were used. The workmen did not seem to know, for he had questioned them. That there was something secret going on in them he was sure; but in what line, he could not decide; nor could he formulate the vague suspicions that the words of the little Scotchman had sown in his mind. To tell the truth, he was sorely puzzled by the conduct of the agent, who appeared so courteous and kindly. Of late he had sought Chamberlain when it would not be noticed by the workmen, and had impressed him with his desire to see the mill folk raised to a higher level. So earnest did he seem, that when with him, Chamberlain believed him to be sincere; but when alone, he found the old doubts asserting themselves, and the fragmen tary sentences of Tam, with the plainly uttered opinions of the laborers, came back in full force and shook his confidence.

After the store had been gutted, he had gone to Lamson and had received his sympathy. In deed, the agent expressed strong indignation, and yet appeared so hopeless of finding out who did it, that Chamberlain even in his presence began to doubt his honesty. Lamson declared that Pfaff was at the bottom of the outrage; but in the same breath said the rascal was so wily that a skilled detective would be baffled by his way of working. Chamberlain made little or no reply to the queries of the agent, as to what he intended to do with the store, and refused to accept the kind offer to relieve him of the lease.

The care of Pfaff, who was in a high fever at Chamberlain's lodgings, made it impossible for him to visit the mill yard as soon as he had planned. Forced to occupy a lounge, on the lower floor of his lodging-house, while the delirious rum-seller occupied his bed, he, how-

ever, took the first opportunity to steal away to
reconnoiter. On this occasion he started at nine
in the evening and made his way boldly through
the mill village, answering the hails of fellow-
workmen, but refusing to stop for friendly converse.
Passing around the ample yard that enclosed the
front buildings, he soon came to the footpath
where first he had become acquainted with Tam.
Having carefully taken bearings on his last visit,
he was able to go straight to the small gate, and
raising it, to enter the forbidden enclosure. Once
within, he carefully let the board down into its
place, and stood looking about him. The yard,
with its heaps of debris, its huge boilers, its
misshapen shadows, had a weird air that greatly
enhanced the romance of the scene. Now that
he was fairly within it, Chamberlain somehow
lost his imaginative expectations, and suddenly
felt that he might after all spend his time in a
fruitless quest. He argued to himself that things
nowadays happen as they should, running in the
everyday, practical ruts, and never turning aside
for the delicious adventures of which one reads.
Even as he entertained these thoughts, so dis-
couraging to the adventurer's cause, he heard a
quick step on the footpath, and then some one
fumbled for the gate-board. Noiselessly Chamberlain moved aside, and concealing himself be-

hind a hogshead, awaited the new comer. A
moment later a figure passed through the narrow
gateway and strode across the yard. Even in
the dim light he recognized Sam Putnam. In
great surprise, Chamberlain followed at a distance,
feeling that he was on the verge of a discovery.
Sam skirted one of the buildings, crossed the
yard, and stopped in front of a shed, upon the
door of which he knocked.

"Enter," said a voice that was easily recognized as Tam's.

"Well, old man, how goes it?" asked Sam,
opening the door and disappearing.

"All reet. So you have n't forgotten Tam?
Well, you are a gude lad, Sam, and the Loord
will one day bless you for your kindness to a
poor, daft body like mysel'."

"I should be a pretty mean chap if I did n't
stick to an old chum," answered Sam, heartily.
"I don't forget the good turns you did me
years ago, Tam; they are all down in my
memory."

"Does Lamson never wish to have me removed
noo?" was the anxious query.

"He has n't said a word about it for months,"
replied Sam. "I told him that when you went,
I went."

"Ye were aye generous. A man with so gude

a heart as you, Sam Putnam, should not rest till he had given it to the Loord."

Chamberlain expected some jeering reply, for he knew of Sam as one who made fun of religion unsparingly, and whose jokes were repeated from one end of the works to the other. He was therefore astounded to hear him say, —

" I would if I . could, Tam; but I am too deeply involved in certain affairs to make it possible. No man can serve the Lord and the devil at the same time, — that is, no man but Lamson."

" He . will reap his reward; let us not trouble about him. The question concerns you now. Do you believe on the Loord Jesus Christ?"

" I fear I do," was the reply, after a long pause.

" Well, then, you never will have peace till you surrender. And mark me, you must give up everything that stands between yourself and God."

Sam made no answer. Tam continued, —

" I do not wish to boast, but did I not give up everything ? "

" You did."

" And such peace as I now possess the world can never bestow. I might have been rich and well looking, but for the Loord's sake I surrendered it all, and lonely though I be, he daily repays me a hundred fold."

"I believe it," was the warm reply. "I believe it, and would willingly change with you to possess that peace."

"Let us pray over it," said the Scotchman.

One of the strange, heartfelt prayers that Chamberlain had before heard from the same lips now followed. It seemed to bring him near to the throne of grace, and he could hardly suppress the amen that rose to his lips as the prayer was ended.

"I must go and look after the polish-makers, but I wish I was out of it," said Sam, at length.

"Poor lad, I'm sorry for you. I wish you were as well out of the rascally business as I am. I will pray for you the night."

The visitor left the hut, and with his easy stride went further into the labyrinth of buildings and yards, Chamberlain following as closely at his heels as he dared. Turning first to the right and then to the left, among heaps of castings, passing around many obstructions, they went till he fairly lost his way. Finally, Sam stopped before the rear door of one of the lofty stone buildings that were now closed as not necessary for the work, and were supposed to be store houses. A peculiar double rap, accompanied by a low whistle, caused the door to be opened, and the giant passed from view. At the opening of the door, Chamberlain caught a glimpse of a well-lighted room, in which about a dozen men were working. Just what they were doing, he was unable to discover in the brief interval between the opening and closing of the door.

For some minutes he stood in concealment, waiting for Sam to reappear, but in this was disappointed. Advancing very cautiously he tried the door through which he had disappeared, but it was firmly fastened. Up and down the length of the building he passed, looking for windows that should enable him to catch a glimpse of the life within, but in vain. Baffled and puzzled, it seemed almost a freak of the imagination, for he could not hear any noise of tools, nor the least conversation. By placing his ear close to the wall of the building, however, he could detect a faint throb, like the beating of his own heart. This, he decided, must come from a small engine; yet no sign of escape-pipe or exhaust was to be seen.

At last, grown bold by his freedom from danger, he decided to make use of the double rap and whistle that Sam gave, and take the risk. It was a fool-hardy thing to do, but a

knowledge of Sam's true character kept him
from fear of bodily harm. Stepping up to the
door, he raised his hand to give the pass rap,
when it was caught away, and a voice whispered, —

"George Chamberlain, are you daft?"

Turning with a start, he stood face to face
with Tam.

"Come awa', man, till I talk with you," said
the little Scotchman.

Astonished by the sudden appearance of the
little Scotchman, Chamberlain followed him in
silence. No word did either speak till they were
safe in the tiny shed. Then Tam said, —

"Master George, what in the world were you
about? Would you put yourself in peril?"

"Why do you call me 'Master George'?" asked
Chamberlain.

"Are you not George Chamberlain?"

"I am his son."

With a sudden, frightened shyness, Tam arose
from his seat as if to flee.

"I thought you were Master George," he said,
hoarsely.

"Do not go, Tam. You were my father's
friend, can you not be mine? · My father, George
Chamberlain, is dead."

"Poor lad," said Tam, forgetting his fear; "I

remember, now, to have heard of the death of your father; but I'm no' quite right in my mind, and I forget much that passes. When I saw you, I thought that you were he. You favor him greatly."

Tam sat fingering the lapel of his coat, manifestly uneasy. Chamberlain watched him, wondering how he could gain his confidence, and learn something of the clandestine work of the night gang that were in the stone building. He saw that the little Scotchman distrusted him, and had half a mind to escape.

"Tam, things are going wrong here in the works. Lamson is playing a shrewd game, by which he makes money which should be turned into the hands of the company. Now what is it?" he said suddenly.

The little Scotchman hesitated, and looked longingly at the door.

"I daur not tell," was the muttered reply.

"But isn't it right that I should know? Am I not wronged by your silence? I am in the mill, daily; I know that something is brewing. You were my father's friend; can you not be mine?"

"Have you ever seen the crucibles?" asked Tam, suddenly.

"Yes."

"Well, you ken that they are made of black lead? After a few heats they become spoiled and are cast aside. You have seen the broken ones in the yard, mayhap?"

"I have," replied Chamberlain.

"It was always the · custom to throw them away, after they had served their purpose, as unfit for further use. Lamson, however, heard of a scheme that was employed in other mills for converting them into stove-polish; so he fitted up a room in the old stone mill, and put a man at work there nights, grinding them to powder. Pretty soon he had another man, then another, till he now has twenty men at work there."

"I should think it would be found out," observed Chamberlain.

"Who is there to find it out? These twenty men are oath-bound. They are supposed to be at the regular furnace-work all night. Instead, they only put in about one-third of the time for the company and the rest for Lamson. They get the highest wages, and far from wishing to divulge the secret, they guard it with jealous care. I don't know what they would have done, had you knocked as you thought of doing."

"Is this polish widely sold?"

"Have you never heard of the Three X Polish?"

"I have seen it advertised."

"Well, that is it. All over the country it is sold, and the profits are very large. Lamson is a wealthy man."

"How did you happen to know all this?" inquired Chamberlain.

"It's a weary tale. I worked in the mill, and Lamson got his eye on me as a mon who could be trusted. One day he tried by flattering promises, to get me go to work at it. I always doubted him, and when I found that it was to be kept secret, I charged him with fraud to Robert Flint, his employer. Oh, mon! How angered he was! I thought he would strike me. He walked up and down his office, and looked as ugly as the Deil himself. He told me that he would be the ruin of me if I did not join with him, and I, foolish man that I was, dared him on."

"Did he ever seek to harm you?"

"He did that, and accomplished it, too. After he divulged the secret, I tried, as I told him I should, to get the ear of Robert Flint and to tell him of the whole affair, but found it impossible. During work-hours, I was kept out of the office, and all letters that were sent to Flint were first opened by Lamson, and wherever I went I was dogged. At length he had his revenge. Do ye note the scars on my face? on my hands? They are the marks o' Lamson's vengeance."

With a shiver, Chamberlain looked at the face so scarred and seamed, from which burned the bright eyes with an almost unearthly light.

"Lamson did it?" said he in amazement.

"Aye, he did it. He was permitted to do it. I bear him no ill will. He can harm me no more, for the Loord has raised up friends for me."

"Talking to yourself, Tam?" said a deep voice, and Sam Putnam put his head into the little room. On seeing Chamberlain he came in with a curious look in his deep-set eyes.

"What is this boy doing here?" he said.

"This lad? Oh, he is George Chamberlain's son. I dinna ken what he wants here, except it is to talk with me."

"I suppose you know, young feller, that no one is allowed in this yard after nightfall?" said Sam.

'Then what are you doing here?" replied Chamberlain.

"That is none of your business."

"I tal you it is his business. He is George Chamberlain's son," asserted Tam.

"Are you?" was the answer, with a piercing look.

"Yes, I am," said Chamberlain.

Sam meditated for a few seconds. It was evident that at first he had thought of him as merely a common workman, who, through love of adventure, or through mere curiosity, had scaled the fence to see Tam; but now he saw his mistake. Manifestly, the news of Chamberlain's relationship to the chief owner of the works made him ill at ease.

"Are you at work here for the purpose of spying on the men?" he asked with a bitter ring in his voice.

"Putnam," said Chamberlain, "I came here to learn the business. My being in the yard tonight is to discover what kind of work is going on at night, when the villagers believe that the men are at the smelting furnaces."

"That is something you had better not find out. Let me warn you, it is dangerous."

"I have told him all. It is right that he should know. I am not oath-bound," said Tam.

Sam knit his brows, perplexed and angry.

"There is another object in my being here in the factory," continued Chamberlain, "and that is to see if I cannot do some good. The terrible state that rum has brought about on Steep Street is as plain to you as to me. There is a fearful daily misery, that calls to heaven for help. It is my honest belief that there are hearts on the street, that even now the Holy Spirit is striving with. It is my wish to point some of those souls to the Way."

Sam listened as if for life.

"Do you honestly believe that the story of the Cross is true,—that Jesus Christ was the Son of God?" he asked.

"I am sure of it. The manner in which he has answered my prayers, and the sweet peace that has filled my soul, assure me of it. There is room for no mistake. The very dignity of truth is in the story."

"You are right lad! You are right," said Tam. "Those who come to the Loord with earnest hearts do not doubt. Their lives are filled so full of His presence that that there is no chance for it. They know His voice and He calleth them by name."

"Why did he not keep Temple from falling?" inquired Sam.

"That is more than I can tell. I believe that John Temple will yet be saved. I know he was in earnest. Perhaps it was that the North Church might have a lesson."

"Mighty little they have profited by it," sneered Sam, the hard tone coming back.

"I am not so sure of that. The church has

voted to banish all wine containing alcohol from the communion table. I believe that Mr. Snow is fervently praying for the Steep-street people, and I also believe that his prayers will yet be answered."

Sam was struggling with a deep conviction of sin. There could be no doubt of it. His whole bearing showed it. Chamberlain prayed in his heart that the Spirit of Truth might triumph. As he glanced at Tam he saw his lips move and felt that he also prayed. Just then the clock struck eleven.

"We must get out of this. The men have their recess in a little while, and it won't do for you to be seen. If Lamson heard of it he would get even with me in some way," said Sam.

"You will not harm the lad, Sam?" said Tam, a ring of anxiety in his voice.

"No, of course not. His pious talk has made me chicken-hearted."

Following the giant, Chamberlain passed through the length of the yard, through the secret gate, and stood with him on the narrow foot-path.

"I should like to ask you a question," said Sam, as they were about to part. "Do you believe that a man whose whole life had been steeped in rioting and sin, who had done scores of things that he could never undo, who loved liquor more than any thing else in the world,

—do you believe that such a man could receive what you Christians call a new heart?"

"The Lord said, 'Whosoever will, let him come.' That means just such a man as you describe, as well as any other. Repent and believe, ask for forgiveness, and turn from sin, and help is certain.

"I have believed ever since my wife died, years ago, but the turning from sin was what troubled me. I can't bear to expose others."

"A man cannot serve the Lord and the devil at the same time," said Chamberlain.

"Well, good-night. I think that you mean what you say, anyhow."

"Good-night, and God bless you," was the reply, and they parted.

Chamberlain had gone but a little way, when he heard his name called, and Sam came hurrying after him.

"There is one thing I forgot to say. You have made a discovery to-night that will change things here without doubt. I am glad of it, but I want it distinctly understood that if any penalty falls on the night gang, it falls on me as well. And, another thing, the little bit that I have talked about religion, to-night, was not to dodge any of my misdoings. I am willing to face the music. Good-night."

XX.

Two · Penitents.

THOSE who are familiar with manufactories, notice that the afternoon jar and roar of machinery has a deeper, heavier sound than in the morning. Possibly the cogs, that shoulder one another in ceaseless rotation, the whirring pulleys, the sweeping belts, weary with the day's labor, take this means of expressing a wish for relaxation. Whether or not this be true, it is certain that the men grow tired, — that their steps are less elastic, and their work moves more slowly. About four o'clock comes the maximum of this afternoon lull, which, as soon as it is appreciated, is followed by a "spurt" that carries things along till six o'clock brings relief. It was in the midst of this portion of the working-day that Sam Putnam stepped into the outer office, and knocked at the door of Lamson's private room.

"What is it?" was the curt query from within.

"Can I see you for a few minutes?"

"Who is it?"

"Sam Putnam."

"I'm busy. Can't you come again?"

"Yes," was the reply.

So astonished was the agent at the quiet answer, that he pushed open the door and looked, a trifle anxiously, at his caller, who was already turning to depart.

"Any thing wrong?" he asked.

"I guess not; but any time that you are at liberty I have several things of some importance to tell you."

"Come in now," said Lamson.

Putnam entered and seated himself, waiting for the other to open the conversation.

"Well?" remarked the agent, impatiently.

"I wished to tell you that I am about to enter the service of another master."

"Who?" asked Lamson, in amazement.

"The Lord Jesus Christ," replied Sam, reverently.

The agent flushed scarlet, then turned white, and seemed, for the moment, completely confounded.

"You astonished me, Sam; I didn't know

you cared for such things. You frightened me, too. Then it won't be necessary for you to leave me. You know I could n't stand that," he said, finally.

"I am not sure of that. My profession is to be an honest one."

"Undoubtedly. You have my heartiest sympathy. It is a wise and commendable step. How is that last file-stock? There has been complaint that it is flawy," replied Lamson, attempting to turn the subject.

"For some weeks I have thought of this, and am now determined to carry it through. My belief in the saving power of the blood of Christ is genuine. It can save me, and has done so. It can save you," said Sam, keeping to the point with quiet calmness.

"Are you trying to preach to me, Sam? You forget that I am a member of the church."

"I remember it, but being a church-member is not being a Christian. That you know as well as I. Do you believe that you are saved from your sins?"

"Are n't you rather too young a convert to be questioning me? How long have you been in the service of this Master?" asked the lawyer, with a forced smile.

"Three days."

"And what has become of the polish-works?" asked Lamson, involuntarily acknowledging that Sam could not consistently continue to defraud the company.

"I dismissed all the men Saturday night."

The agent's face became livid with rage."

"How dare you?" he said, leaping to his feet. "What right have you to discharge any men here? Why, there are scores of orders waiting to be filled!"

"I hired the men, and therefore I could discharge them. You recognize the fact that I cannot do that work any more, and I am glad of it. I would give any thing if I had never consented to it."

"You remember your oath!"

"I do, but it is my belief that all of this will be found out before long, even if I hold my tongue, as I shall under the circumstances."

The agent sat for some minutes in deep thought. Resting his face on his hand, he appeared to study the opposite wall, but when unobserved he was slyly examining Sam's face. The shallowest physiognomist would have asserted, with confidence, that the giant was in earnest. His open face was not a mask behind which lurked any kind of guile. On the contrary, it bore the impress of truth, honesty, and determination. Lamson, with keen eyes, saw all this, and wondered how he should again get the upper hand of this most valuable man. He had little time to decide, for Sam was even then waiting for him to speak.

" Did it ever occur to you that I might possess a conscience?" enquired the agent.

"I suppose every one has something of the kind," replied the other.

"Well, I most certainly have one, and, Sam, this crucible business has troubled me a great deal. I believe from the first a curse hung over it. There has been a quantity of polish sold, but almost no money has come from it. We sell at so small a profit that the bad debts eat up every thing. I am sick of the whole affair, and am glad you dismissed the men. I shall inform our New York agents that after this they must get some other firm to manufacture for them."

"You really mean to give it up?" asked Sam, in surprise.

"I do. It was a temptation to me at first, and I yielded, which was very wrong, but now that you have started to do right, I am going to bear you company. Only, one thing for the sake of my mother, this must be kept a pro found secret."

Sam, with genuine fervor, promised that he would breathe no word of the affair. To tell the truth, he had gone into the office with a prayer on his lips that his former partner in guilt might be influenced to turn away from his sin. And now it appeared as if the prayer was answered.

Accustomed, as he was, to manipulating all kinds of men, Lamson perceived that he had again gained Sam's confidence, and it occurred that here was a good opportunity to learn more of his plans. Putnam, when feeling well, was apt to be off his guard, and, on matters of minor importance, could be easily drained of information.

"Where are you going Sundays? It won't do for you to spend them in the engine-house, as formerly."

"I shall go to Chamberlain's mission, I expect," was the reply.

"Chamberlain's?" repeated his listener, having heard nothing definite of the scheme.

"Yes," was the reply.

"That is a grand idea of his, but it will cost something."

"Only for the settees, lamp, desk, and books," replied Sam.

"Ah!" thought the agent, "Chamberlain is going to fix his store over into a mission-chapel. That was why he refused to throw up the lease." Aloud he said, —

"Young Chamberlain is a fine fellow. I like him better the more I see of him. His efforts at doing good are most commendable. I wish I could assist him."

"Do you mean that?" enquired Sam.

"Certainly."

"Then give us a ten-dollar bill to get some mottoes for the walls," said Sam.

With a look in his steely eyes that boded ill, Lamson wrote a check for the amount, and Sam went off highly delighted. As for Lamson, he locked the door and indulged in a long, silent temper-fit, from which he came out pale, smiling as ever, and several degrees more crafty and unscrupulous.

The confession that Sam had made to Lamson was hard, yet it was nothing compared with one he was already preparing to make. For so many years the leader of the Tigers, and so thoroughly identified with them in their various escapades, he knew that only a manly confession of faith could give the impression he was anxious to give, — could keep out the suspicion that he had been 'bought up' by the church in the upper town. With great anxiety he waited for the next meeting of the engine-company, determined fully to state his new faith, and trust in the Lord to impress the honesty of his repentance upon the hearts of his comrades. At the hour of gathering he was on hand, and, as usual, was at once surrounded by a circle of admirers.

"Pass the elixyer to the foreman," suggested one, and the decanter was in an instant proffered to him.

"No, not any for me," he said.

"Are n't you ashamed of yourself, to ask the president of our 'reform club' to drink, after he has been laboring so many years to 'put down liquor'?" shouted a jolly voice, and, at the remembrance of Parson Snow's mistake, there was a general shout.

"Take a hand at our table?" pressed a couple of the younger men, who were playing cards.

How hard it was to break in on all this real heartiness, and do as he had resolved. No man there suspected the change that had come over him. He almost wished that they were able at that moment to see into his heart and recognize the difference there. The liquor, the profanity, were so loathsome to him now; yet the

hearty admiration of the men, and their friendliness, was more than ever grateful.

" You fellers shut up," said Josselyn, with a
shake of his fist at the card-players, in simu-
lated wrath. " What we all want,· and what we
intend to have, is a yarn, — one of Sam's
stories. Such as no one else can tell. Hey,
boys ? "

" That 's the talk; a yarn ! a story."

"Will you listen to any story that I may read
or tell ? "

" Yes, yes ; go ahead ! The first man that in-
terrupts will be fired down stairs."

Aware that this promise would be rigidly kept,
with a prayer for guidance, Sam drew a Testament from his pocket, and with some difficulty
found a certain chapter, and began to read.
He had selected the story of the Crucifixion, and
and as he read, the silence in the room grew
till hardly a sound could be heard but the
smooth bass of the reader. Slowly, reverently,
distinctly, the foreman read, and the simple eloquence of the story held them all spell-bound.
When it was finished, a little sigh ran round
the room, and the rough faces, for the moment
softened, again assumed their rugged lines. An
old man, a stranger in the engine-room, although
one of the puddlers, said in a subdued tone, —

"Eh, mon, but that is a gude tale. Read it agen."

There was no demurring on the part of the audience, and Sam, with a new realization of the power of the Word, again read the story. The tender pathos, the wonderful love of the Saviour, and the bitter agony on Calvary, so vividly impressed itself upon his mind that he could with difficulty command his voice; nor was he alone in his agitation. The hardened file-workers were also affected, and tears stood in the eyes of men whose whole lives had been spent in reckless sin.

"Boys," said Sam, breaking the silence that followed, "you asked me tell you a story; I have told many during the years we have trained together. You have seemed to enjoy them, and I am sure I have. Of them all, this one has been the best to me; this is true. I have been unmindful of it long enough, God knows; but that shall no longer be said of me. I believe that Jesus Christ died for me, as this book says. His blood cleansed me from sin. He is my friend, and from this time forth I am going to do all I can to live as He tells us to live."

"How is that?" was the inquiry from younger men.

"Just this way: To live without drinking and swearing; to keep the Sabbath; to read the Bible, and pray; to follow His commands; and to try and bring other men to him. And O, how I wish you all might know this Saviour! We have been comrades in sin for so long, why can't we be in holiness? I tell you, boys, there is no slip-up' to this matter. It is all down in black and white. The Bible says, 'For God so loved the world that he gave his only beloved Son, that whosoever believeth in him might not perish, but have everlasting life.' That *whosoever* was what caught me; that did the business. I knew I was mustered in when I read that. When we have scoffed at religion, and made the most fun of it, at the bottom of our hearts there was a feeling that, after all, there might be something in it. We know that this life does not end all. We know, when we are drunkards, and swearers, and wicked, that we shall have to pay for it sometime. Now, why not act on the square, and drop all this folly, and get a new start? The doors are wide open to-night. I wish some of you fellers would start along with me, and own the best Friend man ever had."

When he had finished, there was a long silence in the room. His story had made a deep impression upon the men, but there were one or two who hardened their hearts against any thing religious; among them was Josselyn. As

glanced about at the faces, tear-stained and softened, he flushed with anger, and said, —

"That's a mighty interestin' story, and you
told it well; but it don't wash with me. Do
you s'pose I am fool enough to believe that a
man who loves rum as well as you do, is going
to give up drinking it for nothing? I ain't forgotten how five years ago Bert Thompson, the
biggest drunkard in the works, turned suddenly
sober and started a big revival. I was one of
his converts, and believed that he was genuine;
but three weeks later he was drunker than ever,
and boasting of the good clothes and the money
the 'up-town folks' had give him. That game
is too old. Fool the church folks all you please,
but don't try it on us."

This speech had its effect, and the faces that
had been softened by better feeling grew hard again.

"You are the first man, friend or enemy, that
ever accused me of playing a double game in
any thing," said Putnam.

"I s'pose there is a first time for every thing,"
was the sneering reply.

With a grave dignity, the giant rose to depart, aware that no argument would avail to set
his action in its true light. Only a consistent
Christian life could impress upon this company
the real honesty of the views he had expressed.

He stepped down from the platform, and Josselyn rose and came forward to meet him.

"You are a turn-coat and a traitor. Take that!" he said, slapping him in the face with his open hand.

The men in amazement, almost in horror, that one should dare lay hands on so dangerous a man as Sam had proved himself to be when roused, stood gazing at him. They expected to see the assailant fall under the sudden and terrible "left-hander" that had almost killed the bully of the next village; but Putnam stood calm, motionless, looking straight into the flaming eyes of the other.

"Tim," he said, and his voice held a cadence of such sweetness that the tears started to many eyes. "Tim, there was a time when that blow would have cost you much, but that is all past. — God bless you!"

They stood aside and let him pass, then sat down again to their cards and their drinking. Josselyn seated himself apart and looked gloomily out of the window. When asked to play, he answered with a vigorous oath. Soon he got up and went out.

"I'll bet," said one of the elder grinders, who had been deeply affected by the story, — "I'll bet that Josselyn will be the next to go as Sam has."

XXI.

An · Accident.

BY the foot of Steep Street ran the river.
Through the night and whenever the mills
were "shut down," it was full from bank to
bank; but as soon as the gates of the canal
were opened above the dam, most of the water
was drawn away, and the great boulder-strewn
river-bed lay open to the sight of all. This was
the grand play-ground for such children as were
not in the mill. The little pools of water
among the slippery rocks held many a prisoned
pickerel and perch, and when these more valuable of the finny tribe were absent, the place
abounded in eels, from three to six inches long,
the catching of which afforded unending sport.
Many a youngster spent all day trying to capture the slippery squirmers, handling dozens,
retaining none.

Among those who sometimes came that way

and invariably stopped to watch the lively sport
in the river-bed, was Miriam Whitney.   Driving
as closely as was possible, she enjoyed their
successes and lamented their failures, and soon
came to have quite a knowledge of the little
folks of the street.   Among them all, one in
particular attracted her.   He was a cripple, poorly
dressed, and sadly misshapen, one limb being
shorter than the other.   In spite of this disad-
vantage, he looked the most alert and intelligent
of the party.   His big black eyes saw all that
was to be seen, and his stick descended unerr-
ingly upon the frantic fish that fled for life
down the shallow rivulets to the pools below.
The success that attended his efforts made some
of his companions jealous, and as a result, those
who dared bullied him as often as possible.
Yet he had a friend that any of them would
gladly have secured, in the person of the lady-
watcher on the further bank.

One morning she had become so interested,
that she descended from her phaeton and came
almost to the water's edge, just below the fish-
hunting ground, and stood watching the actors.
As usual, the big brown head of her favorite
was bobbing in the thick of the fray, and his
left hand clutched a fine string of fish.   Suddenly a sturdy, forbidding youngster caught the

fish from his hand and started on a run for the opposite bank, the owner close at his heels. The thief would probably have escaped with the booty, had he not met an unforseen obstacle. A tall young lady stood in his path, with such a look blazing in her eyes, that he stopped in sudden fear. That instant of hesitation was just what the lame boy needed, for springing upon his enemy, he overthrew him and by a quick wrench recovered his property.

"You are a coward!" said Miriam, as the boy regained his feet, and stood looking defiantly at her.

"I am no coward, neither. I lickit the school-mistress, an' I can lick thee!" was the astonishing reply.

"Ye cannot lick her, till ye have me!" said the little cripple, stepping in front of his fair ally. "And ye are a coward, all ye daur tackle is lame folk and lassies."

"Course he's a coward, he dares not tackle a lad of his own size!" yelled the others in high glee.

The little ruffian raised his hand as if to strike, when the cripple with a quick motion tripped him up.

"Wi' ye say ought agin' the leddy?" he asked, standing over him with uplifted arm.

"No," was the surly reply, and the battle was won. The defeated one stumped off, followed by the rest, except the lame boy.

"I 'd like to tal you my thankfulness, Miss," said he gratefully, "yon lad is a sair trial to me. Will ye not accept the fish? They are right gude!"

"My father is very fond of pickerel, and if you are willing to take them to my house, the Whitney Place, I will buy them. By the way what is your name?"

"Jamie Bruce, but I dinna' wish to sell them," he answered blushing.

But the money was already in his jacket-pocket, and his friend had gone, with a bright smile.

From this time, Jamie became a protegé of the fair young lady. Whenever she appeared in the vicinity of the mill settlement,—and most of the attractive drives in Steelville, had their beginning in that direction,—he was on hand to shyly give her welcome. His quaint suggestions as to desirable places for pleasure excursions, together with his unique comments on the life of the mill folks, made him a most entertaining companion. Miriam had already made up her mind to speak to her father about the little fellow, and see if something could not be done to secure for him an education, when there came one of those strange happenings that sometimes fall even upon the innocent.

A fire had broken out in the "packing-room" of the file-works, and all Steelville was in a ferment. The up-town engine, a steamer, had reached the village soon after the first alarm, and was closely followed by almost the entire population of that section. The steamer men were in high spirits at having reached the place nearly as soon as their rivals, the Tigers, and were working with might and main, unreeling hose, coupling, and getting into shape to work.

The grinding-room hands, led by Swinert and Gaffney, formed a line of buckets to the canal, and were doing substantial work. Around on all sides, surging close to the engines, and blocking the way, pressed a dense crowd of people with the characteristic lawlessness of town folk. In a comparatively open spot on the side hill overlooking the scene, somewhat removed from the crowd, stood Miss Whitney and her father. She was watching every move with the deepest interest and pointing out one and another of her juvenile acquaintances, much to the amusement of her parent.

The engines were now playing in good earnest,

the short "chug-chug," of the steamer vying with the clatter of the brakes on the hand engine. The town firemen were working for pay, the Tigers "for fun," and it was hard to decide which put forth the greater exertion. On the leading hose, flat on their faces, where the hot breath of the flames sent the perspiration rolling down in streams, only to be dried by the thick, black smoke, were Chamberlain and Sam Putnam. Thus they lay side by side, holding the restive, jerking hose, that like a canvas serpent, writhed and twisted a if determined to free itself. The foreman of the Tigers had an object in choosing this position. Considerable feeling existed between his men and the firemen of the town. So high had it run at times that it had stopped little short of pitched battles. The file-workers complained that the Steamer men were in the habit of turning their hose on them and ducking them whenever opportunity offered, and of course they retaliated. So many times had these complaints reached Sam, that he had determined to discover which side was the aggressor. He therefore stationed himself just within the threshold of the flame-filled room, held to the hose and waited.

Presently, from the opposite side, where the steamer men were in possession of a shattered window, came a sudden burst of water, striking the wall about a foot above their heads, with a force which, if it had been expended on them, would have swept them out of the door. Soon another dash, then in different places not far from them came the savage swish and hiss of the solid water-column. The town firemen were "feeling for the Tigers," and meant to drown them out, The foreman's eyes, filled with smoke though they were, snapped dangerously. Just then the chief engineer, who was also one of the selectmen of the town, crawled up beside him, and in a moment his experienced eye took in the whole affair.

"It's that miserable Tom Strong," he said to Putnam, "and the other fellows back him up in it. The fire is really under now; let's give him a lesson."

Chamberlain was sent to rouse the tired men on the brakes to a final effort. A word explained the situation, and a stream was sent through the canvas channel that was about as much as Putnam and the chief engineer could manage. When the full force was on, the two men braced in the doorway, turned it point blank on the window. There was a crash, a sputtering yell, and the chief said, with intense satisfaction in his voice, —

"That was a good shot! Tumbled Tom clear out of the window! Now, by the time he picks himself up, he won't have any water to fight with, for I've ordered the steamer to stop."

Meanwhile, not far from where Miriam and her father stood, a little woman in neat, black dress and white cap, was watching eagerly the swaying mass of men and boys around the engines. Several times she glanced at the young lady as if in doubt, and at last advanced, dropped a quaint, old-country courtesy, and lifting a face such as some of the gentle, "gude wives" have, — a face rare, saintly, — said, —

"Lassie, your eyes are young and strong; will ye tal me is that my Jamie doon by the engine yon? You'd ken him; he's the lame laddie."

Miriam looked long and searchingly in the direction named, but could discover no sign of the boy.

"Are you Jamie's mother?" she inquired.

"No'; I'm his grannie, and I'm sair worried about him this moment. It's this day week he started to wark in the mills, 'cause he would na' have his grannie gang oot to service longer. It's in the part of the mill where he warked that the fire is."

"I do not think there is any danger," said Miriam, soothingly. "All of the hands were out before the fire was under way. I heard one of the men say so."

"The Loord grant that it be so; but I'm much straightened about the lad. I went doon and tried to question the man at the engine, but he bade me gang back oot of peril, that the lad was all reet."

At this moment there was a sudden movement toward the blackened doorway, about which the heavy smoke hung like a pall. From the confused murmur, nothing could be learned but that a startling discovery had been made. Mr. Whitney had already left the scene, preferring to walk home; and his daughter and the little Scotchwoman stood alone, anxiously waiting for information as to the sudden excitement. Soon the dense throng parted, and Chamberlain, pale even through the grime of smoke, hatless and coatless, with a slight, limp form in his arms, came toward the bridge.

"Where is the little fellow's home?" he said.

A score of voices responded in subdued accents, and led by him the great crowd abandoned steamer, hose, and every thing, and surged toward Steep Street.

"My heart tells me it's my lad," said the old lady, faintly. "I'm very weak like."

Miss Whitney passed her arm around her, and

and thus they followed slowly the mass of people. When they came in sight of the wee cottage back of the tenements, they saw that the throng had surrounded it. As they neared the place, a way opened for them, and the whisper went round:—

"That's the lad's grannie."

On the tiny bed in the bare, little bedroom lay a still figure. It was indeed her lad!

The little Scotchwoman, with a heart-breaking cry, leaned over him, took him in her arms, and rained kisses and tears upon the unconscious face.

"Oh, my laddie, my laddie!" she mourned; "would to God that I might have deed for ye! My pure bairnie! My wee, broken-winged duve; I ken that yeer better—aye, far better off now. Yeer with the feyther now, and the mother, and thy auld grannie is desolate! Ah! laddie, if ye could but have stayed, that we might have gang thegither; but it's the Loord's will, and we'll no be lang parted!"

The people slowly and sadly dispersed, talking soberly of the young life that had so suddenly gone out. From the position in which he had been found, it was evident that the boy had lingered to shut the tin-clad doors of the lamp room, and been caught by the dense smoke and stifled. Rough men, calloused women, felt the heroism of the deed, lowered their voices, forgot their oaths, and truly mourned.

In her great grief and loneliness the Scotchwoman seemed to cling to Miriam, and the young girl, with the true instinct of noble womanhood, prepared to spend the night at the cottage.

One of the firemen, a broad-shouldered young man, who had quietly cleared the house of all but a few women, was just leaving, when she accosted him.

"Can you find me a messenger, sir? I wish to send a note to my father, Mr. Whitney."

"I should be very glad to be the bearer of any message for you," was his reply, and she then recognized Chamberlain, and the real pleasure that she allowed herself to show was very grateful to him.

"God bless you!" he said, holding out his hand. "You are doing a noble, womanly deed."

The strong hand seemed to impart some of its owner's self-command, and she felt strengthened. She watched him as he swiftly passed through the long street and disappeared, then shutting the door, returned to her self-imposed task of soothing the stricken one, while the "auld wives" tenderly prepared the form of Jamie ere he should be forever laid out of sight.

As Chamberlain passed through the street on his way to the Whitney place, he saw Gaffney and several others earnestly conversing.

"Is the boy dead?" asked the grinder.

"Yes. The physician said that he inhaled the smoke and flame, and must have been instantly suffocated," was the reply.

"Poor, little feller!" said Gaffney, the tears springing to his eyes. "Shure it's many times I've seen him carrying water fer his grannie, and choppin' wood, when you could see that every step and every stroke was pullin' him to pieces of pain! Poor, little Jamie! shure ye'll never have any more backache; the water-pail will never again be too heavy fer ye, — poor, little lad!"

XXII.

ßoiler·ŋumber·Six.

ȴN his tiny room, preparing for the coming Sunday's wrestle with a class of Steep-street boys,
sat Chamberlain. It was no light task to train
the infant-minds of the mill youngsters. Their
views on theological subjects were unique. Not
at all bashful in expressing them, a teacher of
timid habit was apt to be disastrously overcome. The young man was deeply interested in
his class, and they returned his affection, even
going so far as to indulge in shin-knocking and
hair-pulling, for the honor of sitting next to him.

As he digested the lesson, a heavy step
on the stair roused him from his work. The
door opened, and Sam Putnam entered.

"Are you willing to lay your papers aside, and
talk a bit?" he inquired, awkwardly.

"Glad to," was the reply. "Sit down."

The chair groaned as it received its weight;
but Sam, used to wooden protests, did not notice
it.

"Maybe you have heard of my change of base?" he remarked, interrogatively.

"No."

"Well, I thought perhaps the agent told you I had decided to train in the company that you joined not long since."

"Do you mean that you have given your heart to the Lord Jesus?"

"That is just the checker," said Sam, wiping his eyes. "I am in dead earnest. Not a wink of sleep have I had for two nights, I am so happy. It makes me strong as a giant. Why, I believe I could sling a small-sized locomotive over my head and not strain myself!"

"I am so glad to hear it! It will be a help to us all. Do you know, Mr. Snow, Miss Whittier, and myself have been praying for you for a long time? How it will rejoice the others to know that our prayers are answered."

"What possessed you to pray for me?" was the surprised reply.

"Steep Street listens to you, — follows you. We prayed that you might awake to your responsibility."

"I felt as if something or 'nother was stirred up about me. For a long time I fought it off, but at last had to give in. Bless the Lord that I did! The matter about Lamson troubled me

I determined to have it settled all right, so I went to him and refused any longer to do his bidding. He was mad at first, but finally when I told him the reason, he cooled down and told me I done just right. He has given up the polish work altogether. Says there was n't any money in it, and that he is out of pocket for running it. Besides, he owned that it was wrong, and that he was sorry. It considerably aston· ished me when he said that. He is not in the habit of thinking that he has done wrong. Perhaps, after all, he is as good as the rest of us."

"But Tam accuses him of having some fearful revenge upon him because he would not consent to be one of the polish gang. How is that?"

"Have you ever heard the story of Boiler Number Six?"

"No, I have not."

"Well, that is what Tam refers to when he lays his disfigurement to Lamson. I am in no hurry, and if you can spend the time I will tell it."

"Do! I shall be interested," answered Cham berlain, sitting back to enjoy one of "Sam's stories."

"This boiler was pretty near thirty feet long," began Putnam, crossing his knees and entering upon the recital with all the zest of a natural story-teller. "It was built after a plan of Lamson's, and had but a few flues, and those at the sides. As it was very large, this manner of construction left a large tunnel in the centre, capable of holding a score of men in single file. One thing curious about this boiler was its faculty for attracting a sediment. Every little while some of us had to go in with hammer and chisel to chip off the hard, porcelain-like scale. Possibly this was from the defect in the construction. However that may be, there was an everlasting bother with that boiler. Lamson would hear no word against it, and no matter how it acted, how much fuel it used, and how little steam it produced, he stood up for it. It usually fell to my lot to go inside, because I can stand an awful amount of heat. And so jealous was the agent of its reputation, that he did not wish it to be idle a moment hardly, and he would have made me go in to clear it before it was fairly blown off, had it been possible. I have seen the steam at forty pounds in it, and Lamson so anxious not to have it cooled too much, that he put a man at work unscrewing the manhole plate, and blew the packing half across the boiler-room.

"One night word came from the office that I must stay and clear out Number Six. I was

tired out at the time, and went in and made a
row about it. I told Lamson that about half of
my time was spent inside of that boiler, and
suggested that he build an office in it, and let
me stay there all the time. He was kinder provoked, and flared up a little, but when he found
that I was really played out, he ordered Tam
McDonald to help me. I was to do the bossing,
and he the chipping. Tam was a fine, strong
man, although small, and did almost all the piping in odd corners and in tough places, because
he was so hardy. He could stand heat almost
as well as I could, and I was mighty glad of his
assistance."

Sam paused and looked back into the past as
if he had the whole scene before him.

"It was nearly eleven o'clock before it was
cool enough for us to enter. Tam went first,
and I followed. On the hot floor of sheet-iron
we laid a few short boards, to make it more
comfortable. I can recall distinctly just how Tam
looked as he went in with his lantern and his
tools. He was a fine, ruddy-appearing man, with
an intelligent air that won him many friends.
For a long time he worked away, the hammer
ringing like a bell on the sides of the boiler,
and the echoes filling our ears till it seemed as
if we should never hear any thing else. At

length I noticed that he appeared uneasy. Finally
he said, —

"'Sam, I don't feel that all is right. I have
an intuition that Lamson intends me harm to-
night. I wish we were out of this.'

"I had more faith in Tam's intuitions and
second-sights than I was willing to own, and
though I joked at his superstitions, I could not
help looking a bit nervously at the little manhole 'way down at the further end of our prison.
We had not finished our work when Tam grew
so fearful that I consented to go out for a few
minutes, and look around just to satisfy him.
We started, — I was ahead, of course, for there
was not room to pass in the queerly-constructed
interior. I had gone but a little way when I
heard a quick hiss, and knew that steam had
been turned into the boiler. The only thing to
do was to hurry as fast as possible for the
manhole. With all the strength and quickness
that I possessed I darted for the little opening,
Tam close behind me. The steam coming in
faster and faster, no longer hissing, but rattling
against the expanding flues and fast-heating sides.
Swiftly we hurried, but swifter came the steam.
I loved Tam, and would far rather had him in
front of me, for in spite of my fear of the
steam, my faith in my own probable escape from

harm was just what every young, strong man has.

" Queerly enough, a prayer that my mother taught me came into my mind, and repeated itself over and over. The few seconds that we were in passing the length of the boiler seemed like ages. Never in my life have I exerted my self to get ahead, or appeared to progress so slowly. At length I swung myself out of the manhole, and turned to help Tam. He had dropped just under it, right in the steam. Muffling my face, I reached down and drew him out just as one of the workmen shut off the steam.

"For a long time Tam was very sick. When he recovered, he was so disfigured that his own mother would not have known him. The shock also affected his mind, and he seemed unable to reason clearly. He had told me all about Lamson's enmity, and now he insisted that the agent had done this in order to assure his revenge. That was absurd. Lamson had nothing to do with Tam's being hurt, further than his sending him to help me was concerned. And when he heard that Tam charged him with it, he was fearfully worked up, and he did all he could to shut him up. He finally succeeded in having him put in an insane asylum. But he did n't stay long. He escaped, and was not heard of for a long time. At last it was discovered that he was living in the stone-cutters' shed, in the rear of the mill. Lamson was going to have him sent away at once, but one or two of us stepped forward, and gave him to understand that we should not allow any more interference with Tam. So he was let alone, and since then he has lived where you saw him."

"Then it was not really his fault that Tam became so disfigured?"

"Not at all. He knew nothing about it,— but Tam will always believe that it was his revenge."

"If I am not mistaken, Tam was at the fire in the mill the other day," remarked Chamberlain.

"Yes, that is another of his queer notions; he will go miles to a fire. People about here do not know who he is, as a general thing, yet he is always on hand when there is a blaze. He 's a worker, too, when there is any thing to do. I have seen him do things that I would not dare attempt. Did you ever hear tell of the 'Coffin house' fire?"

"No, tell me, please."

"It was several years ago,—soon after Tam escaped from the 'sylum. He used, at times, to see me and talk things over, and was sensible on everything except his own trouble. Any reference to that would rouse him at once. So I used always to avoid mentioning it. One evening, as I was speaking with him down back of the mill, he all of a sudden held his head up and snuffed the air ; just as a horse sometimes does ; then he looked around in a frightened way and says, —

"'Sam, there is a fire up on the street!'

"'Nonsense!' says I.

"'There is, and in a few minutes there will be an alarm.'

"I did n't take any stock in what he said, but sure enough, within five minutes came a rousing alarm, and we were all putting as hard as we could, first for the engine-house, and then for the fire. It was in a queer-shaped old tenement-house that was called the 'Coffin house' from its shape; the name just described it. How many families were crowded into it, would be hard to say, but when we got there the street was filled with all sorts of household goods, half-dressed children, crying women, and swearing men. The house was only an old shell anyway, and in spite of our best efforts, the flames had it all their own way. We pumped all of the wells dry, and finally went to the river, and then had to stop every few minutes to put in a fresh section of hose, it burst so often.

"When the whole building was one mass of blaze, with the exception of the end furthest from the street, word went round that an old, blind woman, who occupied an attic, had been forgotten and was still in the building. The women fairly shrieked when they heard it, and all the men could do was to help on the 'brakes,' or stand and stare. We were n't well provided with ladders, and even if we had been, none could have gone into any part of the upper stories. I had come up from the river to look after the hose-men, when the story was told me, and almost at the same instant I caught sight of Tam.

"He had just been informed that the old lady was within, for he looked about with a wild air, then made straight for a big apple-tree that leaned over the tenement. Its leaves were already crisping, and its twigs curling and sizzling with the heat. Like a squirrel, Tam climbed the trunk, springing from branch to branch, till he reached the big one that hung over the gravelled roof. No tight-rope gymnast could have run along this, easier or surer than he. An instant later, and he stood on the roof, the flames curling up over the eaves on all sides of him.

"Not willing to have him left entirely without support, I climbed part way up the tree myself, and shielding my face with my coat, watched his movements. Whether or not any one had told him which skylight was the right one, I don't know, but he did not hesitate a minute, but ran up to one, kicked it in, and swung himself through. After a little, he jumped out again, and then reached down and drew up the old woman. She was n't bigger than a ten-year-old, hardly, and could n't have weighed over eighty pounds, at the most. Tam lifted her as easy as if she been a baby, and brought her to the edge of the building. Then for a minute he seemed at loss, till he saw me. Before I could decide what was best, he sung out, —

"'Watch out, Sam Putnam!' and tossed the little woman right into my arms. I had my legs wound round the tree with, what I thought, was a good hold, but it almost upset me. Still I managed to cling on and catch the old woman. She was trembling all over, poor body, and muttering prayers, but she never screeched or strug gled a bit. By the time I had recovered myself, Tam was with me, and between us we got her down to the ground in safety."

"The people must have gone wild over such a rescue."

"They did; but Tam disappeared at once, and even I could n't find him for nearly two weeks. I don't know as I would have found him then if he had n't been praying; and speaking of that, his prayers have been to me more than words can express. It was poor Tam McDonald that kept alive in my breast the wish for a better life. He did not know it, but the influence of his life upon me was more than that of any other Christian that I ever knew."

"This fact of our individual influence frightens me," said the younger man, musingly. "It seems always with us, and strongest when we are off our guard."

"Do *you* feel that way?" was the surprised query. "Why, I s'posed that was peculiar to me! And I 've wished with all my heart that there was in the Bible some prayer that I could get hold of, that I might keep a Christian tongue in my head when I *am* off guard."

"'Set a watch, O Lord, before my mouth: Keep the door of my lips,'" repeated Chamber- lain, reverently.

XXIII.

Gaffney's·Luck.

"THERE is never any bad accident happens
to a drunken man," said Swinert, to the
crowd who were sitting on the "casting bench,"
eating their dinners. "Now, there is Gaffney. I
have seen him drunk as a fiddler, in all
sorts of dangerous places, and he always came
out straight. If a sober man had gone through
with one-half of what he has, he would have
been killed a half-dozen times."

"That's true," was the universal assent.

"Now, when he went to McCloskey's funeral,
and drove his team off of the railroad bridge,
killing the horse and smashing the carriage, he
was not hurt a whit. Any sober man would
have been dashed to pieces."

"No doubt of it," agreed all.

"And when he fell under the fly-wheel of the
engine and had the clothes all scorched off of
his back, but came out as lively as a cricket,

—a decent, honest man would have been knocked to inch bits."

"He would that."

"Then there was the time he got full, and tried to hang himself in Bob Jones's barn, and the rope broke three times. S'pose it would have broken with a teetotaler?"

"No, sir!" chimed the audience.

The whistle blew, and the group scrambled down from their seats and hurried away to work. At the end of the procession staggered Gaffney. He had been close by when they were discussing him, but was too drunk to catch the drift of their remarks. There was something a little singular about his numerous escapades. He never seemed to get badly injured, and yet he was continually in trouble. So famed was he for his escapes, that the phrase, "Gaffney's luck," was often used in the mill to express a never-varying good fortune that pulled its possessor through the most threatening disasters.

With a jolly, unstable gait, he followed in the rear of the crowd. He was a privileged character in the mill, and was allowed to go and come as he pleased. With no thought of going to work, he entered the grinding-room, and looked about for amusement. He usually chose this room for larks, as the men were all on piece-work and were not obliged to attend closely to their occupation at all times. Among the grinders was a young Frenchman, whom it was his special delight to torture. He was a good, conscientious workman, but very timid. Whenever he saw his tormentor coming, even though the latter had no hostile design, he turned scarlet, and fidgeted in his seat, and, if possible, escaped. He now saw him, and, slipping down from his lofty seat in the wooden saddle over the whirling grindstone, he hurried off to a safe distance and stood, anxiously regarding his foe.

Gaffney looked at him in ludicrous contempt, and then made his way up to the stone. The great wheel of granite was whirling so rapidly and evenly that it seemed not to move. It was beautifully "trued," and in just the condition to do the best work. With particular care and cumbrousness the drunken wag climbed into the saddle and picked up a file, then glanced over his shoulder, in exact imitation of the frightened Frenchman. The caricature caught the eyes of the workmen, and they roared with laughter. The one to whom the stone belonged came slowly and hesitatingly forward, sorely afraid to venture near, and just as much afraid to stay away.

"Look here, Parley Voo. See me grind for you. You should put the end of the file on the stones, so as to make a decent little groove, like this," remarked Gaffney.

He placed the end of the file as stated, and dug a deep grove in the smooth surface. The Frenchman uttered a cry of anguish.

"Hear him applaud me," said Gaffney. "No bokays, please. I'm a very modest man, I am. Let me do as I wish, and don't compliment me."

The crowd shouted in applause, for the Frenchman, with his quiet, cowardly ways, and his money-getting and money-saving qualities, was not a favorite. To be sure, two or three of the older men spoke in disapproval, but they were not heard, nor did they expect to be. To the undisguised delight of the lookers-on, Gaffney still sat in the wooden saddle, ludicrously imitating the motions of his victim. It was cruel sport. The Frenchman suffered so that he danced up and down in agony. From one to another he looked for relief, with extravagant gestures and unintelligible appeals, but he only met mirthful faces, devoid of sympathy. In the midst, however, of their laughter and shouting, there came a fierce crash. The air was filled with bits of plank, dust, and debris. For an instant none knew what had happened. Then they saw that the swift-whirling stone, over which the drunken man had been seated, had torn loose from its shaft, and, in three fragments, had crashed through the partitions, in a mad flight into the yard. A dozen feet away lay a helpless figure, the blood slowly oozing from his mouth. It was Gaffney. The rough men took him up carefully, and bore him away to a quiet room, where his wounds could be examined, and the crowd kept at bay. After an anxious half-hour on the part of the men, word came that the injuries were not serious, — that he would recover.

"Just as I said," remarked Swinert. "You cannot kill a drunken man; some power protects them."

"Gaffney's luck," echoed the crowd.

There was more truth in the saying than they knew, for that accident was the best good fortune that ever the poor fellow had. He was taken to a cottage not far from the mill, as his home was not fit to nurse a savage in, and his wife was away on a drunken spree. Here he had an opportunity to reflect on his past life. He could get no liquor, and after the first crazy thirst passed away, he began, with the peculiar philosophical spirit that he possessed, to institute comparisons, and think things over, in a manner that would have been impossible, had he been drinking his usual allowance.

One afternoon, when deep in his cogitations, a knock fell on the door, and in came a young lady. The sick man glanced up in surprise, and a frown gathered on his brow. He did n't want to be "missionaried."

"Excuse me, Miss," he said, "but perhaps you did n't know that I was sufferin' from small-pox?"

"No, sir, I did not know it," she said, as she seated herself. "This is Mr. Gaffney, is it not, and how is the broken arm?"

"Better," was the surprised reply. "Say,— Miss, is my name on the door-plate?"

"I think not. I do not believe the house has such a thing."

"I know it did n't before I was sick, but I did n't know but they had put one on it for the use of the ministers, and colporters, and evangelists. It saves their knocking and en-quiring."

"I came from the mission-school. My name is Whitney," said the lady.

"Well, I 'll be blamed! Did you think maybe you might get me to sign the pledge?"

"Perhaps so."

"And give up smoking, too?"

"If you feel inclined."

"Stop cussin' and swearin', of course?"

"Certainly."

"Join the mission-school, and become pious?"

"I hope so."

"Well, I don't know about that. Where is John Temple?"

That question was one that every scoffer in the village asked, when he intended to knock any religious fact to pieces.

"I do not think that is your affair. The Lord knows where he is, and all he requires of you, is to get in the right place yourself."

"Well, I was quite impressed by a little talk that I had with Mr. Chamberlain, not long ago, but when he pointed out Temple as an example, and I found him howling drunk, it rather took the edge off his remarks."

"Let us not talk of Temple. He must answer to God alone. I believe that one day he will be saved, even if he did fall in so terrible a manner. The question is, are you willing to be saved from your appetite for liquor?"

"Certainly, I am, Miss, if it can be done, which it can't," was the positive reply. "You can't argue me into that."

"I cannot argue at all, but I know what I

believe," replied Miriam, with a tremble in her voice. "There are numbers praying for you every day. We want you to know that at half-past six every evening we pray that the Lord will heal your body, and heal your soul, and we believe He is going to do it."

"It's an awful waste of time," said Gaffney. "Now if you prayed for Sam Putnam, who is some good, it would be worth while, but to pray for me! Pshaw! I call it foolishness."

"We did pray for Sam Putnam, and he has joined us, and is praying for you."

"Why don't he come and talk to me, and argue a little?"

"All the argument necessary you will find in this Bible, which is his gift to you. He prefers to spend his time in praying for you."

"Well, I hope you will succeed," said Gaffney, as Miriam took leave.

"We shall," was the reply, with a bright smile.

Moving as much as his bandages would permit, the wounded man reached out for the volume that Putnam had sent. During the visit of the fair, young missionary, he had been regarding it with an interest that amounted almost to eagerness, although veiled by a pretense at skeptical argument. Once in his hand, he sank back exhausted, but with a look of content on his face that his sufferings would hardly warrant.

"So, they are sure of success, are they?" he murmured, a glow appearing on his cheek. "Sure to save me. And they are praying for you, Gaffney, and my old woman, too, God pity her! She was once a decent, tidy body, as fine-looking as any of them. Mayhap if she had got a better man she might have been all right now. Praying for me! Well, that beats every thing. I wish they knew how happy that makes me feel, only I should never have the cheek to tell them, after all I've been and done."

With a motion of affection and reverence, he slipped Putnam's gift under his pillow, and, still holding his hand on it, closed his eyes, not to sleep, but the better to think. Breaking rudely into his day-dreams came a heavy step on the stairs, the latch lifted, and Josselyn came in. His face was pale, and he looked exceedingly disturbed.

"How do you get on?" he enquired of the invalid.

"First-class."

"Be round in time for the monthly meeting?" The other shook his head.

"You won't be well enough to come?" persisted Josselyn, with an accent of eagerness that he seemed unable, wholly, to suppress.

Gaffney eyed him distrustfully.

"I suppose," he said, a dangerous light coming into his eyes, and the muscles on his bared arm swelling as his hand convulsively grasped the hidden volume, — "I suppose if you saw a poor, tired sailor, wrecked, crawling up on a rock, with only just strength enough to get on to it, you would go down and shove him back into the water, and then laugh at his drowning agony; would n't you?"

"What do you mean?" was the choked reply.

"Why, if you saw a man, who had never done you any harm, trying, by the grace of God, to get rid of a habit that was destroying him, and you knew his weakness, you would pull him down and get him back into it, would n't you?"

"I know I am guilty; but if ever a man has suffered for such a sin, it has been me. At the time, it seemed a little thing. I put the boys up to it for a mere lark; and though I in no way justify my action, they carried it further than I expected."

"Yet that plan dashed me down when I had at last climbed upon the Rock, — when I was helped upon the Rock," said Gaffney, a wail in his voice that made the other shiver.

"Then you intend to go to the monthly meetings? You will take up the old life?" asked Josselyn.

"Take it up again, — no!" thundered the sick man, amazed at what he deemed the other's anxiety to keep him among the liquor-drinkers. "I have got my lesson. I shall know enough to keep out of temptation now; I was too sure last time, and I have suffered for it. Now I shall keep away from all sight and smell of liquor, — I 've learned my lesson."

"Thank God!" ejaculated Josselyn.

"What for?"

"That you are saved; that you are not going back to the old life. Do you know that *I* have *prayed?*—that I have been on my knees, asking God to keep you from going to ruin on my account? And I believe he has heard my prayer."

Gaffney grew very sober. Finally he said, —

"I 'm mighty glad for you; but I 've just found out something that makes me feel kinder bad, too."

"What is it?"

"Well, now you were praying for me, and I was feeling bitter toward you. If I had been the least sort of a Christian, I would have been pray-

ing for you. Well, I *believe*, anyhow, and as
soon as I can, I'll ketch on to the rest. Give
us your hand, old man; we will travel this new
path together. And when you go into the mill
to-morrow morning, and some one mentions 'Gaffney's Luck,' just tell them of this last good fortune that has come to me. Tell them to drop
it, and I'll **give them the whole story."**

XXIV.

Lamson's · Triumph.

FOR some reason, a great and sudden change had come over Miriam Whitney. Not that she was less lovable or less cheerful when among her friends, but she seemed to have lost all interest in the affairs at the North Church, and if one could observe her closely, it would be seen that she constantly avoided the places where Chamberlain was likely to be found. As a strong friendship had sprung up between them prior to this, it troubled the young man not a little. After the death of Jamie, the cripple, Miriam had done much to comfort the stricken grandmother, and in her frequent visits found a warm welcome.

"You're looking poorly, dear," said the keen-eyed little woman, laying down her knitting-needles and surveying her visitor anxiously, on one of these occasions.

"I do not feel very strong," acknowledged Miriam, flushing. "I have n't slept well of late."

"Do you lie with yeer head to the Noorth?"

"I don't know," said she, faintly smiling.

"Now, Mr. Chamberlain, the last time he called, were advising me aboot this verra point, as I had been telling him that since Jamie's death I were wakeful. He said that there were those who believed that if one turned their bed so that the head was Noorth, and the foot Sooth, one could sleep better. But he said when he were sleepless, he started out and walked all the neet, and then next neet he slept. And what led me to think of him, there he is yonder, coming down the hill."

The young lady looked up the street. The erect, familiar figure was rapidly nearing the house.

"He won't come in here, will he?" she said helplessly.

"He rarely passes without a word," responded the old lady, complacently.

"I don't want to see him, I can't see him!" said Miriam, plaintively. "What shall I do?"

"Poor bairn, your nerves are all unstrung; ye can slip into the bedroom yonder and lie doon and rest; he 'll not be long here."

With a thankful smile, she gathered up her

wraps, slipped into the cosy room, closed tl door, and in a moment heard the pleasant voic of the caller mingling with that of the Scotcl woman.

"I brought down that volume of Burns Poems," she heard him say, "Burns has always been a favorite of mine. I remember when a youngster, poring over the book by the hour. Indeed I think it is from him that I imbibed my love for the Scotch."

"My gude-mon used to read the 'Cotter's Saturday Neet,'" said Mrs. Bruce, with a slight tremble in her voice. "It's lang years since I've heard it. Would it be asking too much if I wished ye to read a part of it?"

"Not at all, if you can stand my pronunciation," was the reply.

Throughout the whole of the sweet poem, the rich, strong voice of the young man rose and fell in harmony with the matchless thought. The sound welled in through the wide crack over the sagging bedroom door, and the trembling girl in the chintz-covered rocking-chair, fearful almost to breathe, lest her presence be suspected, hid her face in her hands, while the hot tears flowed unrestrained.

"Ye need not tell me that yeer mother was not a Scotch lassie," said the old lady, wiping her eyes. " How else could ye have gotten the dialect so perfect ? "

" I think it must be because I have always enjoyed talking with your people," replied he, smiling, "but my pronunciation does not suit me yet. The genuine, fascinating burr is not there, and I am doubtful if any but a native of Scotland can ever acquire it."

" Ye should hear some of the elocutionary students from the town read it," said Mrs. Bruce. " Eh, it's enough to make one weep. They have it mixed up with ¯Irish, and such folly as they make of it is beyond compreheension."

" I have heard them. They are thought very fine by some audiences, but they should never air themselves before the Scotch."

Chamberlain took out his watch, and, looking at it with some surprise, said : " It is later than I thought, I must go." Then, taking the old lady's hand, · he asked if there was any thing that she lacked, as kindly and gently as if he had been her son.

When the little woman entered the bedroom, Miriam was sobbing bitterly.

" Eh, my poor bairnie, here is trouble of which you friends ken naething ; heartache that nane but woman can bear. Is not that it, lassie ? "

"Yes," was the faint response.

"Aweel, darling, it's our lot to suffer. I have felt at times as if the end had come, as if I could not stand more. Those for whom I would gladly have given life have been taken. I have wept till my tears are all gone. Now I can but pray to the Loord for help."

The little woman soothed, petted, and crooned over her until the storm of grief passed, and then bathed her face and eyes, and arranged her hair.

"Forgive an auld wife's question, dearie," she said, as Miriam stood ready to depart. "Are ye quite sure that you are right in yeer sorrow?"

"Yes," was the answer, with decision that left no room for misunderstanding, "very, very sure."

"Aweel," soliloquized the Scotchwoman, after her visitor had gone. "It's a sore pity if they maun not be brought thegither. So bonny and weel-matched a pair are seldom seen. I must not, I daur not meddle with it, but if matches are made in heaven, the Loord grant that this may be ain."

As for Miriam, although not for the world would she have acknowledged an affection for Chamberlain to any of her friends in the upper

town, yet with lowly Mrs. Bruce she felt wholly
safe. Possessed of a most positive conviction that
there was an insurmountable barrier between
them, — a barrier, not of station, nor of wealth,
but one arising from a clouded and disgraceful
early record on his part. The knowledge that
she had all came from Lamson, and it was not
wonderful that he maligned his rival to the best
of his ability, and did it in a way that made it
seem the merest accident of speech.

During the past few months Lamson had been
a frequent visitor at the Whitneys'. With unob-
trusive persistence he worked his way into the
almost daily presence of the father and daughter,
until he came to be an accustomed member of
the small family circle. Miss Whitney at first
entertained a mild dislike for him, but the courtesy with which he ever addressed her and the
tact he exercised in letting her alone, made her
grateful, and she soon learned to tolerate him.

In place of the sharp pain that she had felt
when she had learned that Chamberlain was so
weak and unworthy, came an indifference to almost
every thing that took the zest and the poetry
out of life. Under the ordeal she had grown pale,
and her voice had a faint, hardly noticeable
plaintiveness that told of tears shed in secret.
it was pitiful, or would have been had one pen-

etration sufficient to read her beautiful face, to note the effort made by her to be interested in those around her, and in quiet charities, and the failure of it all.

Realizing her own weakness, she came to admire the strength of the silent gentleman who was so often before her. By degrees he began to lead her into conversation, in which she, strangely enough, did most of the talking.

The power that he exercised in interesting her in things to which she had thought herself forever careless, surprised, fascinated her. Mingling with the half-smothered pain in her heart, came the distinct assertion of her father, told with pleasure, that this man loved her. It insinuated itself more than once into her mind as she talked with him. It was only when she was with him that she indulged this idea; it was only when his keen eyes were sparkling with power that she felt thrilled by some poet from which he quoted. It was only in his immediate presence that the image of her love grew misty and far away. When she was alone, the old ache was there, and the dreary helplessness that had been lifted for a few moments by the will of the lawyer, closed around again with a deeper gloom.

Gradually the intimacy between Mr. Whitney

and the agent, which had been the excuse for his many calls at the house, grew less, while a new one was formed between the latter and Miriam. Just how it was that the father drifted into the background and changed places with his daughter could hardly be told. That it was, ere he was aware, the established order of things, the gentleman finally discovered, and was far from being displeased.

Resistance to a hidden, unsuspected foe, is out of the question. An individual who gains advantage after advantage, without the least show of exultation, who conquers but indulges no triumph, is an enemy to be feared. Such was Lamson. No sign that he knew anything of the power that he exerted came to the surface. If Miss Whitney was silent and downcast, and did not choose to be entertained, he made her forget her troubles by some word or thought, in which there was infinite skill. When she discovered that in spite of adverse resolve, she was forsaking her clinging misery, and felt a flash of anger against him as the direct cause of her forgetfulness, he was unmoved as ever, and apparently had no knowledge of what he had accomplished. This marble calmness was the fortress of his strength. Once assumed, he was impenetrable. To be sure he recalled the first of his visits at the Whitney mansion, and the coolness with which his advances toward Miriam had been received. He remembered the favor shown Chamberlain, until checked by his insinuations, and the remembrance of it, even in the present plenitude of his power, galled him. He was not suspected of vanity, yet his conceit was overpowering; although so determined was the cast of his character, that it was ever held under and hidden from view. His guile partook of the features of positive genius. Were Mr. Whitney with all of his shrewdness and his keen intuitions questioned, he could not have advanced a single word or expression of Lamson's, that mirrored aught but good. This may have been in part due to the influence that his place in the church inspired. But a more excellent reason was that he had the faculty for playing the part of a Christian gentleman to the last limit of perfection.

In a measure, Miriam felt as did her father. There was nothing with which to find fault. He was so courteously master of himself at all times; never intruding; ever foremost in giving to all charitable enterprises, — she had absolutely nothing to reinforce the vague distrust in her heart, and was at a loss to comprehend it. Often she wondered what she really did feel toward this omnipresence in faultless broadcloth. If she could not divine, he well knew. His finger was on her pulse and marked its every beat. The whole violent nature of the mill agent was concentrated in, not a desire, but a resolve to marry Miriam Whitney. Whatever stood in the way should be removed or trampled under foot. Whoever interfered, let him beware. A single, unflinching resolve is a fearful thing to face. All that grit and pluck mean to the sporting man were expressed in his fixed determination, and he was on that ground alone almost certain to succeed.

The majority of people plod through life eyeless, earless. Broadsides of hints and suggestions as to the character, disposition, aims, and abilities of those with whom they have to do are fired at them, and they know nothing of them. They persuade themselves that they can read character, while they know not the initial letter of its alphabet. Worthies of this ilk pronounced Lamson a perfect gentleman, — a modest, retiring man, whose quietness was akin to diffidence. To the few who could read the average man, he was distant from pride of birth and station; none in the upper settlement knew him as he was. Of all the members of the North Church not one read his character with the single exception of Chamberlain, and he was not likely to bruit his knowledge to the world at large.

All through the summer, — the last summer of Chamberlain's apprenticeship, — this quiet, unsuspected wooing went on. At every move Miriam lost, Lamson gained. In his moments alone his face wore a look of proud strength, — hers one of unrelieved sadness. At times she half realized her position, but was without force to resist. No word of love had this silent visitor spoken, yet he felt as sure of possessing her as if she wore the betrothal ring. His thought was not that he should win, but that he had won.

Since he had become so intimate with the Whitneys, the visits to the mill village had become less frequent. Not that Miriam had lost her interest in the little ones that she taught when opportunity offered, but rather from the excuses made by her father for staying away. It did not occur to either that this was due to Lamson's influence, yet that was it. He said very little about the operatives. The fact that they were wretched from drink and persistent neglect, was sadly acknowledged by him, and he had expressed in words a certain sympathy for them, but he could do nothing to help them. Miriam, in the first flush of her enthusiasm, had appealed to him to do something for Steep Street, and had been quieted by the promise of an investigation, but it never came. None are so hard to combat as those who will not fight. The lawyer quietly held his own way without comment, and his iron will and great tact gradually drew the little family away from the mill folk. With Chamberlain out of the field, it was not hard to make them forgetful of the operatives. For a time it seemed as if all that had been done was to be entirely swept away by the wave of wickedness that rolled in. Lamson, perhaps, more than any other, saw what was going on, yet he viewed it calmly, apparently neither lifting his hand to help nor to hinder.

XXV.

"As·the·Fool·Dieth."

IN spite of Mrs. Bowman's energetic and frequently repeated protests, Pfaff had remained
at her house. At first, he had occupied Chamberlain's room, but that being too near the
noisy street, he was moved to one in the
rear. For more than a week he was a very
sick man. In his delirium, he divulged so much
of the raid on the store, that, had Chamberlain
not known all about it from Sam Putnam, he
would have been fully posted. When he became
sane he was very uneasy, and made one of the
most thankless of patients. Mrs. Bowman exerted herself to do all that could possibly be
done for him, but he was not slow to show his
dislike for her.

Whether he ever had a conscience is a question. No signs of such a regulator were ever
detected by those who were familiar with him.
While he remained there, he did not lack for
subjects to think about; for, during his conva-

lescence, his landlady daily suggested to him the many evil deeds that he had committed, and warned him of the terrible punishment that was in store for him.

Since the mission had been started, numbers of the lady teachers had made it a point to call on the sick in the mill village. Pfaff was not neglected in these calls. No matter what was said, whether he was read with, or prayed for, he preserved the same imperturbable countenance, and his thoughts, if he had any, were never divulged. There were those who scoffed at the idea of calling on the sick in this manner, and inquired what good it did, pointing to Pfaff as an example. Could they have gauged the good will that it brought forth, from the lookers-on among the mill folks, their question would have been fully answered.

As the sick man gained in health, he was tormented by a raging thirst for stimulants. He suggested to the physician, several times, in a whisper, that a little whiskey would do him more good than any thing else, but his hint was quickly rebuked. Not understanding Chamberlain, he attempted to bribe him to bring a pint, offering a fabulous price, and was astonished at his refusal. He tried every way that his ingenuity could devise, but in each case was check mated. A careful watch was kept over him, and, lest he should, in a fit of momentary strength, attempt to go for it himself, his boots and most of his clothes were put away and locked up for safe keeping. Now that he was gaining so rapidly, and entirely free from delirium, a watcher was not needed. Chamberlain, however, sleeping across the hall, left the door of his room ajar, so that he could hear any movement.

One night, when all in the house were asleep, except himself, Pfaff arose, shut the door, and lighted a lamp. With a trembling, nervous strength, he hunted for his clothes, and grew black with rage at not finding them. Urged by the terrible thirst that had for days been tormenting him, he resolved to go to his store and satisfy it, come what would. He had no fear of meeting any one on the street, as it was late and was mid-week. The fact that his boots were removed, only increased the obstinacy of his purpose

He hesitated a little over the absence of coat and vest, and ended by wrapping a comforter over his shoulders. Thus equipped, he stole out of the room. With every faculty quickened by his mad desire, he opened and closed doors, never allowing a knob to rattle, or a hinge to squeak. If doors stuck at the bottom, he firmly lifted up till they swung free. His nervous acuteness forewarned him of a creaking stair, or a loose banister-round, and he descended to the basement as quietly as a shadow of the night.

The last barrier was successfully overcome, and he stood in his stocking-feet, wrapped in the comforter, bareheaded, in the little yard. Feverishly he exulted in his freedom as he sped down the street. Stumbling over tomato-cans, loose stones, and gutter-wreck, but oblivious to pain, he made straight for his store. No one met him. No arm was stretched out to save him. Passing around to the rear of the building, he entered through a window that he alone knew how to unfasten from the outside. Again he stood in his own bar-room. Once more he could, with unlimited resources, quench the burning thirst. He had circumvented his watcher; had braved the doctor. With an insane, half-articulate chuckle, not stopping to light a lamp, he groped his way behind the counter, and drank.

Morning dawned, and Mrs. Bowman, as usual, with anger in her heart, and dire admonition on her lips, entered the sick room, bearing the invalid's breakfast. The bed was empty!

In great surprise, she stood, looking about, hardly able to credit the evidence of her senses. He had gone, and so had her best comforter, as her quick eye discovered. Gone without paying his board, and she slaving day and night for him, just to please the mission folks! With a most emphatic tread, she went back to the kitchen, and began her day's work, without mentioning her discovery. Soon Chamberlain came running down-stairs.

"Is Pfaff here?" he demanded, looking about the room.

"No, he is not."

"Where is he?"

"How should I know? When I carried up his breakfast, a while ago, he was gone, and I am glad of it. He stole my best comforter."

"But his clothes are locked up."

"Mercy! so they are! and his boots, too!" said Mrs. Bowman, awaking to the fact that it might be more than the mere removal from one boarding-house to the other.

To assure themselves, they went to the closet, and found his things resting quietly in their places, not having been disturbed.

"Most likely he took some one else's things," said the landlady.

But a search and close inquiry revealed no such appropriation.

"He must have wanted to go dreadful bad, — barefooted, and in his shirt-sleeves, — after all I've done for him," remarked Mrs. Bowman.

"It was rum he was after," said her son. "A rum-lover will go through any thing to get it. I bet at this minute he is at some of the shanties down-street, dead drunk."

"If he is, it will kill him," said Chamberlain.

"Oh, I guess not. It is wonderful, what a drinking man can stand. I don't know but it will be a good thing for him. He has been pining for it for some time. Perhaps, after all, it was what he needed. Nature knows," remarked a neighbor, who had dropped in, with a feeling that all true Steep Streeters had, "that there was something goin' on."

"Nature knows," almost screamed Mrs. Bowman. "It isn't *nature* that makes a man love drink! It is the devil, and his own appetite, that he has for years cultivated! And I tell you, if I hear any more of your bar-room sermons, I'll show you that this isn't a saloon, or a family rum-store, but an honest, temperance house."

Considerably abashed, the man slunk away Soon after, the doctor came. He looked very grave, when they told him about the patient.

"Where would he be likely to go?" he inquired, of Rev.

"To McShares," was the answer. At once they all went to this shanty, but were told that no trace of the sick man had been seen.

At first the physician was inclined to doubt, but the honest air of the proprietor of the house finally assured him that he was speaking the truth, and that they must look further.

Somebody suggested the store, and the little party of searchers went toward it. When they reached the place, and knocked on the door, quite a crowd collected, to see what was going on. Up and down the street, the people, seeing the gathering, threw up windows, and thrust out uncombed heads. The gamins, running from all sides, packed close to the doctor, who was making the building ring with his vigorous knocking.

"Say, Mister, they is a winder opin round back of the store. I seen it," called a youngster.

Learning that the statement was true, the physician went round to the rear and climbed in, leaving Chamberlain to keep the crowd back. A minute later he came to the window.

"He is here," he said.

"Why does n't he unlock the door? We want to drink his health," said one of the crowd.

"He is dead," said the doctor, gravely.

It was even so. Behind the counter, in a little pool of liquor, that had run out of a half emptied bottle, his face resting against a cask of ale, lay the rumseller. His thirst had been quenched, never again to be awakened.

The news fell upon the gathered crowd with startling effect. The few who forced their way in, and saw the bloated, disfigured face, the half-dressed form, the shoeless feet, came back and told it with genuine horror. Never had such a temperance sermon been preached in Steelville as this mass of degraded clay now preached. Every teller of the story, whether liquor-lover or hater, was doing good work for his neighbors, if not for himself. Steep Street, at last, had a lesson that equalled its needs.

Pfaff was buried. As was the custom in the mill village, there was a large funeral. Those whom he had most injured, — the hard drinkers, — were loudest in their expressions of regret. In the little cemetery, back of the village, he was laid, — to be forgotten as all supposed. When his death was announced, relatives appeared and claiming his property received it. They attempted to continue the store, but through the efforts of Chamberlain, backed by a strong public sentiment, were refused, and the " Hole in the Wall" was forever stopped up. After the division of the property no money remained for a headstone. Mrs. Bowman, indignant that it should be so, said that at her own expense she would erect one. No one objected. Three weeks afterward, a slab, carefully cased, was carried to the cemetcry and erected. For a day or two, no one had curiosity enough to see what it said. At length, one Steep-street gossip languidly strolled over and after standing before it, in amazement for ten minutes, almost ran back to the village. Soon others came. Then others. The graveyard never before had so many visitors. Even the Wilson monument, of Scotch granite, had not attracted so much attention. Scores came from the upper village. From far and near, from the outlying districts, people journeyed to read the inscription that was on the plain stone, which the hand of charity had erected ; it read : —

" Here lies the body of

" Jacob Pfaff, — rumseller,

" Murderer of John Bowman, Jacob Randall, William Seaforth, Gabriel More, Edmund Johnson, Patrick White and Wife, Timothy Sedgwick, Randall Wilson, Tom McCarty, John Ferguson and four Sons, Tobey Escott, Richard Gobbin, Jacob Vrail, and many more whose names cannot be recalled, both of Men and Women, Fathers, Mothers, and Little Children.

" When he shall be judged let him be condemned. — Ps. 109:7.

" Let the extortioner catch all that he hath, and let strangers spoil his labor. — Ps. 109:11.

" Because that he remembered not to show mercy, but persecuted the poor and needy man, that he might even slay the broken in heart. — Ps. 109 16."

XXVI.

Down·the·River.

BOUT this time, Mr. Lamson received a telegram, which, to judge by its effect upon him, did not contain good news. After its perusal, he paced the floor for an hour, his beetling brows bent in deep thought. As one result of this hour of reflection, the rest of the day was spent at home in burning certain papers and the few business letters that he had preserved. He then sent an answer to the message that had so agitated him.

At ten that evening, a man emerged from the grove at the rear of the house, and advancing cautiously to a side door, entered. With accustomed step he made his way to the lawyer's study, and was at once welcomed.

"You received my telegram?" said the stranger, taking off his slouch hat and revealing a foxy physiognomy, that alone might have stamped him as a sharper.

"Yes," was the reply. "Why could you not get cash?"

"I did at the last moment."

"Has the sale indeed been made?" was the delighted inquiry.

"Yes, I have the cash here in my bag."

"Good! now all will be right. I can make the investment that I wished, and reap a golden harvest."

The other made no reply, but watched the agent's face with the keenest attention, as if feeling that his partner was about to do something' in which he was to have no share. He kept this attentive air through the evening, as they talked on various topics. Lamson was, as ever, quiet and controlled in his expressions, yet a bright spot burning on each cheek, and the dilated pupils of his eyes, showed that he was laboring under excitement. His friend talked with a purpose, keenly alive to every hint that voice or countenance might suggest. The other knew that he was being closely observed, that the man before him was schooled in reading men, and the knowledge made him restive. He had found it necessary to take him into partial confidence, and had purchased his co-operation at a large price, but he also had plans that he did not intend to divulge. He therefore guarded

every word, although speaking with assumed can-
dor. It was quite late when the stranger departed, and although weary to the last pitch of
endurance, Lamson collected a few papers and
a large bundle of bills, and prepared to go out
into the night.

When all was prepared, he slipped out of the
back door, quietly locking it, and stood for an
instant looking up at his mother's window.
After a mute farewell, he dashed away a tear,
and noiselessly crossing the yard, entered the
grove at the rear of the estate, and was soon
threading its broad paths towards the river.

Had any of his friends encountered him at
that moment, it is doubtful if they would have
recognized him. Clad in a suit of the coarsest
material, his beard and mustache shaved off,
his thick hair cut close, hands and face purposely roughened, he was no longer the easy,
polished gentleman, but had become a flat-footed,
heavy-visaged laborer. His disguise was perfect,
and with the great self-command and abundant
mimicry that characterized him, there was little
fear of detection.

The grove sloped gradually to the river below
the mills. Taking a well-kept path, he soon
gained the neat wharf, to which was tied a
pretty wherry. One might reasonably presume

that this boat was to aid in the flight, but it was not. A few rods further down, where a dense thicket pressed so closely to the water's edge that its advance guard stretched over and dipped its branches in the stream, was a small canvas canoe. With some difficulty, it was drawn from its security and laid alongside the wharf. Carefully the valise was placed in it, and then with more skill than one would expect from so heavily built a personage, he stepped in, gave the wharf a powerful shove with the paddle, and was floating in mid-stream.

There was hardly any current in the black, narrow river, and letting the boat drift, he waited to discover, if possible, whether he had been followed. Fully aware that he could not trust his partner in the polish business, and anxious to destroy every clue to the manner in which he had left Steelville, he waited until sure that no one was watching him from the deep shadows of the pines in the grove.

The last doubt dispelled, he dipped the paddle into the still water and moved down stream. A few strokes, and rounding a bend, he was alone — alone on the river, dead to the Steelville world.

The stream upon which he had embarked was the same that furnished power for the file-fac-

tory, and from where he floated he could hear
the water roaring over the dam, a half mile
away. It was a deep, inky river, and from boyhood Lamson had known every part of it. He
had waded in the bubbling mud of its 'lagoons
for water-lilies, fished in all its pools, bathed,
boated, and skated its entire length; hence
when his eyes became accustomed to the darkness, he was as much at home as he would
have been on the highway before his house.

Shut in by the walls of trees that grew down
to the river's edge, he moved along with no
sound but the quick plunge of the startled muskrat, the hoarse double bass of the bull-frog,
and the many voices that are audible only at
night. Such sounds make silence more profound.
There is no loneliness so complete as that which
comes over one in the midst of noisy, unsym-
pathetic life. So the fugitive, listening to the
uncouth language of reptile and insect, which
mingled with the gurgle of the water as it was
parted by the sharp prow of his boat, felt oppressed, as if he were threading an unknown
river in a planet which none but he had ever
before visited. It was this overpowering loneliness that made him suddenly cringe when the
swift wing of some bird of night cut the air
close to him, or when the wheeling, invisible

bats snapped their sharp teeth over some appe-
tising insect that the reedy banks afforded.

The first half mile of the liquid trail was
between thickets of trees. Their brooding shadows, even in the darkness, shrouded the river
in a denser gloom. Here and there the whited
skeleton of some forest tree, from which the
water had sucked all vitality, stood a rigid, familiar landmark. An occasional phosphorescent
stump glowed uncannily on the margin of the
stream. At times, the forest sentinels leaned far
over, till one seemed to be gliding through a
tunnel, and again they opened wide and allowed
the faint color of the clouds above to sift down
between their ranks. With carefulness, the voy-
ager felt his way along; turning perilous corners,
dodging snags that would have pierced the painted
canvas and defeated all for which he was working. Guarding against every danger, his whole
attention bent on the few feet that were visible
in front of the canoe, he paddled cautiously on-
ward.

Following the prodigal curves and bends that
doubled the distance, the light craft soon slipped
out of the dense woods into a tract of country
where only occasional clumps of oaks, interspersed
by thickets of alders and dwarf willows, obtained
foothold on the banks. On either side, leading

from the main stream, were shallow bayous crowded with lily-pads, and in the season, holding thousands of lovely Nymphæ. A short distance below was a low bridge of poles, used by the farmers when getting wood or hay. Below this the banks were entirely free from trees. On both sides stretched square miles of prairie meadow. The broad fields, as far as the eye could reach, were alive with twinkling fire-flies. Far up on "Flint Hill," a lofty eminence in the rear of Steelville, gleamed a solitary light. Looking ahead through the gloom, a ghostly shroud of river-mist could be barely discerned, marking accurately the course of the stream.

With more confidence, and less of overwhelming loneliness, the fugitive dipped the paddle deeper and oftener, sending the boat at a more rapid rate on its way. Yet, even here the dangers of navigation at night were not trifling. There were sudden shallows where the keel grated ominously; drift-wood logs that stuck endwise up-stream, as if trying to shoulder the crowding water back; masses of matted river-grass, that clung with obstinate tentacles to the boat's side, wrapped themselves about the paddle, and required vigorous efforts to shake them off.

Down-stream still, past forests of flags, where the bulrushes lifted their cockades like ramrods

in blossom; past the reedy houses of hundreds of
red-winged blackbirds. Does one ever forget one's
boyhood? Was it strange that unsentimental
Lamson, weighed down by a sense of isolation
and danger, should recall minutely the kingfishers' nests? the pickerel that he had captured
in certain shallows? the night-fishing with torches
for the wallowing horn-pouts? the best swimming
places?—all that made his early life so free and
happy?

At length he passed beneath the stone arch
of the railroad bridge. The river now ran close
beside a high ridge, a continuation of that upon
which the Whittier house was built. This ridge,
densely wooded with pine, maple, and oak, over
grown by tangled seines of thorny squirrel vine,
although so near the lower town, was not often
visited.

In its shadow the boat slid along till within
an eighth of a mile of the town, and then, where
a break occurred in the ridge, through which
trickled a tiny brook, Lamson stopped. Laying
aside the paddle, and catching the branches of
the thicket that completely hid the deep mouth
of the rivulet, he worked his way in with difficulty. Erelong the ashen keel of the canoe struck
bottom. Standing erect, his head buried in the
mass of vines and leaves, he felt along the steep

bank. In a moment he had discovered a stump clinging determinedly to the gravelly slope, and beneath, with one of its huge, bare roots for a threshhold, an untenanted muskrat hole. A few moments' work sufficed to enlarge the mouth of the miniature cave enough to admit the valise. Then, when it was carefully concealed, he pushed out into the stream again, aud paddling to the well-known " swimming hole," just below, landed.

It took but a short time to ballast the boat with stones, float down almost to the mill pond, land, cut two or three slits in the cloth sides, and send it out into deep water to sink with a remonstrating gurgle. The only clue to the manner in which he had left Steelville being thus destroyed, Lamson went to the little village and had breakfast. After lounging about for a little while, he bought a second - hand carpet - bag, transferred the contents of the valise to it, and started to walk the score of miles that intervened between him and the city. Why he feared to take the cars when so well disguised, does not appear. Perhaps it was from the impression that most defaulters, when apprehended, were found either on a train, or in some railway station.

Leaving him following the turnpike road toward the metropolis, we will turn back to the town from which he so hastily fled.

A sweet-faced lady, scrupulously dressed, was walking up Steep Street. Her appearance created a deal of attention, of which she was unconscious, as no one accosted her, except a few of the "gutter snipes," who challenge everybody. The walk was rather fatiguing, as her quickened breathing, and cheeks faintly tinged with red, suggested. At length she reached the upper end, and stood looking back over the wretched tenement-houses, the more distant mill buildings, and finally far away to the blue hills that were heaped up on the horizon.

"I will lift up mine eyes unto the hills from whence cometh my help," she murmured.

In the blue eyes was a pain that only the kindest eyes can express. An unselfish, loving look they held, that many a boy can recall when he thinks of his mother. Advancing to the Bowman cottage, she knocked.

"Is Mr. Chamberlain in?"

"Yes 'm. Won't you come in? I 'll call him."

Rob, with clumsy civility, led the way into the sitting-room, pushed forward the calico-covered rocking-chair, stumbled over the mat, and went for the lodger.

When the latter entered the room, the little woman rose, and with a sweet, anxious smile, asked, —

"Is this Mr. Chamberlain?"

"It is."

Without further words, the visitor stood before him, in unaccountable embarrassment. Chamberlain was too much surprised by her agitation to do more than seat her, and wait in silence for her to speak. He had seen her face before; where, he could not remember. She did not look like the kind of person who would come with a tale of trouble, or solicit alms, for her dress was rich. The more he looked, the more absurd this fancy seemed; for he could not but see her gold eye-glasses, costly lace, and expensive dress.

Fully aware that it was no ordinary matter that was thus overcoming her, by neither word nor act did he strive to hurry her confidence. At length she spoke:—

"You must pardon me," she said, in a voice a little broken; "but I have just lost my boy."

Chamberlain bowed sympathetically.

"I hardly know why I have come to you; but my boy often mentioned your name, and I thought possibly you might help me get trace of him."

Chamberlain, with quick perception, reasoned that the lad had run away.

"It is easy as a rule to trace runaways;

:hey either start for the prairie, or the sea. I do not doubt, if you put a good detective on his track, he can easily be found, and will be glad to return. How old is he?"

"You do not recognize me?" said the lady, a look of surprise on her face.

"I remember your face very distinctly, but I cannot recollect where I have seen you."

"I am Mr. Lamson's mother."

Then Chamberlain remembered and at once apologized, but was gracefully interrupted.

"You have met me but once, and then only for an instant. It would have been wonderful if you had remembered me. I am to blame. Had I not been troubled by my loss, I should have introduced myself. Do you suppose there is any means by which I can get word to my boy? He was your friend, can you not suggest a way?"

Chamberlain reflected. He had never known that Mrs. Lamson had a son other than the agent. He pictured a fifteen-year-old, with the same general make-up as the elder brother. The mother, as a matter of course, was troubled and anxious, but as he had told her the probabilities were that the boy could be found, not far away and all ready to return home. He was about again to assure her of this probable happy ter-mination, when she handed him a letter.

"This is a note he left," she said.

He opened it slowly, the troubled mother keep-ing her eyes fastened upon him to catch every expression written on his face. Surprise was the first emotion he experienced, for the letter was in the agent's well-known chirography. It was written on the File Company's letter-sheet, and must have been penned at the office. It read : —

"*Dear Mother,* — Business troubles have overwhelmed me, and I am forced at once to leave Steelville. Please do not worry. There would be no help for me if I remained here, as certain business transac-tions to which I was party, would be misconstrued and made to appear frauds. You know, my mother, that my integrity remains unshaken. I shall one day return free from all suspicion. You may not hear from me for some time, as it will be best not to give any of my enemies a clue to my where-abouts. Remember this, dear mother, if I am in any trouble that you can allevitate, you shall know it. Let this thought comfort you.

"Your loving son,

"EPHRAIM LAMSON."

Chamberlain's eyes were opened. It was not a younger son! It was the agent! The whole thing came before him in a flash. The "busi-ness troubles" were the discovery of his secret manufacture of polish, out of materials owned by the company, by help paid by the company. This was a most serious affair, for he had, during the weeks past, been making careful estimates of the amount of stock thus consumed, and found it was very large. Lamson's profits in the business must have netted him a snug little fortune. Since Sam had dismissed the night gang, there had been nothing done in the file-works in that line, and Chamberlain learned, by writing to the city agency, that the right of manufacture had been sold to a rival firm.

Just what to do in this crisis he did not know. As soon as he had discovered exactly how things stood, he wrote a letter to the attorney of two of the other members of the company who were, at the best, but small stockholders, requesting that the matter be looked into at once, and advising secrecy, that Lamson might be apprehended, and the stolen money refunded. In doing this, as was natural, he had many doubts, for it is easy for one to make a mistake, and accuse an innocent person. He was sorely puzzled by many things that came to light about the agent. At one time he had thought him a fraud, and at another believed that he was all right, and the reports about him were malicious slanders. Now, however, his sudden disappearance was an acknowledgment of guilt. From his reverie he awoke to the fact that the mother was patiently waiting for him to give her some encouragement.

"Do you know where he has gone?" she inquired.

"I am sorry to say, I do not," was the reply.

"Has he not made a great mistake, in going away like a criminal? Will not people say that he has done wrong and been forced to flee to save himself from punishment?"

"I fear they will."

"Mr. Chamberlain, a few days before my son went away, he told me of your hopes with regard to the mill. He said that you had learned the business thoroughly, and that in less than two weeks your probation would be up, and you will be the heaviest stockholder and virtually owner of the mills. You are acquainted with all the facts. Can you not prove to people that my son's intentions were good? He may have been unfortunate in some of his undertakings, but he certainly was not dishonest."

Chamberlain remained silent. There was now no doubt in his mind as to the rascality of the son, but he could not say so to the trusting mother. He could not shake her confidence in

her "boy," so he agreed to do all he conscientiously could to keep people from maligning
him. Even as he talked with her the probable
effect upon the business, of the sudden flight
of the agent, would obtrude itself. The works
were fortunately shut down for a week's repair-
ing. Before they started again, all must be
straight. The sensation of a new and heavy
weight of responsibility settled over Chamberlain. He knew that the agent was a man of
ability, and had managed the affairs of the
company so that they had prospered. He had
sometime expected to see to many things in
Lamson's province, and naturally wished for a
longer training in that particular line. He was
aware that a carefully systematized business,
with competent clerks, will run itself for awhile,
in the absence of the head, but he also knew
that it was unsafe.

The sweet-faced mother of the agent rose to
go, as she saw the young man so deeply
engrossed with his thoughts. She trembled as
she crossed the threshold, and Chamberlain,
stirred by the sight, caught his hat, and insisted
upon accompanying her home. On the way she
was cheery and chatty, although with a shade
of sadness in her voice that could not be entirely dispelled. When they reached her home,

alleging business engagements, he excused himself from coming in.   She held out her hand,
and, keeping his, said with tears in her eyes, —
   "Will you pray for my boy?"

   Pray for Lamson!   Chamberlain was startled.
It had never occurred to his mind that he
might pray for him.   And then like a blow
came the recognition of his own lack of faith.
Pray for him!   Certainly, and he felt rebuked
that when he had discovered his dishonesty, he
had not asked the Lord to soften his hard
heart, and give him true repentance.

   "I will, Mrs. Lamson, pray for your son, that
God may forgive and save him from sin."

XXVII.

Tam's·Temptation.

IT was August. Torrid, dusty Steep Street sweltered under the burning sun The "Arabs" spent most of their time in the river. It was almost too hot to go to Sunday-school, and for a while the mission languished. Business at the file-works was none the less pressing, and the men worked away steadily, suffering less inconvenience from the heat than did the hammock idlers in the town above. Among the changes that had come to the mill settlement, was one that was a great surprise. It was the appearance of Tam McDonald. He came quietly, as if he had been gone but a week, and the village folk received him with few manifestations of surprise. At the east end of the File Company's domains, was a large old-fashioned house, where lived a man who was half gardener and half farmer. Among his other possessions were

twenty head of cattle During the life of Robert Flint this man had been a favorite, and
was allowed many privileges. Among others he
fitted up an extra building that adjoined the
"packing-room," for a barn. When Lamson
came into power, he tried in many ways to dislodge this man, as for some reason he had a
most decided grudge against him. Finding that he
could neither buy him out nor scare him away,
he built a high fence between his barn and the
"packing-room."

With this man Tam took up his abode. The
exposure to which the little Scotchman had subjected himself during his term of hermitage,
left him with a hard, dry cough. Chamberlain,
who had grown to have a strong liking for
the strange man, was troubled about this
cough, and finally persuaded Tam to allow the
doctor to examine his throat. The physician
prescribed a mild tonic, and furnished the first
instalment himself in the shape of a bottle of
old cider. Tam at first demurred, but when he
considered the small amount prescribed, he concluded that his fears were groundless, and took
it as ordered.

The first bottle was finished, and the racking
cough had grown less frequent. The farmer, in
whose ample kitchen he had a place, seeing

how much he was improved, persuaded him to taste of *his* old cider, and ere long, it was the regular thing to have a drink each evening out of the brown pitcher.

The jolly, bluff farmer had been a former friend and fellow-workman of Tam's and promised him that whatever happened, Lamson should never again have a chance to send him to an asylum. Tam, with his old pertinacity, believed that his disfigurement was due to the agent's hate, and avoided the latter accordingly. There was no need of his caution, however, for the lawyer made no attempt to trouble him. He therefore remained, doing odd jobs in the garden and on the farm, and taking long tramps, occasionally disappearing for three or four days at a time.

One evening, when the farmer's family had retired, Tam sat in the great kitchen, getting his mind calmed for the night's sleep. After moving about uneasily for a while, he found that he was very thirsty. As usual, of late, he went to the brown pitcher. It was empty. The pump was near by, but he scarcely thought of it. Cider seemed the only possible thirst-quencher. His thirst increased. The parched throat called for one drink and *would* have it. His dark eyes burned with the strength of his desire. Dimly conscious that this was an awakening of the old appetite, he tried to fasten his mind on some Scripture thought, and failed. At length, seizing the pitcher, he started for the barn.

Fully aware of what he was doing, for the same temptation he had felt in former years, he hurried through the yard, skirted the fence, swiftly crossed an open patch of moonlight, which was in full view of the farmer's bedroom window, and in the shadow of the huge barn made his way toward the door next the cider-room. It was locked. The three doors on the other side were also locked. There was yet another way to be tried,—the barn cellar, which was always open, and from it he could reach the cider-room. With the perseverance of madness, wholly under the control of his appetite, Tam entered the thick darkness of the barn cellar. His remarkable memory for places led him directly to the steep stairs, and then up into the barn. As he raised his head above the floor, all the noisy silence of a room, containing twenty head of cattle and several horses, burst upon his ear. He climbed over a plow and the shafts of a hay-wagon and stood in the middle of the floor. The moon shone in through the line of window-panes, above the great doors, partially lighting the large enclosure. On one side, the palisades of hay reached from floor to rafters; on the other, the shelving mass overhung ' the long row of ruminants, whose heavy breathing, uneasy movements, and chewing, warned him of their position.

The cider-room was on the other side of the cattle. Standing as closely as they did, he knew that it would be somewhat difficult to pass between them, even in daylight, unless he happened to hit the passage used by the farmer. His memory, however, again served him, and he remembered that next to the passage was the loft-ladder. This found, he secured a hay-fork, and explored the space ahead and on both sides. Finding the exact position of the cross cow on one side, and the nervous heifer on the other, he went on, crossed the dangerous place in safety, and reached the cider-room. Having seen the farmer draw the coveted beverage, he was familiar with the place and cask.

Filling his pitcher, he turned to go back. On reaching the little square window opposite the passage, he saw on the floor something white, perhaps a handkerchief. He stooped to pick it up, then jumped suddenly back, spilling half of the cider, for he had seized a hind foot of the nervous heifer, and narrowly escaped receiving a vicious kick. Feeling the wall for some distance

further, he discovered a hoe, with which he per
suaded the heifer and cross cow to stand far
enough apart to allow him to pass. This they
did, after several angry kicks into empty air,
and Tam went through unharmed. Carefully
carrying the precious pitcher, he again climbed
over the shafts of the hay-wagon, passed the
plow, and went down the stairs into the cellar.
The door at the further end was the only opening in the whole vast apartment. Through it
streamed a flood of light. Sitting on the lower
stair, with the one fierce idea still holding his
mind in thrall, he raised the pitcher to his lips.
He was about to gratify his thirst. It was
right for him to do this, he argued, for
had not the doctor ordered it? There was
a nervous, frantic joy in the thought that
in an instant he would satisfy the clamoring
appetite.

He raised the pitcher and then lowered it
without tasting. The thought of what he was
really about to do, swept over him with a force
that made him reel as if he had received a
blow. He was about to drink, and, as he acknowledged to himself, not a little, but again
and again, till he lay in one of the old, sense-
less stupors. *He*, a man redeemed from drink
by the power of God, was again courting the

drunkard's curse. With a mighty prayer, "O
Loord, help!" he set the pitcher down, too
weak to pour it away, too strong to yield to
his desire. Praying with all his might, keeping
his hands resolutely away from the accursed
stuff, Tam slowly gained strength, and finally,
with a great effort, reached out his foot and
kicked the pitcher over, although it almost broke
his heart to do so. Once settled, he felt better. The tempter vanquished, fled, and Tam,
trembling at his narrow escape, sat rejoicing and
weeping. For some time he staid on the lower
stair, musing on his temptation. Occasionally he
murmured, — "O Loord, help me!" and each time
received new strength. In long review passed the
incidents of his life. He recalled his many follies,
and remembered how often, when he was deliberately planning sin, the Lord had made it
impossible by removing the opportunity. Close
by was the factory, — so close that he could hear
the sighing of the exhaust-pipes on the boilers.
So near the places in which so large a portion
of his life had been passed, it was not wonderful that he sat and listened and forgot the
barn full of ruminants, and remembered only
the ever-present noises of the mill. How many
times had he wandered away from the Lord
when in that mill, and how many times he had

been lovingly brought back! In his humiliation, he acknowledged that the punishment received in Boiler Number Six was just.

Kneeling reverently, he prayed long and earnestly. Not aloud, as he had when sure that he was alone in the deserted mill-yard, but in broken whispers and with choking sobs. Poor Tam! Almost broken-hearted, he did not know that his temptation was to be the means of saving another. Rising from his knees and turning toward the doorway, he saw, with a thrill of surprise, the figure of a man, looking eagerly back over the lighted fields.

The moon shone full upon him, showing him to be vigorous, well-built and muscular, while the slouching, dogged, nameless air bespoke the rough. After surveying the landscape to his satisfaction, he stepped within the door, out of the light, and was lost to view in the blackness that filled the cellar. Up to this moment Tam had not moved, but now, with instinctive caution, he stepped quietly back, behind the stairs, and waited the turn of events. He had hardly done so, when a noise and a smothered oath, not two feet in front of him, made his heart leap to his mouth. The stranger had run into the stairs. The shrill voice of a startled rooster brought another invective, and as the

unknown crept quietly up the stairs, his arrival
at the plow was made known by still another
unhallowed expression. Determined to know
what the visitor wanted, Tam softly followed
him. As he raised his head above the level of
the barn-floor, he saw the dim outline of the
plow just in front of him, and, further off, the
faint silhouette of the hay-wagon. The silver
ladder of moonlight that lay on the floor half
an hour before was gone, the cattle were
quieter, the man was nowhere to be seen. He
listened intently, but heard no sound like a
human footfall, nor was he directed by any more
profane signals. He had a feeling that the man,
or tramp, was, as he had been, in search of
cider, so he turned his attention to the well-
remembered passage between the cross cow and
the heifer. There seemed to be no movement
in that direction, and, tired of waiting, he had
just gained the barn-floor and softly climbed
over the plow, when he heard, close by him,
the familiar oath. For a moment he supposed
that he was discovered, but a little delay showed
that he was not. The stranger had caught his
foot in the shafts of the hay-wagon and had
almost fallen. It was easier to follow him now,
as he moved around, for the loose litter on the
floor rustled under his feet. Instead of at-

tempting to reach the cider-room, the intruder went in the opposite direction, down to the farther end of the long barn. Here he paused some moments, and listened intently; then, with increased caution, unhasped the door at that end of the building, and partly opened it. Retracing his steps, he passed his unsuspected follower, and went on till he reached the centre of the barn-floor. Here he paused, and, with considerable noise, began to collect the litter into a pile. "To make a bed," his observer thought, with some surprise. A moment later, however, he saw his mistake, for the tramp, stooping low over the pile, lit a match, and held it closely in his hollow palm till it should be fairly ignited. By the light of that match, Tam read the purpose of the stranger. He was preparing to fire the barn! Half a minute's delay might be fatal. The little pile of inflammable material, placed near the overhanging mow, would, in three minutes, settle the fate of the barn, and then of the mill-buildings. Scarcely stopping to think, the impulsive Scotchman sprang forward, struck the shielding hands together, extinguishing the match, and in an instant more was rolling in desperate combat with the incendiary.

Neither uttered a cry; both put forth all of the strength they possessed. Back and forth over the floor they rolled, startling the cows from their contented reclining, as they came almost under their horns, and then bumping up against the mows on the other side. The man was naturally strong, but had not the skill or suppleness of his wiry antagonist, and finally relaxed his struggles, and lay still.

Knowing that he could not rely upon any such forced condition as a signal of defeat, the excited Scotchman suddenly seized the two wrists of his antagonist and crossed them quickly over his back; he thus had him at his mercy. Holding him in this manner, he raised him to his feet, and pushed him out through the open door, guided him around the barn into the large yard; through this to the door, past the growling watch-dog, and into the large, old-fashioned kitchen, where the light was still burning. Here he released him. Looking eagerly into his face, Tam saw John Temple. The incendiary recognized the half-insane stranger—one of the file-workers. The deep-toned oath that he uttered showed his utter astonishment. In another instant his face was livid with passion.

"Curse you! Curse you!" he said. "There's one way I'd like to settle with you."

"Can ye tal me one thing that I have done to harm you?"

"Aye, that I can. This affair to-night will be the ruin of me. If I had known it was *you* that was wrestling with me, I would have killed you! Where did you get your strength?"

The speaker looked over, in his great anger, at the puny, wizened figure, in amazement that he had been able to conquer him.

"The Loord gave me strength," said Tam.

"If you are going to talk that way, I'm going," said Temple.

"You'll stay where ye are, mon," said Tam, decisively. "We canna' rastle here as we did in the barn without waking the man of the house. You'd best stay where ye be."

"What do you want of me?" asked Temple, sullenly.

"I wish to know what grudge you hold against the owner of this farm, that ye were trying to fire his barn?"

"I had no grudge against him. It is with Lamson that I am angry. He knew when I was upon my last 'bat,' and he offered me a job nights; but I did n't want to take it. Then he refused to pay me the money that was my due on an old debt between me and him. I did n't care for it when I was sober, but when a fellow gets full, he needs more money to keep him happy."

"And why did you try to set fire to the barn?"

"To get revenge on the agent. If that barn burned, the packing-room would go, and the office, and lots of other buildings. The fire would get right into the midst of a nest of wooden buildings, and Lamson would be ruined. I tell you, I hate him! More than any one else, has he been the cause of my ruin. Any time I would risk my life to injure him."

"Do you think burning the mill would hurt Lamson?"

"Yes."

"Well, it would n't. Lamson has little or no interest there. Instead of hurting him it would hurt one whom, if you have a spark of manhood left, you still love."

"Who?"

"Thomas Chamberlain."

Temple bowed his head and thought for an instant, then he said, —

"I don't see how it would hurt him, but it does n't signify much. I would do any thing to help Chamberlain. It is on his account that I have kept out of sight."

"He would give any thing to see you, lad," said Tam, tenderly.

"He never shall!" was the fierce reply. "Have

I not disgraced him enough? Don't tell me! He hates the very thought of me, and I don't blame him."

"Tell me how you come to fall so suddenly."

"No! no! It's too hard and cruel a story. I was so near, — I felt so thankful. The appetite that had held me, I felt I was able to conquer, till I *tasted the wine*, then I was crazy! I could think of nothing else. The days right after my fall are blotted out. I went on a terrible spree. Just as things were running *so* nicely — just as the store was beginning to prosper a little. Oh, Tam! Tam! if you only knew the hell that I live in when I think that what I did is probably keeping many in the mill back from the right!"

"Thank the Loord that ye can feel so! Did ye know that the North Church use no more alcoholic wine at the Communion?"

"No! Is that so? I'm glad of it. Perhaps some poor fellow like me, with that means for help, may be able to pull through."

"They are holdin' prayer-meetings for you, so I hear."

"Why do you tell me such things? It is like telling a lost soul of the salvation he has forfeited! Why do you torture me?"

"If I believed you lost, I would na' say ı

word; but I *know* that you are not. As sure
as there is a Saviour for me, you, John Temple,
may yet be saved."

"It is too late, I tell you! No man can have
sinned as I have. There is no hope!"

Tam's voice was as calm 'and steady as ever.

"There is salvation, and you know it. Now,
why not drop your pride, and accept it?"

"Pride! Where is the pride? I am willing
to do any thing!"

"Are you willing to kneel, and ask God now?"

"It would be mockery."

"Cannot God see into your heart? Does he
not *know* that you do not mock? Put down
your pride, now, and lay hold on salvation."

"You can not comprehend my appetite, — my
weakness, — the helplessness of my struggle ——"

"Listen, mon," replied Tam, intensely. "Do
ye ken why *I* was in the barn when I foun'
you? It was to get a pitcher of hard cider to
quench the thirst that I have so many times
promised the Loord never again to indulge. I
was there to get drunk! I was saved from it.
Noo, by the Loord's help, you can be saved
from going farther in the wrong. We are both
terrible sinners, but I have faith to believe that
there is help for us. Let us, then, lay hold on
it."

Temple's face lost its look of deep despair. Under the light, the haggard, hollow lines showed plainly. His spree had taken years out of his life.

"Can there be hope?"

"'*Whosoever* will, let him come and take of the water of life freely.' That is the only thing in this world that can quench a thirst such as we have. Noo, brother, we have sinned. Only God Almighty knows the depth of our wickedness. We can not hope to do the good that we might, had we always lived pure and good lives, as many have; but we can perhaps save one. Let us kneel and ask God to help us."

Temple shuddered.

"I can't go back, Tam," he moaned. "I can't go back and fail again. Oh, why did n't I go to the river, as I planned, and end it all?"

"Will you allow the men in the mill to say, as they do, that the power of the Loord Jesus Christ is not equal to any case of rum-drinking? He wants you for a witness. If you trust in Him, there can be no failure. Will you do it?"

Putting his arm about him, the little Scotchman drew the form of the half-crazy incendiary down beside him, and prayed. Oh, that wonderful, melting prayer! It melted the heart of the listener till he sobbed like a child. Broken, contrite, he poured forth a petition of his own. Then were the heavens opened, and the rain of peace descended on his soul. He rose, sane, sober, redeemed from the bonds of appetite; willing to take up his heavy cross and appear again before the world.

XXVIII.

Mr. Whitney's Proposal.

THE afternoon sun slanting in through the staring windows of the factory buildings, shone full on Chamberlain's back, making him even more uncomfortable than did the heat of the room. He was dead in earnest and was not cognizant of what was going on near him, till a pleasant, cultured voice said, —

"Is this Mr. Chamberlain?"

Glancing up, he saw Mr. Whitney regarding him with an expression that was far from hostile.

"Yes, sir," he replied.

"I have been looking for you, but fear I should not have succeeded in finding you, had I not been directed by the men. Are you at leisure for a few minutes?"

"Certainly, sir."

Leading the way to a part of the room that **was less** noisy and not quite as hot, Chamberlain seated himself on a bench by the side of his visitor, and waited for him to open the conversation. After speaking of the weather and general topics, he said, —

"I never have had the pleasure of greeting you before, Mr. Chamberlain, although I have often seen you. My life among business men has led me to decide quickly as to a man's capacity or attainments. I must say, that it has been a surprise to me, that you were here in these works among the lowest class of laborers. You must know that you are fitted for something better. Are you anxious to leave this place?"

Chamberlain hesitated, for he at once guessed the kindly errand upon which the gentleman came. His questioner was Miriam's father. It would be a most awkward thing for him to refuse aid, or to accept it. How could he explain?

"The surroundings are not as pleasant as I could wish, yet I think my duty bids me stay here," was his answer.

Mr. Whitney pondered. At length, he said, —

"Mr. Chamberlain, I wish that I could in some way serve you. There are numbers of young men from Steelville, for whom I have been instrumental in securing good positions in

the city. My business relations are large. I enjoy giving a young man, who is worthy, a lift.
Is there any thing that I can do?"

There was a sincerity in the tone that could
not be doubted. Chamberlain wished that he
were in a position to be helped, but there was
no need of personal assistance.

"There is abundant opportunity for any help
that Christians can offer, in the line in which
I am working," replied he.

His caller made no reply, asked no question.
Possibly he did not understand the allusion to
the mission work. There was a moment of
silence, during which each was busy with his
own thoughts. The young man, in some perplexity, wondered at the proud man's coming to
see him, when he had so lately opposed him in
the debate at the church meeting. Could he
have looked into the other's heart, he would
have seen that, while he was keen and quick
in any business matter, and lordly in his bearing, there was at the same time an absence of
vanity that was admirable.

Mr. Whitney was in many respects a remarkable man. Very pronounced in his conclusions,
full of the quickest insight into practical matters,
he had the rare quality of bearing no enmity
toward those who opposed his opinions. He was

possessed of a shrewd, business-like charity, that was as sweet and wholesome as it was original. People often misunderstood him. They thought him proud while, in truth, he thought of himself but rarely. They called him close, — "snug," the countrymen termed it, — because he refused to pay more than an article was worth, yet he gave largely to various chari-ties, and had done more for the young men of the place and vicinity, than any other man of his time.

A rich man's son, of great natural ability, he had been successful in whatever he undertook, and this fact was, possibly, the chief grievance that his neighbors had against him. He had been brought up to use wine, and without in-vestigation believed it to be right. Very rarely was he befogged by it as Chamberlain had seen him, and he doubtless tried to think that he was only a trifle excited.

"Is there no way in which I can help you?" he asked. "We have a situation in our count-ing-house, that I should be glad to see you fill. It would put you among people of your own kind, and give you an excellent opportunity to improve. You should be where you can grow. You certainly are not satisfied with your progress here?"

"No, sir, I am not," was the honest answer. "But if I went away, what help should I be to Steep Street? It is my ambition to see liquor-selling and liquor-drinking entirely banished from this settlement. I wish to see, instead of the drunken, brawling, Sabbath-breaking workman, a peaceable, honest, temperate man, who will serve the Lord instead of the Devil."

"That is a most commendable ambition," said Mr. Whitney, approvingly, "but one, I fear, that cannot be realized. Now, I take it, that it is for the interest of the manufacturer to keep the help down. That is one reason I should never wish to be a mill-owner. There can be no money made where the help have every thing at their command. A drinking man will work for less wages than a sober man. He is more under the thumb of his employer. While this is so, there will be no reform in the file-works, at least while Lamson is at the head of it."

Surprised at this view of the question, Chamberlain stopped and thought for a moment.

"There is truth in what you say," he replied, "and yet, I cannot see that it is an advantage to the mill-owner to employ degraded help. More work is spoiled by the drunkards in the mill in a year, than would suffice to pay them half a dollar a day more for wages. The last fire, that cost nearly ten thousand dollars, was the result of a spree."

"I have not studied the question with any great care, as I am not specially interested in it, but to my knowledge, the little tumble-down mills, knee-deep in dirt, in which work a set who are as bad, if not worse than the file-men, pay the best dividends, while the handsomely furnished mills with the neat tenements and nicely tilled gardens and genteel help pay the smallest. While this is so, the money-makers will fight all reform."

"For nearly two years I have studied this subject, having been daily among the men, and I am convinced that your deductions are wrong," was the respectful answer. "Let us look at it from a business standpoint. One family of drinkers use, say, fifty cents' worth of liquor a day, and that is a small estimate. In a year they would consume one hundred and eighty-seven dollars and fifty cents' worth. Three hundred such families would be fifty-six thousand, two hundred and fifty dollars a year. Now, that is what Steep Street pays for liquor. It is, of course, a damage. It neither feeds nor clothes the operatives. It renders them unfit for work; after a drunk the work is slighted in a manner that an outsider would hardly credit. The mill pays out that money for the hands to throw away, and then is obliged to pay them for food, clothing, and all the costs of living besides. How does that help the dividends?"

"To tell the truth, I have only repeated what some mill-owners have told me," was the reply. "I am not specially interested in the subject, yet I should think that a sober man, who saves his money, would be more independent, and more likely to leave, under a forced reduction of wages, than the improvident, hand-to-mouth sort."

"The men who leave suddenly, unreasonably, when the work is going to rack and ruin for need of their help, are the drinkers," returned Chamberlain. "If they have *no* money, *no* credit, *no* hope for future employment, they plunge ahead, when a sober man would be thoughtful and prudent. Your friends argue that they dare not leave, being drunkards, because they can get work nowhere else; but do they find the hard drinkers very loth to go to the poor-house? And are not the mills, in their taxes, obliged to support a set of thriftless, useless creatures, that otherwise would be self-supporting?"

"Do you believe, Mr. Chamberlain, that the file-works would be benefited if they constructed new tenements, stopped the sale of liquor, and hired only sober men?"

"I am sure of it. My experience has shown that the drinkers are continually damaging work, stopping important jobs, and making themselves most unreliable just when they are most needed. And there is another way to look at this matter. No Christian has, I believe, a right to tolerate any evil among his help, that he can in any manner remove. A follower of Christ, who hires drunkards because they are cheap, puts a premium on sin and disgraces his profession. An employer should feel great responsibility concerning his help. If the bosses of the mills only took an interest in the young men, and aided them in doing right, and removed opportunities for doing wrong, there would be a change in the laboring classes that would make the whole nation smile with prosperity and peace."

"You are eloquent," laughed the other.

"I am in earnest. There are in the works men from all parts of the country, who have worked in most of the large mills, — not alone file-workers, but in cotton, rubber, woolen and other manufactories and foundries. I have frequently questioned them about things in those places, and find that the works here are a fair average of what may be found throughout the Union. People of the better class, even if they saw it with their own eyes, would contradict it, because they *cannot* see, as do those who are inside of the lines."

"Really, I am getting interested. Do you intend, single-handed, to combat this state of affairs?"

"I intend," answered Chamberlain, slowly, "one day to be a manufacturer. My mill shall be run carefully, frugally. Every man shall be required to do his duty if he can do it. No drunkard shall find lodgment within the gates of the mill-yard, and no drop of liquor shall be brought into the mill settlement. As far as feasible, I shall know what my men do evenings, and shall give them plenty of opportunity to indulge in pleasant and profitable amusements. The whole place shall be run in the fear of the Lord."

"Do you think it practicable?"

"I believe that the fear of the Lord is the beginning of all wisdom, whether it be running a mill or a Sunday-school."

"So do I," assented Mr. Whitney. "By the way," continued he, "you have not yet told me what I can do to help you out in this?"

Then came the moment of trial. Rather would he have been silent; but a voice within him gave him no choice but to obey, so he said respectfully, —

" Mr. Whitney, I staid last night with a man who has been a very hard drinker, and who was hurt in the mill. For some time he has been willing to lead a better life. He hates the thought of 'giving up his liberty' — as he terms it. Even on the verge of delirium-tremens he will urge that the aristocrats have their wine, and why should not he have an equal liberty with whiskey ?"

"But he should know that he cannot control himself."

" Exactly; but such men reason queerly. He says, when I plead with him, that when a certain man in the upper town is willing to give up his wine, he will leave off drinking, and not until then."

" Who is the wine-drinker ? "

"Mr. Whitney," said Chamberlain, growing a trifle pale; "the man who is going to destruction, for the sake of this whim, is Swinert, the drunkard; and the gentleman, whom he daily quotes and glories over as being a moderate drinker, and able to hold his own, and stay in the church, to serve the Lord and drink fine wines at the same time, — is yourself."

XXIX.

Breaking·the·Ring.

"IT's a mighty good man whose place can't be filled by somebody," Gaffney remarked, as one after another of his friends had dropped into the little bed-room, and told him of Lamson's flight, and the uneasy feeling that pervaded in the village.

Among those who most enjoyed Lamson's absence, and hoped it might be indefinitely prolonged, was Chamberlain. He was at once sorry and glad, for he looked ahead of the avalanche of cares with no little anxiety. After the flight, he had received a call from another lawyer of the town, who announced himself as one of the gentlemen who were to assure themselves that Chamberlain's part of the contract was carried out. He was pleased at this, as he could not but worry a little over his approachnig trial, when he knew that the one to whom in particular his uncle had entrusted the management of the plan had so signally failed in his duty.

Several days after this, Chamberlain was walking rapidly away from the hamlet toward the distant hills. It was the last day of his trial as laborer. Suddenly he heard his name called. He had reached a considerable elevation where he could look back, even on Steep Street. For an instant he was puzzled to know from what direction the voice came; it had a familiar sound that made his heart leap with joy. How well he had learned the varied music of that voice! Scanning the roadside with rapid glance, he saw beneath the bending branches of an apple-tree that had managed to live its whole life outside of the civilized restraints of stone walls, a pony phaeton; in it sat Miss Whitney. Her black horse was contentedly eating the leaves from the tree, and switching flies at the same time.

"I am afraid I did wrong in speaking, you looked so preoccupied; but I wished so much to tell you some good news," she said, with a deep blush.

"I am very glad you did speak; and good news is always welcome," replied Chamberlain, coming under the canopy of leaves.

"Do you remember—of course you do—that queer Swinert, whom you wished some of the teachers in the mission-school, myself among the number, to call upon?"

"I do."

"He said that he would give up his liquor when my father gave up wine. Father, at first, after you told him of it, was quite disturbed. He thought the man insufferably impudent, and I doubt not, still thinks so; but he reasoned with himself about it, and what do you think he did?"

"I guess——"

"Don't guess, I wish to tell you. After some little debating with himself, like the grandly upright man that he is, he wrote Swinert, telling him that if his drinking wine caused him to stumble, he would never drink another drop. I saw the letter; it was courteous, polite, splendid. Oh, it made me so happy! I don't know of another man in the world who would have been so considerate of the feelings of that poor wretch, whom he had never seen, as my dear, old father. I am proud of him."

"That is indeed glorious news. Now, if Swinert will only keep to his promise, your father will have the satisfaction of knowing that he has saved at least one from a drunkard's grave."

"Swinert answered at once, signing a queer pledge that he himself had drawn up. In it he promised several things; among others, to give the mission-school, 'God bless it,' a good, solid lift by his weekly presence."

"I am very glad," replied Chamberlain.

"Do you know, Mr. Chamberlain, that there is altogether a different atmosphere in this village than what there was before you came? Father remarked it. It should make you very happy to feel that you can do so much good among the workmen."

"As I look back over the two years spent here, I am filled with wonder. Certainly, God uses any willing instrument. I have prayed and struggled in a poor way, and he has given his blessing. But the prayers of Pastor Snow, and your Aunt Whittier, were not unheard. It seems to me, as I think of it, that one who doubts the efficacy of prayer, after having seen what it has accomplished in Steep Street, must indeed be blind '

"You are right. I would that I had more faith. I believe I see a work opening among my boys that leads me to covet power in prayer. I cannot tell you, Mr. Chamberlain, how much happier I am since I have tried to do a little for the factory people. Why, before I knew them, I actually despised them. I am sorry and ashamed that I ever entertained such feelings, but I think it was the prejudice arising from ignorance."

"The future of Steep Street depends on the people of the upper settlement and the owners of the file-works," said Chamberlain.

"And Sam Putnam."

"Yes. There is another signal answer to our prayers, — the conversion of Putnam. His influence with the men is unbounded. There is little doubt, so I hear, that the engine company will really become a temperance organization."

Chamberlain stood for an instant in silence, looking into the fair face before him. He saw reflected in it his own enthusiasm, and, as the brown eyes fell beneath his gaze, he hoped he read something more.

"Could man or woman have a grander life-work than raising such a village as this from its sin and ignorance into the marvelous light of the Gospel?" asked Chamberlain.

"I think not," was the low reply.

"And even though a man labor with his hands, when he is striving to win souls, it does not degrade him?" said he, with tremulous voice.

"Saint Paul was a tent-maker, and a greater than he, — the Lord, — was a carpenter," was the gentle response.

Chamberlain reached over the wheel and clasped the little hand that fluttered for an instant, and then lay still in his firm clasp.

"Can we not join hands for life in this work?" he said.

The brown eyes were raised to his face with a grave, earnest expression, as she said, simply and without a falter, —

"Yes."

He drew from his watch-chain the curiously-chased ring, so worn that it was but a shell of gold, and crushing it between his strong fingers, broke one side, leaving the band in one curling piece.

"It is an old, perhaps a forgotten custom," he said, holding it out to Miriam.

She understood, and with the same sweet gravity broke with him the ring, retaining half as a seal of betrothal. Tenderly, almost reverently, he kissed the red lips, thanking God in his heart for his present overflowing happiness.

As the sun was already setting, Chamberlain walked as far as the village by the side of the phaeton, and then, with a pressure of the hand and a look eloquent with true affection, took leave, to finish his walk. It seemed as if he had reached the climax of his life. Happy that Steep Street already was showing signs of spiritual life; that no rum-shop flourished there; that the people were bountifully supplied with pure water; that Temple had returned and proclaimed his intention of serving the Lord; that Sam Putnam and Gaffney were henceforth to be true soldiers of the Cross, — happy in all this, he felt that the only other thing that he could ask, — the love of Miriam Whitney, — had been granted him. With great thankfulness, he knelt in a nook by the roadside and prayed earnestly. Then he rose and walked on toward this new life, determined, with God's help, when he was "village king," to be, also, His village laborer.

XXX.

A · Lesson · in · Chemistry.

IT was raining. A genuine north-easterly storm, that for twenty-four hours had threatened and lowered, at last in good earnest was fulfilling its menace. Cold as the spray of the ocean, driving in slanting lines over sodden fields, "lodging" acres of heavy grass, beating off leaves not yet yellow, soaking every thing, till fences, tree-trunks, and even stone walls took on a water-logged appearance ;—it was the typical "three-days' rain" of New England. Along a country road, splashing through the many puddles, came a traveler. He was to all appearance a laborer, on his way from one village to another in search of work. Over his shoulder he carried a stout stick, which was thrust through the handles of a small, shabby valise. The uncomfortable weather apparently had its effect upon the lonely pedestrian, for an ugly scowl was on his face. From time to time he looked about for a farm-house or

barn that could afford shelter, but without success. As he journeyed, night fell, and still the
long reaches of woodland, the ill-kept mowing
lands, and the alder-circled meadows stretched
out as if there were naught else in the world.
Wet to the skin, and chilled to the bone, he
plodded stolidly on; more and more discouraged
at not finding a habitation of some sort. At
length, far away across the fields, he descried a
solitary light. Thinking it would proffer a warm
supper and a bed, he eagerly turned toward it.
A "short cut" in the night, across uneven
fields, hedge-bound and half-cleared, means hard
work. The uncertain light hides the hollows, re-
duces distances, and leads one into sudden, dis-
locating steps, that are painful if not dangerous. When the light was reached, the traveler
was not a little surprised to find himself on the
borders of a great salt-marsh, and facing a number of brick buildings enclosed by a high fence.
What kind of manufactory it was, so far from
human habitation, with no clustering tenement-
houses, with a weed-grown cart-path leading to
it from the distant road, he could not imagine.
Yet it promised shelter, and on the whole, perhaps, the fact of its strange isolation might make
the watchman the more accessible and ready to
entertain a wayfarer. As he drew nearer, a pe-

culiar odor was discernible, that he remembered before to have known, but where his weary memory could not recall. At the gate he knocked loudly with the end of his heavy stick, and awaited answer. None came, and again he knocked. The light shone calmly from within, yet there was no sign of life; and it looked as if he must, after all, be disappointed, and spend the night in the lee of the fence, when, in response to a third attack with the cane, that filled the empty yard with echoes, a wicket opened, and a thin voice said, —

"Who's there?"

"Can you give me a bed? I am wet through, and not able to go a step farther!"

"Who be yer?" was the suspicious query.

"My name is Lam—" began the tired traveler, but stopped as if influenced by a sudden thought, with a look that might mean self-accusation of great stupidity.

"Wal, Mr. Lamb, you may be all right, or you may be all wrong; I don't know. You kin come in," said the voice, and the side gate swung open.

The other accepted the invitation with alacrity, and entered the yard, the gate closing after him with a vigorous thud. While he stood looking around to see with whom he had been speaking, the door of a low, brick building opened, a faint light streamed out, and the same voice bade him enter. He did so, but had hardly crossed the threshold when he recoiled, a real terror impressed upon his features. Before him stood a man, clad in a red flannel shirt and canvas trousers, his scrawny, skeleton-like arms bare to the shoulder, the veins swelling and bulging in a horrid net-work that the absence of flesh made the more apparent. The great hands — one resting on his hip, the other holding a lamp — were nailless. His face and head were without hair; his huge mouth toothless. An unhealthy complexion, inde-scribable in its color, and a pair of prominent eyes that seemed straining to get out of their feverish sockets, completed the make-up of this monstrosity.

"You are welkim," he said.

"What kind of a place is this?" demanded the stranger, in a shaky voice.

"Kimical-works."

"What is it smells so?"

"The acids. Dretful onhealthy place. Guess you ain't used to seein' folks that work in these places, be yer? Look kinder scared; but, bless ye, I ain't a sarcumstance to the old man that was here before me. Why, when he went to town, the women folks used to faint away, he looked so skeery; but then he had begun to unj'int."

"Unjoint?"

"Yes. The acid had worked on him so long that it eat him clean up. They was n't hardly enough of him to bury!"

The visitor glanced from the livid face down to the slippered feet, from which protruded a couple of toes, from which the nails had fallen, and shuddered.

"You are a-shiverin' with cold," said the other, hospitably. "Come into the furnace-room."

The stranger followed him in, and was soon dressed in dry clothes, and enjoying a cup of hot coffee made over the coals. Even the kindness of his host did not serve to dispel the horror that his uncanny looks inspired; and to avoid betraying his feelings, the guest kept his eyes upon the glowing coals, and away from the grim visage. There was, however, a fascination that drew his gaze, again and again, back to the face, which lost none of its frightfulness as it grew more familiar.

Besides its use as a furnace-room, the further end of the apartment was a store-room for the products of the works. Across a long, frail platform stretched a line of glass carboys, nearly all of which were filled with a greenish-colored liquid.

Whether it was the color of the thick glass, or not, that tinged the contents, the observer could not decide.

"There is acid enough there to burn up a town," remarked the host, observing the look. "It's dretful powerful. Drop most any thing into that, and it will eat it clean up."

"Why do you work in such a place as this? It is killing you. A few years hence, and you will be in your grave. Why don't you leave?" broke out the visitor.

"Leave? Do you know, Mister, I git eight dollars a day for what I do?" was the triumphant reply.

"Eight dollars a day! What would a hundred dollars a day be in comparison with what you lose? It's wicked! You have no right, for a little money, to throw away your life."

"Oh, sho! I've heerd folks talk afore now. Unless a man kills himself jest in the fashionable way, he is doing a wickedness. Why, there ain't a third of the business men but what dies years afore they'd oughter. And as fer killin' *yerself* fer money — that's nothin'. It ain't to be compared to crowdin' the widders and the fatherless, or to sellin' rum for money, or stealin' from those that trust ye."

The visitor winced, and lapsed into silence,

looking fixedly at the uncouth bottles that held in solution such a dangerous force.

"Be you interested in kimistry?"

"No; not especially."

"If you be, I kin show you some curous things about the acid. I tell ye, it's jest like a ravening beast when it gits to eatin'. I'd like to show ye in the mornin'."

The other expressed a languid interest, and then inquired about his bed. With true hospitality the watchman made him up a "shake-down" at the further end of the furnace-room, where he could lie with his feet toward the fire. Back of him, in a double row, stood the long lines of carboys. With his valise under the mattress that was laid on the cement floor, the visitor disrobed and was soon sound asleep. The watchman, after attending to the fires, wandered off alone to smoke, and a stillness, only broken by long-drawn, bubbling sighs from the "vats," enfolded the furnace-room. After an hour the stranger suddenly woke, and starting up, felt under the mattress for his valise. It was safe, and he sank back, and from his couch looked keenly about for the watchman. He was nowhere in sight, and stirred by a second thought, the stranger drew the valise out and slipped it into a mammoth rubber pail that stood in front of the carboys. A sheet of rubber cloth that lay on the floor was carelessly thrown over the whole, and with a satisfied look he returned to bed, and in a few moments was soundly slumbering. A half hour later the watchman came in, stirred the fire, glanced at his guest, and again went to his little office in the adjoining building.

The sleeper did not waken when the "slicer bar" rang on the bricks, or when the slippered feet scuffed noisily across the cemented floor. Neither did he waken when the frail support that held the carboys began to creak ominously and to bend under a weight that had long been too heavy to be borne in safety. Slowly three of the mammoth bottles tipped forward a fraction of an inch at a time, till the sudden snap threw them entirely over, their long necks resting on the stout guard that was used as a "pouring-rail." After rolling and clashing one against the other for an instant, they were still, and the danger that had threatened the sleeper, should their burning contents be thrown over him, appeared to be arrested. The rubber stoppers held back the liquid that leaped eagerly into the bottle-mouths. The stoppers held at first, but soon from one came a single drop of acid. Then another and another, till the loosened plug gave way, and a stream was flowing out, not upon the flôor, but into the rubber pail. Beating down the cloth cover that the stranger had with such artfulness disposed so as to conceal his valise, it rapidly filled the vessel and then spread out over the floor.

Untroubled by any dream of danger to himself or his belongings, the stranger slumbered peacefully on. Occasionally through the night the watchman entered, replenished the fire, and scuffed out again. Once the traveler turned over, partly roused, but with a deep, weary sigh dropped back into dreamland. The chemical-works rats,— for even this place was not free from them, although according to the traditions of the workmen, they lodged somewhere else,— scampered about, and even mounted the bed, but did not disturb the sleeper.

Outside, the rain still fell heavily, and as the wind had risen, it was flung against the side windows. That the sleep of the wayfarer was not without dreams, his occasional disjointed sentences and feverish breathing testified, yet none of the sounds of the night served to impress him with a remembrance of his surroundings.

The morning had given place to noon ere he roused from his stupor and awaked to the fact that it was time he was pursuing his journey, As he dressed, the watchman, who seemed to

work night and day, came in, and greeted him
with a good-natured smile that made him look
like a genial fiend.

"Slep' well?" he inquired.

"Yes, very. I was thoroughly tired out. What
time is it?"

"Quarter-past twelve."

With an exclamation of surprise at the lateness
of the hour the stranger turned to his treasured
valise. As he saw the three carboys tipped so
far over, the one almost empty, and the rubber
pail brimming with acid, he uttered a half shriek,
half groan, and sprang toward it. But the watchman, till now so obtuse, suddenly awoke and
was before him, holding him back with a terri-
fied look on his face, that made him if possible
more ugly than ever.

"Are yer crazy?" he said to the struggling
man.

"My valise is in that pail," gasped the stranger.

"Well, I will get it; you stand back. Do you
want your hands burned off?"

The fit of frenzy over, the other stood passively
back, and allowed the watchman to search with
a short poker through the mammoth pail for his
property. First the rubber cloth came up, black,
shiny, and dripping, not in the least injured by
the acid. Then he poked further, fished further,

and at length brought up a queer skeleton frame, with burned shreds of leather hanging to it, that looked not at all like his property.

"That's yer valise, all except the sides, and yer change of clothes," remarked the man.

"But — but get out the rest. There was money," came in a weak voice.

"Bills?"

"Yes."

The watchman put the poker in again, and poked and poked, at last bringing up a black mass that fell upon the floor — a shapeless, useless bunch of pulp.

"All eat up," he said.

The stranger sank down on the bed, white and trembling.

"Look — look again!"

"No use, Mr. Lamb."

"Lamson," corrected the other, mechanically.

"Thought you said it was Lamb; but never mind. There ain't no use lookin' furder; the acid has eat it all up. Sorry if its strapped you. If you're specially hard put, I can lend ye a dollar."

"A dollar!" almost shrieked the sufferer. "Do you know what I have lost? There were forty thousand dollars in that bag! I have spent years in gaining them. I have lied, cheated, lived a hypocrite, struck hands with sharpers and thieves, and oppressed the helpless, to gain that, and now it is all gone!"

"That's worse than bein' a laborer in the kimical-works," was the remark.

But his sarcasm was not heeded. The other, with bowed head, with a look of unrelieved hopelessness, went and sat down in front of the furnace, buried his face in his hands, and indulged in bitter reflections.

XXXI.

Trying · It · On.

GREAT changes often come quietly. With a certain apprehension the file-hands received the news that Chamberlain had been placed at the head of the business. There was, at first, a feeling that he had been playing the spy, until it was known that Robert Flint had arranged the whole affair, and then they were satisfied. "Old Skinflint" always got ahead of the help when he was alive, and, though dead, he still kept up his reputation, was the universal thought. That the advent of a new "boss," up in all the mysteries of the trade, acquainted with the many means of shirking that were among the men, aware of the "soft jobs" and the lax habits, should affect them all, was highly probable.

To many, the fact that Chamberlain was a "church-member" was most unpleasant. Some sincerely believed that all piety was a sham. Their learning, drawn from such living epistles as Lamson, was faulty, but honest. Divided in opinion, the operatives held long and serious consultations. The boiler-room, the coal-yard, the slag-heaps, were debating grounds, where word-battles raged with varying success. Sam Putnam, Gaffney, and Tam McDonald,—the last-named having returned to the mill,—were the champions of the new order of things. They had many opponents. Even before a single change had been inaugurated, the operatives felt aggressive. They longed for an opportunity to show their feelings. The changes, however, came so gradually, so differently from what they expected, that they did not do themselves justice, so they thought, which nettled them the more. In addition to this, the older men were indignant that a boy should presume to assume control of a corporation that gray heads had heretofore managed. If their advice was asked, they intended to let him know how they felt. But the opportunity, much to their chagrin, did not present itself. The days passed, the work went on, and the men found other things to grumble about. The wave of excitement spent itself without doing damage.

When the business was well running again,

and all seemed propitious, Chamberlain one evening sent word to the various heads of departments, that he wished to meet them in the packing-room after the whistle blew. It was with some uneasiness that most of them gathered in the spacious room. They were not kept waiting long. Advancing from the office, the "new boss" stood before the group, and at once plunged into his theme.

"It is customary," he said, "for all concerns doing business to have certain rules, — not to crowd the help and get as much as possible out of them, but that they may know just what they are expected to do. The employés have their rights, and the corporation has its rights. A schedule of minor rules has already been drawn up and printed. It relates to the time for coming and going, the rights of time-workers and piece-hands, and has already been seen by those of you whose departments it touches. There is, however, one rule that I have not caused to be printed, but the enforcement of which I deem most important."

Chamberlain paused for an instant, and measured the men before him with a keen glance. He saw an enmity in some faces, an indifference in others, a fear in a few. One or two looked friendly.

"The rule of which I speak will, doubtless, seem to many of you to be arbitrary, but to the management it is believed to be necessary. It is this: After this week. no drinking men will be employed by this company, in any capacity. We have, as I have already stated, weighed this matter with extreme care. Any thing that we can do to break the chain of habit that binds some of the help, will be done, but from henceforth, this corporation intends to discourage the use and the sale of ardent spirits to the very best of its ability. Sober men will be valued — will be assisted in every way that is in our power. Unsteady men, 'spreers,' can neither expect work in the mill, nor shelter in the company's tenements. This rule has not been drawn up thoughtlessly. Its enforcement will, we trust, result in the greatest good that this village has ever enjoyed. The love of liquor is a disease, the worst disease this world has ever known. To eradicate it thoroughly from Steelville, stern measures are required.

"I have gathered the superintendents and foremen of this establishment, not to harshly announce a rule that may seem to abridge personal liberty, but to claim your sympathy and assistance. No sane man could live on Steep

Street a day, and not appreciate the curse that broods over it. No reasonable man in all this great establishment will deny the harm that the drinking habits are inflicting upon the operatives. The wrecks of homes, and the wrecks of human beings, men, women, and even little children, can be daily seen. Steep Street, the most wretched settlement the sun ever shone upon, poisoned, degraded, by continual drunkenness, calls to us for help. We alone, under God, can give it assistance.

"If there are any here who are not willing to help, who will see souls perish rather than throw the weight of their influence on the right side, let them assert it. We shall understand, by your presence in the mill, that you bind yourselves to carry out the rules of the corporation. And not only that, but we shall expect from you all an earnest sympathy, an untiring vigilance, and all possible aid in furthering this best gift to those under your immediate charge."

Chamberlain paused, having spoken longer than was his first intention. A rigid silence had prevailed in the room throughout it all. The faces of the men, whether stolid or expressive, told of surprise, and, in some cases, of rebellion. When he had ceased speaking, there was an uneasy movement, and then one who had been, for years, a department superintendent, stepped forward as if to speak. He was a tall, broad-shouldered, noble-looking old man. He was known as an impressive speaker, a keen debater. Clearing his throat, he said, in a deep, resonant voice, and, perhaps, a touch of condescension, —

"Mr. Chamberlain, I think that the energy of your character, that your earnest wish to be a reformer, is leading you into a serious mistake. You are fresh from school. It is natural that you should look upon the men gathered here as school-boys of a larger growth, but there you are wrong. A school-boy can claim no liberty beyond that granted by pedagogue or parent, — a laborer can. He has arrived at man's estate, and is jealous of all his rights and privileges. Any attempt to curtail his liberty in the slightest is immediately resented. There are, among us, men from England, from Germany, from Russia, from oppressed Ireland, who have come here to be free. Your laws might do in a land where despotism prevailed, but here they can never succeed. All will rebel. I am an old man, Mr. Chamberlain. My gray hairs will protect me in saying what younger men could not say. I, too, have the interest of the operatives at heart. I, too, despise the rum-bottle. It is my belief, however, that a man has a right to destroy himself by debauchery, if he wishes. In this country he is his own master. You have made a strong and beautiful garment of these rules, Mr. Chamberlain, but it won't fit Steep Street, and I beg that you will not try it on."

There was a tendency to applaud among the small audience, but Chamberlain's reply checked it.

"Every man has a right, in a certain sense, to degrade himself as much as he wishes. That, however, is not germane to this question. We are discussing, rather, the rights of the corporation. We claim, and justly, that we can hire whom we please. We choose, hereafter, to employ sober men. All are at liberty to drink if they wish, but not in our work-rooms, in our tenements, nor in our village."

"Mr. Chamberlain," said Wilcox, a black-eyed, wiry little man, a hard worker, and an occasional hard drinker, "are you not coming down on us a little bit suddenly? We thought you were our friend. A good many of the boys have been thinking seriously of leaving off drinking, but I am afraid this will anger them. You can't drive a man into goodness. If he goes at all he must be led."

"Mr. Wilcox, were you aware that the fact that the liquors that are drunk in the mill cost us yearly a large sum for insurance? That we pay a heavier rate than any other file-manufactory in the country? Did you know that respectable companies were afraid to insure our tenements, occupied, as they are in some cases, by families made crazy through drink? Do you remember the fire in Number Nine, that cost us ten thousand dollars? The right to drink rum in the mill was the cause of that fire. Do you remember when the 'three-chimney tenement-house' burnt, sacrificing two lives? It was set by a drunken file-grinder. It cost the company two thousand dollars. Were you aware that in the past two years thousands of dollars' worth of file-stock has been wasted and destroyed by workmen, who were skilful when sober, but bunglers when drunk? Are not these reasons enough to warrant any business house in protecting itself? Let me assure you all most earnestly that my interest in the men has not ceased, that I will do all I possibly can. Every man in the mill may consider me his personal friend. I earnestly believe that the most confirmed sot among us will be benefited by this rule."

"Going to be pretty tough on them that live on 'iquor," remarked another. "There are men in the mill here, to my certain knowledge,—good, reliable fellows,—that can no more do without their daily drink than they could without their daily breath. If they gave up liquor they would die in a week. They have worked faithfully, year in and year out, till they have grown gray in the service. They have done much to build up this 'ere business. Seems as if they might have some tapering-off rule."

Sam Putnam answered this,—

"Boys," he said, in his old-time, hearty way, "what bosh it is to talk of a man dying for want of liquor, and you know it! When these old rummies, that are fairly pickled in whiskey, are 'up for thirty days,' do they die? Yet they have to do without liquor. The fact of it is, more than half of us have got an awful hankering after the ardent, and we are ashamed to own it. We might just as well be men and face it and fight it, and thank God we have got a boss to help us. It is time some sort of a change came to Steep Street. I have done my share in dragging the folks of this village down, and now I am going to turn round and drag them up. It is a fight with me every day of my life, to keep free from liquor. I never, till lately, realized that I had such an appetite. That it can be conquered, I have daily proof. I don't believe in molly-coddling a set of old men into poisoning themselves to death, and you don't. I don't think that anybody's liberties are trampled on when rum is forbidden, any more than I do when a law is made against picking pockets, or committing murder, and you don't. If we don't kill rum, rum will kill us."

As there seemed nothing further to say, the men, with Chamberlain's permission, dispersed. When they were fairly outside of the mill premises, the restraint that his presence imposed, gave way. Very freely they talked,— most excitedly they debated the question. The almost unanimous verdict was against the new method of procedure.

"I tell you," said Chapman, stroking his gray beard, "that boy don't appreciate the situation. He is puffed up by being boss. His scheme won't work. Just let him try it on."

"He will try it, he is gritty enough to do most any thing," said Wilcox.

"Yes," was the sage answer. "No doubt he will try it, but how long will it last? Not two weeks. It will begin with a great rush and crash and clang, and then die right down into nothing. Men will have rum. Nothing, in my opinion, can quench the appetite. This boy boss of ours thinks a few threats will scare the taste out of the guzzlers' mouths. That is a taste that has come to stay."

"I tell you, Chapman," interrupted Sam Putnam, "you fellows that don't drink a drop, and yet are always helping others to, are, in my estimation, the meanest sort of men. You are worse than the rumsellers. They advise a man to drink that they may make a living; you do it for nothing. You talk about rum-drinking coming to stay; there is something mightier than that has arrived. The temperance movement, under the leadership of the Lord Jesus Christ, has arrived here in Steelville. It has not come for a little while. It is n't going to stop only just as long as our boss is interested in it; it has come for good; it has come to stay."

"Amen," said Gaffney.

It was four o'clock in the afternoon. The regular, pulsing throb of the mighty engines, the confused din of the steel-working machines, came at intervals through the opening and closing doors of the factory, to the cosy office of the young mill-owner. Work was pressing. Scores of orders, as yet unfilled, covered the pages of the order book. The puddling furnaces, running to the utmost of their capacity, kept every man busy.

A gray, grizzled Scotchman, a man of powerful build, but bent and warped like some knotty plank of oak, his face seamed with time-scars and sin-scars, the great muscles bulging on his bony arms, his whole face reeking with perspiration, strode to the office door and loudly rapped.

"Come," said Chamberlain.

Pausing on the threshold, he looked aggressively from beneath his bushy eyebrows.

"I'm come to tal yer that the men will no wark without their liquor," he said, emphasizing his statement with a vigorous nod.

"Do you mean they cannot, or they will not?" asked Chamberlain.

"Baith."

"The heats have been very severe-this week," said Chamberlain, reflectively. "It is hard work. I appreciate that as much as any one. I ordered coffee to be served to the men an hour ago. Was it not done?"

"Aye," was the savage answer. "They brought us some milk-and-water stuff, that weakened the men rather than strengthened them, so we poured it over the slag-heap. What we want is the real stuff, and we'll have it, or your wark will no be dune."

"Did the men wish you to speak to me about this?" inquired Chamberlain, quietly.

"They did that, and they bade me tell yer,

if the liquor was not on hand within the hour, the furnaces would take care of themselves. Do you hear that?"

Without answering, the other took up a pen and began to write. For fully five minutes his pen scratched busily over the paper; the puddler watching him with an ugly frown. Becoming uneasy, at length, he said, —

"What'll I tell them?"

"Who?" was the absent inquiry.

"Why, man alive! the men who are aboot to strike."

"I don't know that there is any thing to tell them. No liquor shall be drunk in the factory, if not another file is ever made."

With an angry growl, the Scotchman stalked away. When he was fairly out of sight, Chamberlain stepped to the outer office and handed a slip of paper to one of the clerks. The young man, taking it, read it through, rose hastily and went into the small telegraph office that was connected with the mill. Placing his finger on the key he wrote, —

"Send the spare puddlers on the night freight.
                                        CHAMBERLAIN."

Meanwhile, around the furnaces, were gathered an excited company. The puddlers, with one or two exceptions, feeling that they had the mill-owner at their mercy, were determined here to make a stand and assert their rights.

Without them the mill could not run. Brawny men, hard drinkers, hard workers, they were, and as they grouped themselves about their leader, who was none other than the Scotchman, they felt able to battle against all the capital that Steelville possessed. They were not particularly angry with the "young boss," as they called him. They were, on the contrary, pleased that they should have opportunity gently and effectually to squelch him. After canvassing the matter at length, it was decided that the puddlers, of all men in the mill, could best afford to lead the strike. The new rule was specially hard on them. Heretofore they had been accustomed to drink liquor by the quart. Their work being difficult, they received high pay. There were none others in the mill who could fill their places. It was therefore decided that they should quietly and unostentatiously absent themselves until the obnoxious law was repealed It was further decided with deep craft, that all the other operatives should be in their places punctually at the usual time, should use up their stock as rapidly as possible, then stand round sad and empty-handed, yearning for work.

The morning came. The puddlers remained at home, complacently smoking. By noon, they calculated, the stock would be used up, and the machines stopped for want of work. But the dinner-whistles blew, the engines started again, and all through the afternoon the white rings of steam, puffing from the exhaust-pipes, proved to the outside world that the strike had stopped not a single wheel. When night came, and the operatives returned to their homes, it was to discuss the strangest thing that had ever befallen them. All who had been near the furnaces agreed in telling the same story. A band of men, athletic and vigorous, even more so than the former company, had suddenly and mysteriously filled the places of the strikers. With accustomed hands they accomplished the work, displaying an energy and dispatch that won the respect of all beholders. A silent company they were, answering no questions, asking none. For drink using oaten meal and water, in the strength of which they accomplished a third more than had their liquor-drinking predecessors. The story had flown from lip to lip throughout the mill. All who could possibly do so, made excuses for passing by the furnaces. Even the superintendents and foremen were as much astonished and as curious as any.

Several of them took occasion to visit the office, hoping that Chamberlain might throw some light on the subject. But he was so polite, reticent, and business-like, that none dared question him. When evening came, therefore, the whole village knew the story, but not one could imagine where the strangers came from, or when or how they had arrived. The very mystery of the thing struck a chill to the hearts of the operatives. They were willing to strike if sure of success, but if their places were filled as soon as vacant, by better men than themselves, without a word of protest, it gave the affair a different aspect. The condescending pity with which they had regarded Chamberlain, was transformed into a most decided respect. The whole village stood, hat in hand, waiting on his pleasure, where, the day before, it had merely tolerated him with partial good-nature. The strikers saluted him sheepishly, having left their confident airs at the feet of their successors.

On rolled the wheels of the great mill; busily throbbed the engine; like silver bells rang the myriad hammers, and the work went steadily on. Except for the occasional discharge of a drunken man, there were no new developments. From the moment that the mysterious puddlers stood in their places, the victory was won. How much anxiety Chamberlain felt in this matter no one can ever know. How many times he had locked himself in his office and prayed that ignorant, arrogant Steep Street might now learn a healthful lesson; how eagerly had he scanned the faces of the operatives, as they thronged out through the open doors, to read, if possible, the success of his experiment! That it was a master-stroke, the bearing of each employé showed. Now all that he waited for was the submisson of the striking puddlers. A week of idleness and reflection was enough to bring them to terms. One or two single men, it is true, sought and found work, but the main body of them were family men, dependent upon the day's wages, with nothing ahead except a few bad debts.

It was the brawny Scotchman who made the first advances towards reconciliation. With no trace of the former aggressiveness, he again appeared at the office. This time he was neatly dressed, carefully shaven, exceedingly subdued.

"Good-morning, Mr. Chamberlain," he said, with an awkward cough.

"Good-morning," was the pleasant reply.

"I thought I would come in and speak with ye a moment."

" Yes."

A long silence ensued. Chamberlain, although deeply interested in the visit, did not think it advisable to smooth the path that the strikers had roughened.

" Mr. Chamberlain," said the old man, at length, "rum makes fules of mony men. I 've a wife and bairns at home. They have no bread. Sic a fule as they have for a provider, who threw up a good job at the call of his worst enemy, rum! Have you no wark that you can give us foolish fellows about the mill ?"

" You are willing to abide by the rules?"

" We are."

" Be in your places Monday morning, all of you. Good-day."

Thus dismissed, the Scotchman ponderously withdrew. The next Monday morning the puddlers, subdued and thankful, took their old stations, and the work went forward as before. The strangers, with whom none of the operatives had been able to form acquaintance, who had boarded at the teamster's, adjoining the mill, had disappeared as suddenly as they arrived.

The mystery connected with them wonderfully impressed the mill folk. It gave them an impression of unlimited resources at the disposal of their employer. Most thoroughly was their lesson learned. A long stride in the right direction was made by this management of the affair. There was, of course, a certain amount of liquor consumed by stealth in the mill settlement, but in comparison with that formerly used, it was as nothing.

As the people became sober, their interest in the mission increased. The little room that had once been Temple's store was crowded. Pfaff's building, which was larger and more convenient, was therefore taken. Among those whose testimonies swayed the audience, and brought many forward as signers of the temperance pledge, were Temple, Gaffney, and Putnam. To these might be added Tam McDonald, Chamberlain, and the Rev. Charles Snow. These six speakers were always heard and welcomed.

Daily the interest grew. Steep Street, at last aroused to her condition, was vigorously bestirring herself to shake off the shackles of sin. Those who had never heard a sermon were attending the meetings. Aged reprobates, whose lives had been spent in scoffing, were on their knees. The work was begun. Earnest, prayerful hearts were pledged to carry it on. No failure could come except through their want of faith.

XXXII.

Results.

A STOUTISH man, with steel blue eyes and red whiskers, dressed in a suit of faded blue, wearing linen that bore the stains of travel, was walking up the main street of a New England factory village. With an air of easy assurance, he looked around at the neat cottages of the laborers, at the carefully-kept gardens, at the rows of shade-trees that adorned the level road. Stopping in front of a cottage a trifle more pretentious than the rest, he spoke to a man who was busily pruning a tiny hedge.

"Is this the mill-village of Steelville?" he inquired.

The person to whom this was addressed straightened up, and said, with good nature,—

"Yes, sir; that's just what it is."

"I never should have known it," said the stranger. "I was tolerably familiar with the place ten years ago."

"Perhaps you know me; most of the people in the village did. My name is Sam Putnam. Did you ever hear it?" said the other.

The other shook his head slowly, saying, —

"I have a poor memory for names."

"But I have an excellent one," returned Putnam. "Might I inquire yours?"

The stranger drew from his pocket a soiled card, and handed it over the fence. Upon it was printed "Mr. J. Winslow Smith, Phrenologist."

With a look of contempt, Sam handed it back.

"What was your name ten years ago," he asked.

The stranger started, but recovering himself, said, with gentle suavity, —

"I was then J. Winslow Smith, book-agent. Ten years of study in foreign lands have fitted me to practise my vocation. Having some acquaintance in Steelville, and being on my way to the great metropolis, I concluded to make a call upon this, my old home."

"What were the names of your friends?" inquired Sam.

Mr. Smith made no reply. Instead, he sighed deeply and glanced toward the spire of the church showing faintly through the trees.

"There have been remarkable changes here," he said.

"Well, I should rather think so. This does n't look much more like old, dilapidated Steep Street than the New Jerusalem looks like the City of Destruction."

"It must have cost something. How was it done? Who paid the bills?" inquired Smith, with a touch of acrimony in his voice.

"Oh, the File Company in part, and the people in part," said Sam, answering the last question. "As you no doubt remember, the old settlement was on a steep hillside,—so steep that people had to wear spikes in their shoes to keep from sliding down into the river. There was no chance for gardens, nor room for any thing out doors but children and goats. Mr. Chamberlain, who had just taken charge of the file-works yonder, saw that on this side of the river was room for the most beautiful, level village that was ever laid out. It was, to be sure, covered with thickets and away from the main road. He had the land surveyed into house-lots, laid out roads, built a new bridge, and had the thickets cut off, and began to put up cottages. These he rented to the help. Mighty glad they were to get them. As fast as the old tenement-houses were emptied they were pulled down. 'Bug Palace,' the worst of the lot, burned one cold winter night."

"I suppose he built the church," said Mr. Smith, with a sneer.

"He helped, but the people did most of it."

"Steep-street people build a church!"

"Certainly; why not?"

"I should as soon think of Satan preaching the Gospel. Why, they were the most drunken, degraded, unchristian set that were ever drummed together."

"I know they were, but it was rum that did it all. When that was removed, the people were all right."

"Wasn't it a difficult thing to stop the drinking?"

"It was that. It took two years to get it fairly under, not to speak of the two years that Mr. Chamberlain put in before that, under old Lamson," said Sam.

"Who was this Lamson?" inquired J. Winslow Smith, with interest.

"He was the agent, who took charge of the mills after the death of Robert Flint."

"Was he smart?"

"Not very; he was too much of a hypocrite. He had an idea that he could cheat the Lord as easily as he could his fellow-men; but a judgment fell on him. He got found out, and had to leave the country."

"Good enough for him!" was the pious rejoinder.

For some minutes after this, neither of the men said a word. Putnam resumed his work, and the clipping of the huge shears was the only noise that broke the stillness.

"Would it be possible for a person to get a little liquor for medicine, here?" finally asked Smith.

"No, sir! Not a drop of liquor can be obtained in the village. Why, the people hate it now worse than the young boss does. I believe they would mob a man for bringing a quart into town!" was the emphatic reply.

"I don't understand how this came about," said Smith, with a ring of sincerity in his tones.

"It is a problem that a good many gave up," replied Putnam. "Lots of people think liquor-drinking can not be successfully handled, either by law or by moral suasion. Mr. Chamberlain's experiment with this village has proved them wrong. He made use of both. Where persuasion would not avail, he substituted the strong arm of the law. This is now a gospel-temperance, prohibition town. It has its schools, its library, its debating club, its literary circle, its church, and not a single liquor-saloon. This village has risen in answer to prayer; not that we prayed, and did nothing else, but prayer and work went hand in hand, and God blessed them, as he always does."

Mr. Smith was somewhat uneasy under this temperance lecture. He fidgeted as if it made him uncomfortable. When it was finished, he asked one more question.

"Are the file-works making money?"

"More than ever before. The goods that are now turned out are first-class — the best in the market, and command a good price. Orders are 'way ahead. I tell you, stranger, there are few men that possess the honest purpose, and the real ability, that Boss Chamberlain has."

Thanking the good-natured giant for his information, Dr. Smith walked slowly on through the village. As he neared the neat iron bridge that led over the river to the file-works, a buggy drawn by two spirited horses passed him. In it were a gentleman and lady and a little boy of five or six. The gentleman, with all the courtesy of a village king, bowed to the stranger who looked so eagerly and keenly at him. The salute was not returned. The benignant doctor, his heavy brows lowering with an ugly frown, strode across the bridge, by the busy factories, and out of sight.

In the stately study of the old Flint mansion sat Tom Chamberlain, older than when we last saw him, thicker set, but still young, vigorous, prosperous.

"Miriam," he said, addressing the lady who was reading near him, "whom do you suppose Putnam declares he saw in the village to-day?"

"I'm sure I can not tell."

"He says our old friend Lamson paid us a visit."

"What did he want?" asked the young wife.

"I imagine he expected at first to find Steep Street as ignorant and degraded as ever. He is going about the country as traveling phrenologist, calling himself Doctor Smith. Putnam's opinion is that he expected to examine heads here, but finding rum and ignorance had departed, had not the courage to practise his quackery."

"It could not have been he," said Miriam. "Putnam must be mistaken."

"I think he is right, my dear. He never forgets faces, or voices, and he is very positive in his assertion."

"How fortunate that his poor, dear mother can never know! Do you remember, Tom, how her last prayers were for her boy?"

"I know it. The mother-love never changes. Perhaps those prayers may yet be answered. Who knows?"

"How can it be possible that he has fallen so low?" mused Miriam.

"I suppose it is an old-fashioned belief that such things come as judgments, yet I cannot but think that Lamson's failure is directly traceable to wrong-doing in business. The opportunity was given him to raise fallen Steep Street. None knew the right way better than he. Deliberately, he turned his back on it, and the Lord gave the work to others. Not that it is an unusual offense. This sin of neglect seems to be one of the greatest, as well as the most common. Its punishment is as sure as those of other sins. Even in this world, swift retribution overtakes it.

www.ingramcontent.com/pod-product-compliance
Lightning Source LLC
Chambersburg PA
CBHW031101110726
47900CB00003B/1012